SLAVE-
OF V

By the same author:

WITCH QUEEN OF VIXANIA

SLAVE-MISTRESS OF VIXANIA

Morgana Baron

This book is a work of fiction.
In real life, make sure you practise safe sex.

First published in 1995 by
Nexus
332 Ladbroke Grove
London W10 5AH

Copyright © Morgana Baron 1995

Typeset by TW Typesetting, Plymouth, Devon
Printed and bound by
BPC Paperbacks Ltd, Aylesbury, Bucks

ISBN 0 352 33054 6

All characters in this publication are fictitious and any resemblance to real persons, living or dead, is purely coincidental.

This book is sold subject to the condition that it shall not, by way of trade or otherwise, be lent, resold, hired out or otherwise circulated without the publisher's prior written consent in any form of binding or cover other than that in which it is published and without a similar condition including this condition being imposed on the subsequent purchaser.

One

The Seneschal asked Lady Laylanda if she would kindly disrobe. The maiden knew the proper response. She had been rehearsing her small role in The Rite of the Morning of Liberation for eight full days. Now the moment she'd been dreading was here. This time a dumb-show of the actions and a rote recitation of the words would not suffice. This was real.

For the first time in her young life, Lady Laylanda's virgin body was going to be exposed before the lustful eyes of men. That alone made her fearful, in a strangely excited way. The demeaning manner in which she was to be stripped naked somehow made her feelings much more intense.

Was she perverse? Did other maidens find that the thought of being shamed inflamed their senses? Could it be natural, to quiver and tingle in anticipation of suffering humiliation before base slaves?

And there would be pain. How did she feel about that? Lady Laylanda was not sure. She knew she dreaded it, but her trepidation was mixed with another emotion – one she dare not name.

The ritual demanded that she show fearful anticipation. That was easy. Her limbs had been trembling since long before sunrise, when the slave-girls had woken her by the perfumed light of shockingly phallic candles.

They'd bathed her, oiled her, given her aromatic leaves to chew, that her breath be sweet, brushed her unruly mane of cinnamon hair into some semblance of order, and dressed her in a manner that mortified her to her very soul. Even so, when she'd glimpsed herself in the tall silver mirror there had been a moment of pride. Her reflection had been uncommonly comely.

Lady Laylanda was used to covering her young body modestly, as befitted the virgin daughter of a Duke. Today, she had been denied her silken pantaloons, her satin shift, her layers of underskirts, and her surcoat. Today, they had allowed her but a single loose garment, and that of a muslin so fine that the rose-pink crests of her barely-budded breasts could be seen quite clearly through it.

The transparent fabric had swirled about her legs, and clung to her hips' curves. Certain humid dreams she'd had, of the happy day when she would finally become a bride, had come to her mind.

But this was not the night of her wedding.

The Seneschal coughed, reminding her that he awaited her ritual response.

'As I am of noble blood, I decline to disrobe,' she managed to chant.

'I ask for the second time,' the Seneschal intoned. 'Will you disrobe, willingly, My Lady?'

She crossed her arms over her breasts. 'As I am of noble blood, and proud, I decline to disrobe.'

'I ask for the third, and final time. Will you disrobe, willingly, My Lady, that you may fittingly serve your Queen, Vixia the Insatiable?'

'As I am of noble blood, and proud, and yet a virgin, I decline to disrobe.'

'Then,' the Seneschal responded, 'I offer to you this goblet of spirits of wine, that you may be fortified for the ordeal to come. Know, O noble, O proud, O virgin, this very morn you will be stripped naked, whether you will or no. Your high station will be brought low. Your vaunted pride will become abject humility. Your treasured virginity will become such a burden to you that you will surrender it in an instant, if you are given Her Supreme Depravity's leave so to do.'

Lady Laylanda prayed that those particular words were also mere ritual. She valued her maidenhead. To Laylanda, it was her ultimate treasure, a gift for her to bestow with love to her groom, on the night of her union, when that blessed eve finally came. The thought of tossing that treasure aside wantonly was repugnant to her.

Laylanda took the golden goblet from the Seneschal's hands, and drained it.

A girl, naked except for the stiff leather collar that held her head high, took the goblet. Another handed the Seneschal his ceremonial wand. It was black, chased with electrum, as long as a tall man's leg, and thin as a whip.

'Stand ready, My Lady,' the man ordered. 'I would not want to mar your lovely skin more than the Rite requires.'

Lady Laylanda lifted her arms out from her sides and spread her legs wide. Her bare toes curled to grip the flagstone floor. 'I am ready.'

The Seneschal was a cruel man. Unlike his three-times predecessor, Pasnar-of-the-iron-member, Krotor enjoyed inflicting pain and terror. Custom did not demand it, but he circled his victim four times, slowly.

Krotor didn't walk. Each step he took was a measure in some slow and elegant dance, drawing out the girl's apprehension until the long muscles in her thighs knotted from it. He pointed his feet. He twirled. The stiff brocade skirts of his uniform swirled wide. He dipped and swayed.

He finally paused. His head was cocked, as if in contemplation of which banquet dish he should sample first. His wand touched her three times, once on each nipple, and once low on her trembling belly. He took a pace backwards, raised his arm, hesitated for two heartbeats, and slashed down.

The rod whistled, but Lady Laylanda did not flinch, not even when the sharp tip slashed a path between her breasts, slicing the gauzy fabric that was stretched between them.

Krotor used his wand's tip twice more, to flick the torn cloth to either side, baring the girl's maiden bosom to his burning gaze, and to the eyes of the assembled slaves.

He licked his lips. She was barely come to womanhood. Her breasts betrayed her innocence. They were just soft sweet swellings on her chest, pink-crested. Well could he believe that he was the first male ever to behold them. She was blushing already, from the insult of his lewd eyes. The flush spread from her smooth cheeks, down her pretty neck, and suffused her chest.

It was delicious, the way shame painted her body. And her degradation at his hands had barely begun.

The tip of his rod lifted her skirt. It caressed the tender skin high inside a slender young thigh. 'You are aware of the duties that are required of you, My Lady?' he asked.

Lady Laylanda swallowed and managed to croak, 'I am to serve my Queen, as handmaiden, for a ten-day.'

'And your duties?'

'To be obedient in all things.'

'Very good.' His rod pointed at the floor, and then whipped up. The girl's gown was slit to her crotch. The wand's breeze stirred the soft down that was but a mist upon her pubic mound, and still her body gave no outward sign of fear.

Slash, and slash again. The skirts of the gown were in tatters. They hung in ragged ribbons from her waist.

'Do you know the exact nature of your first task, in Her Malevolence' service?'

'No.' Was there a quiver in her voice?

A crosswise cut opened her gown from beneath her right nipple to beneath her left. Now she was almost naked, in front. Her firm young thighs were fully exposed. The cleft at their juncture was bare. Strands clung to her belly. Threads dangled from her shoulders, concealing no detail of her tender breasts. The slow uncrinkling of her virginal nipples betrayed the erotic excitement that underlaid her fear.

By Krotor's skill, the back of her gown was still intact. The Seneschal walked around her, and touched one tight-clenched buttock with his cane. 'You will commence your duties by awakening Her Viciousness from her slumber, My Lady. You will perform that task in the manner prescribed by the Ritual of the Bed Chamber.'

'Which is?'

'You will be instructed by example. Your second task will be to assist her, at her robing. Your third will be to

4

simply attend her during her morning duties, observing, a
performing such small errands as She might require of you.

Laylanda's shoulders relaxed a trifle. The duties of a Lady in Waiting? Even though she'd be naked, those tasks would not be unbearable, surely?

The tip of the vicious rod cut a vertical line between her buttocks. So exact was the Seneschal with his weapon that the wand's point passed between the firm ripe mounds, and they felt the wind of its passing, but it did not so much as graze Laylanda's delicate pink skin.

Not then.

A dozen more flicks removed the last few shreds of muslin. Lady Laylanda's gown had been whipped from her body, as the Ritual demanded.

The wand caressed her nape, her shoulder, her back, trailed down her spine to her buttocks, and lingered there. Krotor was forbidden to touch his victim with his hands, so his wand became his finger, slyly stroking the pad of muscle that covered her tailbone, and drifting slowly down, tracing the secret division between her tense cheeks.

'Listen to my words,' he intoned. 'Heed them well. Know this, Lady Laylanda, that you have been chosen by Her Majesty to be the heir to your Father's Dukedom, to have it and to hold it, to rule it and command it, as Queen Vixia's loyal vassal.'

'But my Father? My brother? My elder sister?'

'Will step aside, at Vixia's command. That is why you were summoned here, My Lady, that you might be prepared for your new duties, as well as to celebrate the anniversary of our Queen's liberation of our land.'

The wand's tip dropped, and rose again, between her thighs, to tap a gentle threat against the puckered lips of her virgin coynte.

Lady Laylanda squirmed. Never had she been subjected to such indignity. If the Seneschal spoke truly, and she was to be elevated from 'youngest daughter' to 'Duchess', then her first act of power would be to demand of Queen Vixia that the man be punished. Something with sand-crabs might be appropriate, or perhaps very tiny red-hot hooks.

'You will be transformed, My Lady,' he continued. 'In ten short days you will learn how to rule in the manner that Queen Vixia requires. You will become her slave, body and soul. You will learn to be cruel, and depraved.'

Lady Laylanda prided herself on her kindness, and her chastity. The man was wrong, totally wrong. No matter what they did to her, she would return to her home the same sweet child as when she had left it. Wouldn't she?

'Are you ready for the next stage in the Ritual?' he asked.

The girl braced herself. 'I am.'

Those who would mete out punishment,' he droned, 'must first know its sting. Three strokes are prescribed. I warn you, My Lady, I am most diligent in my duties. If you request it, there is a second goblet at hand, to my left. Its spirits would numb your senses and lessen your pain. Would you drink?'

As the Ritual prescribed, she responded, 'I would not.'

'There is a leather gag at hand, to my right. Would you take it, that you not disgrace yourself by crying out?'

'I would not.'

'There are strong slaves at hand, behind me. Would you have them hold you, that you not disgrace yourself by fleeing the rod?'

'I would not.'

'Then I await your leave to comence, My Lady.'

This was the hardest part of the Ritual, so far. It was bad enough that she had been humiliated by being stripped naked by this monster, before lowly slaves, but to be required to give the signal that would initiate her further shame, and pain, that was what she had been dreading the most. The words clogged her throat and were bile in her mouth, but she somehow forced herself to whisper, 'Begin.'

The rod cracked deep agony into the ripe flesh of her buttocks, where they were fullest. Pain pulsed in expanding waves, rippling through her entire body. Lady Laylanda's knees buckled, but she did not fall. Her mouth distorted into a rictus grin, but she did not cry out. Her eyes filled with tears, but they did not spill.

The second cruel cut paralleled the first, a hand's width above it. The part of Lady Laylanda's mind that could still think resolved never to inflict such torment on any miscreant, no matter how great the crime, except, of course, if that criminal was the Seneschal himself.

The third and final vicious stroke was laid lower, exactly into the creases between Laylanda's thighs and buttocks. She tasted blood from the lip her teeth had bitten, but still she did not cry out.

Through the roaring that filled her ears and eyes, she heard Krotor's hoarse voice. 'There is salve at hand, My Lady.'

She shook her head, not yet able to speak. The thought of a slave's fingers touching her so intimately was worse than the pain. Pain fades. Shame lives with you.

'It is part of the Ritual,' the Seneschal said. 'You may not refuse.'

Lady Laylanda stiffened her shivering limbs. She tried to think of other things. Coolness touched her burning. Gentle fingers smoothed. The fire became a tingling. Burning pain was transformed into a strangely pleasant warmth.

She had been taught to be gracious. Once her power of speech returned, she told the slave, 'I thank you for your kindness.'

A tenor voice replied, 'I but do my duty, My Lady.'

Lady Laylanda whirled on the Seneschal. 'This slave is a man! Your Queen shall hear of this! No man has ever touched my naked skin. I have been defiled. This is not prescribed by the Ritual, I am sure.'

The Seneschal smiled a secret smile. 'No man, My Lady. He has not been a man since the day his clumsiness displeased Her Majesty, My Lady.'

Strangely, it was the thought of the poor man's maiming that finally spilled the tears that she could no longer blink back.

'You weep for him?' Krotor asked. 'My Lady, it is nothing. Our Queen was merciful that day. Take heed. An application of the Tongs of Castration is the least of Her punishments. Be careful, when you attend Her Magnificence, that you do not displease her and discover for yourself how imaginative She can be.'

Lady Laylanda drew herself up with as much dignity as she could muster, naked. '*I* should take care? I have endured this Ritual because it is prescribed by custom, but the poor man is but a slave and without rights. Surely those of noble blood need not fear Queen Vixia's wrath?'

Krotor grinned. 'Yes, he is a slave, now. Before he fell, he was proud to call himself Lord Randus of Elewhone. It was during this same Ritual, three years past, that he fumbled in his duties and was reduced to his present condition.'

All colour left Laylanda's face.

'I warn you, My Lady,' Krotor continued, 'Our Queen is rarely so merciful with those of your softer sex. Should you fail to please her, in any wise, you will find yourself envying this sexless slave.' Krotor folded his arms on his narrow chest and eyed Laylanda speculatively.

'Now, My Lady, we must continue to prepare you for your first audience with Her Supreme Cruelty, Vixia, Witch Queen of Vixania.'

The collar that they triple-buckled around Laylanda's delicate throat was half as tall again as those worn by the slaves, but buttery soft. It had been tanned from the skin of an unborn kid. The cuffs that circled her wrists were made from the same supple leather.

The chains that dragged her arms up between her shoulder blades and drew her hands so high that her fingers touched her nape, had been forged from pure platinum. Lady Laylanda's bonds were of such worth that they could have purchased a small village, but they were still bonds.

'Is this necessary?' she demanded.

Krotor made a sweeping bow. 'It is as the Ritual requires, My Lady. Now follow me.'

Flagstones bruised her feet. As she stumbled after the Seneschal, she asked his back, 'How will I properly serve Her Majesty, so cruelly restrained?'

'You will follow the lead of the others.'

'Others?'

'Nine have preceded you. Today is the day of celebration, but the Ritual runs for twenty – ten preceding and ten following. On the first day, I prepared the son of the Earl of Highfast. On the second it was the turn of Daphnis, daughter of Lord Brax. You are the last, My Lady. Think yourself fortunate. Shared, the tasks you will be set will be less onerous, for now.

'On the morrow, after the Revels, the new Earl of Highfast will be released from these particular duties. His training and transformation will be complete. His position in the Court will be elevated to that of "guest". As this is a time of joyous celebration, he will remain with us until the revels are done, and then return to his Earldom, to rule in Vixia's name. Each day thereafter another new noble will be proclaimed, unless any fail.'

'There will be noblemen there? I am to tend my Queen, naked before the eyes of men of noble birth?'

'Nudity is common, here in Vixia's Court. You will become accustomed to it.'

Laylanda bit her lip, tasting blood again. 'I doubt that, Seneschal. It is not the custom of my people to go unclothed.'

'Queen Vixia has noted the customs of your people, My Lady. That is one of the reasons that you have been brought here to be trained. When you return to your little rustic Duchy, you will take back new customs, I assure you.'

'My people are proud. They will not change their ways easily.'

'So too are you proud, My Lady, and yet this very morning you have submitted to my wand. Now you are naked, and in chains. Where now is your pride, My Lady?'

'I have allowed certain indignities, to be sure. I have done so at the command of my Father, the Duke. He has been forced to sacrifice my dignity, lest the Queen send soldiers to ravage our land and our people. I endure this martyrdom for their sake, Seneschal, but I assure you that whatever indignities and pain you inflict on my poor weak body, my spirit will remain unbowed.'

Krotor stopped, turned, and looked at her. 'My Lady, you prattle. You bore me. This is my first year as Seneschal, but before that I served as assistant to three of my predecessors. Once every three years I hear the same boasting from each of the ten chosen ones. You weary me. Hold your stupid tongue.' He chuckled. 'Conserve its strength, My Lady. It will be needed.'

Lady Laylanda stamped her bare foot, heedless of the bruising that the stone floor inflicted on her tender heel. 'How dare you!'

Krotor sighed wearily. 'How dare I? Lady Laylanda, it will be my duty, tomorrow morn, to repeat this day's Ritual. *And* the next day, and the day after, for ten days. My wand will kiss your pure white skin twenty-seven more times before you depart. Would you make me your enemy?'

She swallowed, and said nothing.

They came to an antechamber. It was bare and empty, except for the nine nobles, five youths and four maidens, who had preceded Lady Laylanda. All were as naked as she, and similarly restrained. Each collar had been fastened to a chain that dangled from the groined ceiling, so that the captives had no choice but to stand erect.

She looked at her feet, avoiding the obscene exhibition. Never in her young life had her eyes been exposed to the nakedness of others. She resolved that she would not look at any of them, least of all the men, but curiosity overcame her. She peeked up from beneath her eyelashes. They were beautiful, all five youths, even their – their male parts. She was amazed. All were pale cylinders of flesh, domed, and marked with thick blue veins, and yet no two were alike. Some were longer, and some shorter. Some were thicker, and some thinner. One, she noticed, was mottled for its entire length. Another was pure white to its mid-point, and blush red from there to the purple plum that sat at an odd angle as a jaunty crown.

Was it natural, she wondered, the way each member strained upwards, thick and throbbing? Surely not. Had that been their natural state, she would have noticed, for no robe could conceal such proud pillars of flesh as these.

Krotor took hold of Laylanda's collar, drew down a chain from above her head, and tethered her in the same manner as the rest. Pain stabbed between her shoulder blades. Her neck ached. A cramp bit into her right shoulder.

Two of the chained girls had their backs to Laylanda. She could not help but observe the weals that stripped their rears. One had six, three faded, three fresh. All were perfectly parallel, alternating new and part-healed.

The second girlish rump was marked by more welts than Laylanda could readily count, one above the other, from mid-way up the backs of her thighs to the small of her back. No two livid lines touched.

Laylanda shivered. In a day, her own bottom would resemble that of the first girl. In eight or nine days, it would be as marked as that of the second. What agonies these noble maids had endured for the sakes of their peoples!

'The candle has one measure left to burn,' Krotor said, looking at the single flickering light. 'I shall return.'

As soon as he was gone, the plump pale girl who was standing closest to Laylanda turned her blonde head and whispered, 'I am Fotis, Princess of Iliam. Listen to my words carefully.'

'A princess?' Laylanda asked.

'My people's Island fell to Vixia six moons past. I am to rule in my Mother's stead, once I leave here. Never mind that. I am lost, I know, but perhaps my words may save you.'

'Save me? How?'

'Listen! You must do everything that they require of you, no matter what. Obey, and do so as if you are eager, do you understand? It is your only chance.'

A handsome blond man, likely from the North, nodded. 'Heed her. We nine are already doomed, but you may still be saved.'

'Saved? By utter obedience? By total surrender?'

'It is the only way,' Princess Fotis said.

'But if they seek to rob me of my maidenhead? Am I to give it up willingly?'

Fotis snorted. 'Your maidenhead? Consider it already riven to shreds. That is the least of what you will lose. Discard your modesty with your hymen. Abandon your self-respect. Vixia will make a whore of you, whether you will it or not. Pretend that you embrace harlotry willingly. If you do not, it will be forced upon you in such a way as it will be no pretence at all.'

'But what is left? You ask me to give up all that I value the most dearly.'

'How about your sanity? How about your soul? Do you not value those more?'

'My sanity? You think they seek to drive me mad?'

'As mad as I now am. As mad as we all are. Crazy with the vilest lusts. Insane with perverse desires.'

'Never!'

'Never? Your words echo my own. Two short days ago I was as innocent as you are now. Now I am as debauched as any follower of Sloona, Goddess of Desire. I crave – I crave things that I have no words to describe, little virgin. You will lust also, I promise. There is no escaping it. You must salvage what little you can. If you are obedient, there is some small chance that the madness you endure may someday pass from you. Resist, and Vixia will kiss you.' She paused to lick her lips. 'One kiss, my innocent one, and your soul will be forfeit, as mine is.'

Laylanda tried to ease the cramp in her shoulders. 'Kiss? Is a kiss what you fear? My mother has kissed me, often.'

'Not as Vixia kisses, I promise. And you ask if I fear her kiss? No, not any more. Now there is nothing I desire more. That is the danger. All of us here are slaves to the taste of the Vile One's sweet mouth. Once those cruel lips ...' She paused. Bootsteps echoed towards them. 'It is time,' she said. Her voice was at once fearful and eager.

Krotor unhooked them, one by one. Laylanda was disgusted to note that Princess Fotis twisted her plump rump against the Seneschal's stiff robe as he released her, as if eager for the coarse caress of brocade against the tender weals that marred the rounded beauty of her buttocks.

Bronze doors opened. The line of naked bodies passed

within, Lady Laylanda at the rear. There was a bed, broad enough to sleep five. Jade satin covered a diminutive sleeping form. Laylanda took a deep breath. Could this tiny figure be the fearsome Queen of Evil?

The chained ones stood five to a side beside the bed, males to the left, females to the right. The two nearest the bed's head bent. Their faces touched satin. Their teeth gripped. The others stood back to let them pull down the cover from the Queen, and there she was, sprawled face-down, in naked splendour.

Laylanda gasped. The Queen was small, and beautifully formed, slender at her waist, but voluptuous at her hips. It was not the loveliness of the Queen's tapered and dimpied back that astounded Laylanda though. It was the unnatural colour of her skin. It was yellow, and not the golden tint of the peoples of the spice lands, but rather a true strong yellow, perhaps jasmine, or even the bright shade of a meadow buttercup.

There was a perfume in the air. Laylanda did not recognise it, but it was potent. One breath of it inflamed her cheeks and made her mouth water. A second inhalation prickled at her nipples and tingled her sex.

She looked sideways at the girl to her right. The long-legged ebony beauty was slack-lipped and drooling! What foul sorcery was in this subtle scent? Whatever, she would resist. She would surely resist. Her resolve was strong.

Fotis stood to Laylanda's left. Her lips were soft with desire. She looked down at the naked slumbering form with eyes that glistened. 'Do as we do,' she hissed from the corner of her mouth, 'for your soul's salvation.'

Awkwardly, because of the confinement of their arms, the nine young aristocrats braced their thighs against the edges of Vixia's bed and arched their bodies over her. Fotis' foot nudged Laylanda's, urging her to follow suit. Laylanda obeyed, puzzled at this strange ritual. What significance could a kow-tow have, when the one bowed to was asleep?

Heads dipped lower. Tongues extended. Laylanda copied. From the corner of her eye she saw the tall blond's tongue stretch out to its greatest extent, and lick at Vixia's tiny toes. Laylanda averted her eyes from the obscenity, and saw what the rest of them were doing. They were – it was vile. Each and every noble captive was tonguing the Queen's skin. Was *this* perversion the manner prescribed for the Queen's ritual awakening?

Two eager mouths, one male, one female, nuzzled into the hollows of Vixia's neck. Two tongues slithered wetly into Her Majesty's armpits. Two pairs of lips sucked on toes of the Witch's feet.

Fotis, and the youth across from her, were both slavering the backs of the sleeping Queen's knees. Directly opposite Laylanda – it was the most obscene obeisance of all! A curly-headed youth was mumbling one cheek of the Vile One's lush bottom.

Fotis kicked Laylanda once more, hard enough to unbalance her. Laylanda toppled, face first, onto the soft cushion of the Queen's yellow-skinned rump.

It – the Queen's skin – was the source of the strange perfume. With her nose pressed to Vixia's buttery cheek, Laylanda had no choice but to breathe it.

It was delicious!

Without volition, her tongue licked. The taste was – it was the taste of ecstasy! Shamed by what she did, quivering in her soul from the depravity of it, she slavered and lapped, sucking the essence of desire out through the pores of the Queen's skin.

Laylanda's eyes lifted to the face of the youth opposite. He was edging forward as he licked. His tongue slid, savouring, but each wet dab was closer, and closer, until it reached the cleft between Her Vileness' buttocks, and squirmed into that soft crevice, thirstily.

One part of Laylanda recoiled in horror. Another part hated the boy, for he was drinking from a more intimate source than she was, and she envied him beyond all reason.

Laylanda's lips spread, covering as much of that delectable golden skin as they could. Her tongue flattened and laved. She heard the disgusting slobbery sounds that her own mouth was making, and heeded it not.

The crazed part of her plotted. The way the youth had burrowed his face between the Queen's buttocks, it had to be impossible for him to breathe. The moment his face lifted to suck air, that would be her opportunity.

Lady Laylanda had no name for what she desired above all things. The word 'anilingus' had never been uttered in her presence. The idea of it had never occurred to her, and yet, at that moment, she would have traded her soul for the chance to squirm her tongue just once into that tight little pucker, and lap out whatever warm juices she might discover.

The soft flesh beneath her mouth flexed and stirred. It was pulled from her. Laylanda almost screamed her frustration, but then the Queen rolled onto her back and there, just a finger's length from Laylanda's mouth, was the ultimate source of liquid desire.

Laylanda, all dignity forgotten, put her thirsty mouth to the Vile One's nectar-oozing coynte.

Two

Twenty-one years before, Vixia the Witch Queen had come from out of the Sea of Lur, leading a rag-tag swarm of degenerate pirates. At that time the land had been known as Arcadia. The war lasted three days. Arcadia was strong. Its defence was in the powers of its four rulers, one representing each of the Elements of Order; Earth, Air, Fire and Water. Furthermore, it was guarded by the secret Order of the White Lodge. Girded by such powerful white magic, it had been thought impregnable.

Vixia had a potent ally – the gibbering God of Chaos, in its aspect of Havoc. Vixia had paid a terrible price for the alliance. No sane human can commune with Havoc. Vixia had chosen the form of her own insanity. Lewd and salacious by nature, she had deliberately addicted herself to the aphrodisiac pollen of the yellow bees that hive in the foothills above what was then Port Arcady.

Crazed with unslakable lust, she had drawn to herself one slender mental tendril from the sleeping God of Disorder. Filled with that demented power, she had laid waste to Arcadia, slain its rulers, and scattered the last seven survivors of the White Lodge. Reigning supreme, Vixia had renamed the pleasant land of Arcadia, calling it Vixania, in Her own honour.

Her dominance was not totally secure. When the White Lodge had fled, its members had borne with them the last infant survivors of the four Royal families, one from each. Her Depravity's power would not be secure while they yet lived.

Vixia had a constant reminder of Her danger. In the Throne Room, surrounded by the thrones of Earth, Water,

Fire and Air, stood the indestructible White Pillar. A prophesy was engraved on its alabaster side.

> Four shall die, and four times three,
> Slain by a Witch, from out the Sea.
> Four shall live, sought by Fives,
> Hidden by Seven, from seeker's knives.
>
> The square's a circle, the circle's a ring.
> Compass me round, and make me sing.
> Nought vibrating, with love's song,
> Turning the weapon, righting the wrong.
>
> The Witch Queen dead, the people free,
> When Four are joined, elementally.
> Love conquers Hate, Chaos takes flight,
> When the sweetest Queen descends from her height.

The first part of the riddle was clear to read. Vixia was the Witch, from out the Sea. She had slain the Four Rulers, and a dozen of their families – 'four' and 'four times three'. Four babes has survived, snatched from Vixia by seven members of the White Lodge. The Fives were the groups of sorcery-assisted harlot-assassins that Vixia has dispatched to seek out the babes.

The rest of the prophesy seemed to threaten Vixia's doom, but in what manner she could not discern. When Vixia discovered that neither her magic, nor any force she might apply, could destroy the White Pillar, she had the Throne Room sealed away.

After twenty years, one Heir-hunting Five had come close to its prey. It had discovered Theocritus, guardian of the Heir to the Earth Throne, Brod. Theocritus had died in agony without revealing the whereabouts of his regal charge, now a young man. Ironically, at the time of Theocritus' torture, Brod had been coupling with two members of the Five, Suisuma of the python thighs, and magic-voiced Raven, a novice assassin, who was, although she did not know it, the Heir to the Throne of Air.

It was that sweaty swiving that had awoken Brod's powers. It is the nature of the Throne of Earth that its heirs be male, but that their powers be drawn from females. Every woman or girl who climaxed while in congress with Brod fed his strength. Each female orgasm fortified his iron thews, added height to his towering body, and increased the size of his male member.

Brod, learning of his heritage from the dying Theocritus, vowed vengeance. In the following months, he defeated Gowan, the Amazonian leader of a band of female brigands. With her aid, he harried and destroyed Queen Vixia's patrols and forts until at last her magic trapped his force, at Fort Calamity.

Just as defeat had seemed sure, Brod and his band had been rescued by Dendri, leader of the rebels.

Meanwhile, Rena, a servant at Vixia's Court, displeased her Mistress. She was condemned to be tattooed with magic runes by Karina and Betohl, also in Vixia's service, but secretly working towards her downfall. The runes were designed to turn Rena into a nymphomaniac, with erotic powers beyond that of any normal woman, but the Rune Gravers deliberately sabotaged their own work, leaving Rena with her sexual prowess enhanced but lessening her erotomania. When Vixia gave Rena to a dozen of her guards for their sport, Rena managed to escape, and made her way to the rebel camp, where she now serves as the first among Brod's many mistresses.

Raven, heir to the throne of Air, was discovered by Vixia. In the course of her sexual torture, she found her first special voice – the Voice of Chaos. The triple note struck Vixia and the other four of Raven's Five unconscious. Raven was spirited away by Pasnar, who hated Vixia because she had turned his male member to insatiable unfeeling metal. His aid was not entirely altruistic. Raven's magic voice had vibrated his iron penis. That was the first sensation it had felt since Vixia had enchanted it.

Raven was nursed back to health by M'ree, Pasnar's slave. The diminutive Tiblan – a race whose women are valued for their beauty, the length of their prehensile tongues, and for their renewable virginities – was an enigma. Pasnar had found her, years before, mindless, wandering the foothills. Her tiny-waisted torso is sealed in an impregnable golden corselet.

When Pasnar ravished Raven with his metal cock her scream of ecstasy laid him unconscious. Raven escaped. M'ree, mindless once more, wandered off. Pasnar was arrested, and now suffers eternal torments in Vixia's dungeons.

Brod and his allies, under the guidance of another survivor of the White Lodge, blind Hypocrate, are concealed just a few leagues south of Vixia's Palace, in the cone of a dormant volcano.

Vixia knows this. The jet-studded iron circlet that Brod wears around his forearm is enchanted. Where it goes, Vixia can see. She is content to leave the puny rebel force alone. Its members are scouring the known world, seeking the other three babes. Once they succeed, and gather the Heirs together in the volcano's cone, then Vixia will invoke Havoc's power. The mad God of natural and unnatural disasters will cause an eruption that will engulf all of Vixia's enemies at once.

Three

Laylanda's coynte craved. Her clit throbbed. Her breasts felt heavy. Her nipples ached. Her mouth thirsted. She strained forward against her leash, but the giant Styxian slave who had dragged her mouth away from Vixia's dripping core was too strong.

The Queen sat up. Laylanda had never before felt unnatural urges. She had no name for woman–woman love, and yet now the sway of Her Evilness' bell-shaped breasts, their deep ochre peaks, the curve of her sculptured ribcage, the crease of her folded waist, and the swollen pout between her long slim thighs, all were so infinitely desirable in Laylanda's eyes that her very soul hungered.

'It will pass,' Fotis whispered. 'The madness will pass.'

'What?' Laylanda's gaze refused to desert the Queen.

'By the morning, you will be yourself again,' Fotis told her. 'The aphrodisiac that oozes from the Queen's skin will lose its power over you. Come dawn, you will be able to feel shame once more, unless she puts her mouth to yours. Once she does that to you, as she has done to us all, you are lost forever.'

Laylanda's mouth ran wet with the thought. To kiss that lush mouth? To taste it? To drink? For that delight, she would endure Pasnar's wand again, and again, until weals stripped her soft skin from her nape to her heels. Even should it be demanded of her that she face the rod, and feel its fire sting across the tenderness of her belly, and even her delicate breasts, she would suffer it gladly, if a sip at Her Viciousness' mouth be her promised reward.

The Queen was drinking a steaming yellow liquid. She

set her goblet aside and instructed a slave, 'Barbaric, today, I think. In the Styxian manner.' She took her own nipples between cruel fingers and pinched their perfect cones obscenely flat. 'Yes. And thorns.'

A Tiblan knelt beside the Queen's bed, a salver held high above her head. Queen Vixia selected two from an array of thorns that lay on it. 'The nectar?'

Another slave, male, presented a dish of thick ointment. Vixia dipped a thorn, coating it yellow, pulled one nipple to its greatest length, and stabbed the thorn through it, from side to side.

Laylanda sucked air. Surely that piercing had to be agony? But the only sign that Vixia gave was a brief convulsion at her loins, as if the pain had been some sort of intense erotic pleasure. Laylanda strained her neck to see the better. Yes! Incredibly, the lips of Her Vileness' coynte had parted by themselves, exposing the ochre of their inner surfaces, and that secret flesh was glistening.

The second coated thorn punctured Vixia's other nipple. The Queen's coynte oozed. A dark stain spread across the satin beneath her. Its aroma reached Laylanda, giddying her.

Through lust-glazed eyes, Laylanda watched in avid fascination as a third slave brought a tray of jewelry. Vixia chose a tiny emerald-crusted clip. 'Prepare me,' she said, spreading her legs wide.

The tiny Tiblan knelt up on the bed, between Her Majesty's thighs. Laylanda swallowed envy. Would that she was that slave! She would have traded her Duchy and her freedom for one moment of the privilege that the collared serf was about to enjoy.

The girl's mouth pursed. She leaned forward. Her lips encircled the Queen's clit, where it gleamed golden at the mouth of its hood. Her cheeks hollowed. Her head tugged backwards, drawing the small polyp from out of its protective sheath.

'Enough,' the Queen commanded. 'Hold it there.'

Her fingers pressed the clip's teeth apart. Reaching down, she applied its jaws to her clitoral shaft, just behind its head. When the Tiblan's mouth withdrew, reluctantly, the golden pearl was left clamped and exposed, unable to retract.

Laylanda tugged at her own hair. She craved sensation, any sensation. The lust she felt was unbearable. Her thighs slithered together. Her shoulders shook, quivering her girlish breasts.

Half a watch before, her virginity had been her most precious treasure. Now, now that she knew desire, she would have impaled herself on any cock, or anything else that was stiff enough to rend her despised maidenhead, given but the least chance.

The Tiblan slave took up the dish of ointment, and was handed a small brush, such as scribes use. The Queen lay back, toying idly with the thorns that pierced her nipples. The Tiblan licked her brush to a point, dipped it, and bent to the Queen's core once more. The brush's tip, no more than three soft hairs, painted the head of the Queen's clitoris.

Laylanda couldn't even imagine what teasing torture that touch must have been, but she knew that had she been the one who was subjected to it, her soul would have fled her body, screaming lust into the void. Not only would each stroke have tickled unbearably, but it was applying a distillation of that potion that, in dilute form, had transformed her from a shrinking maiden into a sex-crazed harlot. A virgin-slut, as yet, but none the less whorish for her maidenhood.

Her Majesty's toilet was completed by the strapping of high-heeled sandals to her high-arched feet, the tight knotting of a strip of ocelot hide around the fullness of her shapely left thigh, and the buckling of a collar around her exquisite throat. It too, was of ocelot hide, and spiked with the wild feline's curved fangs.

Queen Vixia rose from her bed. She sat upon an ivory stool. Painted eunuchs dressed her hair, entwining ebon tresses around the tall black plumes from the tail of a Nyx.

When the Queen stood, high on her heels, her locks a fantastic inky spray above her Imperial head, she was no longer tiny. She towered.

Krotor entered, a scroll at the ready. 'Your Lewdness,' he read, 'the Revels commence at noon. And if it please you, Your Majesty, there is a small matter to be attended to first. There are three criminals to be tried and convicted.' He licked his lips. 'If Your Magnificence so ordains,' he said, 'your humble Seneschal could attend to this trifling duty on Your behalf?'

'A girl, a mature woman, and a young man, are they not?' Vixia mused. 'No – I'll not be remiss in my Regal duty. Lead on, Krotor.'

The leashed and chained young nobles followed the Queen from her bed chamber, and to the Hall of Justice. Being collared like a bitch-hound and led by a base slave should have shamed Laylanda unbearably, but she found herself revelling in her own debasement. It was for Her that she was demeaned, after all. For Her, Laylanda would endure anything.

The Hall was large enough that chariots could have raced within its confines. Laylanda and her companions were forced to kneel in a row on silken cushions. The nearest wall had been painted with an intricate mural. It depicted depravities that would have disgusted Laylanda but half a watch before. Now, under the influence of the Queen's essence, she found them fascinating.

Hairy-legged satyrs copulated with delicate nymphs. A horned and hoofed minotaur sodomised a fragile pointy-eared elfmaid. Ethereal fairies fellated grotesque goblins. Sloona, Goddess of Lust, was shown at her martyrdom. She was depicted shackled, standing, spread-eagled. A thick-linked chain emerged from the ground beneath her feet, entered between the lips of her Divine Coynte, and emerged from her upturned gaping mouth. Demons with yards as long as Laylanda's legs stood watching, masturbating two-handed. A four-breasted giantess flailed her own sex with a jointed rod that was tipped with a bunch of stinging nettles.

A slave released Laylanda's wrists from her nape. She swallowed her scream as prickly blood flowed back into her hands. She blinked at the mural. The flail had been but half-descended, had it not? And yet – now the nettles were but a handspan from those swollen lips. The minotaur's thighs had been tight against the elfmaid's buttocks, but now his glistening pizzle was part-withdrawn.

Laylanda blinked again, as her attendant drew her wrists down behind her, between her ankles, to an iron ring that was set in the stone floor.

Yes! The mural moved! The tiger-man's worrying of the six-armed Goddess' left teat now elongated a straining nipple between his teeth, where before it had crushed the soft mound flat to her chest. And Sloona! Another link had entered her from below, and a fresh one was emerging from between her tortured lips.

Were those flat, painted creatures somehow living? And was time, for them, governed to a different rate of passage? Laylanda wondered whether, should she return on the morrow, the mural would then depict an entirely different set of bestial couplings, or if the wall's prisoners were condemned to repeat the same depravities, over and over, for eternity.

'You may sit back on your heels,' the slave told her, 'but with your body held erect.'

Laylanda sat. Her heel nudged between the cheeks of her bottom. Its hardness pressed, and parted her. The crease at the tops of her thighs, where her lowest weal still tingled, touched her ankle. Laylanda wriggled, savouring the tiny discomfort. She squirmed some more, pressing back and down. The edge of her heel slid from between her buttocks, across the sensitive skin that separated anus from coynte, and pushed its way into the wet softness of her sex's lips.

Laylanda writhed, slowly, languorously, on her own heel's too-shallow impalement.

Krotor had laid his wand aside. He now bore a tall ebony staff, gold-knobbed. It struck the floor thrice. The Seneschal turned to where Vixia sprawled on her nightblack throne.

'Your Lewdness,' he announced, 'the accused await.'

Styxian slaves brought in three naked prisoners, a girl of Laylanda's age, a youth who was perhaps two years her senior, and a young woman.

'The charges?' Vixia demanded.

'These two,' Krotor indicated the young couple, 'are charged with the offence of Pure Love. Each reserves all desire for the other. Worse, your Majesty, both are yet virgin. On questioning, they confessed a mutual pact, to remain untouched by any until their terms of servitude to You be done, and then to wed, in the manner of their primitive tribe.'

The Queen said, 'Guilty. The other?'

'If you recall, your Majesty, this is the slave who served you your morning potion, yesterday. It was too cool.'

Queen Vixia tapped yellow powder from a tiny jewelled box onto the back of her hand. She sniffed it up, and said, 'Guilty.'

'The sentences, your Wickedness?'

'To fit the crimes. Prepare them.'

Slaves fastened an iron collar about the young woman's throat. Two chains from it were run through floor-set rings, and pulled, forcing the prisoner down to all fours. More manacles fastened her wrists to the same rings.

Vixia cupped her own breasts, her fingers forking beneath the thorns that spiked her nipples. She kneaded for a moment, and then lifted her hands, tugging her nipples away from her chest by their impalements. 'A leash,' she said. 'I would have the woman's head upturned.'

The Queen rose from her throne and took a yellow flask from a grotesquely carved wormwood stand. Her victim, head tethered so she could not turn it, watched Vixia from the corners of eyes that were as fear-crazed as those of a mouse between a cat's paws.

Vixia loomed over her. The Queen unstoppered the flask. A low moan escaped her prisoner's lips.

Fotis, chained next in line to Laylanda, whispered, 'Now you will see the power of her kiss.'

Vixia's fingers stroked the woman's cheek. The captive squirmed and distorted her mouth, twisting it sideways away from the Queen's touch.

'You find my caress repulsive?' the Queen purred. 'That will change.' She put the flask to her own lips, and tilted it. Her victim's lips clamped tight. With her mouth full of the liquid, Vixia bent. Her lips brushed the woman's. The woman stiffened. Her lips compressed. She tried to shake her head. The Queen let a tiny yellow drop fall from her mouth to glisten for two heartbeats on her victim's lower lip. The captive's nostrils flared. Her tongue licked, and then she opened her mouth wide.

Laylanda watched in jealous fascination as a golden stream poured from Vixia's pouting lips into the woman's gaping mouth. Vixia's tongue followed. The woman writhed against her bonds. Her hips juddered. Her chest heaved. Muscles twitched and spasmed in her legs and in her belly. She quivered from toe to head, as if her skin had a frantic life of its own. As Vixia slowly withdrew her tongue, the woman strained after it.

'Will you kiss my fingers now?' Vixia asked.

The woman nodded violently, though the movement must have choked her.

'You'll suck anything, won't you?' Vixia goaded, 'anything at all.'

The woman made a wet noise that might have been speech. She drooled golden ichor, and sucked it back as if fearful of losing a single drop. The Queen's nectar had reduced her to a slobbering animal, crazed by the needs of her mouth.

'Not my finger, though,' Vixia mused. 'Fasten the youth to a pillar and bring him to her.'

Guards pushed in a wooden post that was mounted on a wheeled platform. They took the naked young man and strapped him to it, neck, chest, arms, belly, and thighs. His terror had shrunk his member until it was a soft thing, no longer than Laylanda's smallest finger, though thicker by far. The platform was trundled to the kneeling woman, and placed so that the youth's cock was but a palm's width from her gobbling mouth. She strained towards it. He shrunk back.

'Closer,' Vixia ordered.

The guards pushed.

'Enough!'

The chained woman, by extending her neck as far as she could and stretching out her tongue, found the man's loose foreskin. She exhaled, bathing his cock in breath that was laden with the aphrodisiac essence. Her tongue flickered, barely touching. Despite his resistance, the man's staff began to thicken, and straighten. It grew.

Laylanda watched, fascinated. This was a process that her elder sister had giggled about, in dead of night, but which Laylanda had never witnessed. It was like magic. The tiny soft thing strengthened, and lengthened. It reared up. Its sheath retracted, exposing an engorged knob that was bigger than Laylanda would have dreamed possible. Now the woman's mouth could reach it. She sucked its purple dome into her mouth. Her cheeks hollowed.

'Back!' Vixia ordered. 'Stop!'

The man's shaft spanned the gap between his body and the woman's face. The space between them was such that no matter how the woman stretched, no matter how hard she sucked, just the tip of that glistening ball of flesh was between her avid lips.

Fotis whispered, 'The essence is on him now. He needs her mouth as much as it needs him.'

'Will he climax?' Laylanda mumbled under her breath.

'I doubt it. As I understand it, such a caress will tease, unbearably. Stronger contact, and friction, is needed for a man to reach the peak of his pleasure. In any case, the essence works in two ways. It increases desire, but delays orgasm. Once it is in you, you are suspended in that heartbeat of glad desperation that precedes the ultimate joy, but are unable to relieve your need.'

Vixia had left the first two of her victims to their erotic torment. Now she was supervising the preparation of the lad's sweetheart. The wretched girl had been doubled over the padded horizontal of a trestle. Both her wrists and her ankles had been spread and manacled to the legs. Her head hung so low that her hair brushed the floor. The split curves of her girlish rump were uppermost, pulled taut and wide enough that their secret crease was parted, exposing the dark pink crater of her anus.

'Will she be whipped?' Laylanda asked Fotis.

'Our Queen is not so merciful. Look!'

Vixia had taken up the horn of a unicorn. The twisted ivory cone was smooth, truncated, and hollow. 'You seek to retain your virginity?' she gloated. 'You confine yourself to but one man? Very well, I will not sunder your precious maidenhead, and nor shall he, and yet your vaunted purity will be soiled beyond any cleansing.

'Tell me girl, did you not lust for each other, you two young lovers? Did you not yearn for more delicious sensations than mere childish kisses and fumbling caresses? Of course you did. Well, my dear, your Queen is going to instruct you in a manner in which you may enjoy each other's bodies, without tearing that treasured hymen of yours.'

Her Viciousness' talons teased her victim's blushing cheeks, drawing thin red scratch-lines across their pristine plumpness. She turned to an attendant and demanded a dish of butter.

'Fear not,' she told the maiden. 'I shall be as gentle with you as he, your true love, would be. You will feel no discomfort at my hands, though the moment will shortly come when you will beg for pain.' She dipped her hand into the butter and smeared it along the girl's crease. 'There – isn't that nice? Doesn't it soothe? And so slippery! See how easily my finger penetrates you now?'

Laylanda held her breath as the tip of the Queen's finger pushed against the girl's knotted sphincter, forced entry, and slid deep into her rectum, even as far as its second knuckle.

'Relax, child,' the Queen scolded. 'Let yourself open to me. Enjoy my Royal touch.' The finger withdrew. Vixia took the horn, presented its blunt tip to the girl's knot, and pressed. The hard smooth cone penetrated, opening the girl's anus. She whimpered as Vixia twisted it, screwing it slowly deeper and deeper, until as much as a hand's length was buried in her tight little rectum.

'And now,' the Queen said, 'comes lust.' She unstoppered her flask once more, held it high above the maiden's rump, tilted it, and let a single drop spill. The golden droplet fell precisely into the open end of the horn.

Laylanda's mind could see it, creeping down the inside of the funnel. It would trickle slowly down the spiral path, for the liquid was thick. It would take a long time to reach the end, and then it would gradually soak into the captive maiden's most intimate flesh.

The girl screamed and spasmed, rattling her fetters and arching her body against their restraint. Her buttocks twitched, and knotted. She ground her belly down against the pole that supported her. She arched against her bonds. The long muscles of her thighs bunched. Tiny beads of sweat appeared at the small of her back, and ran down towards her neck.

'Isn't lust wonderful?' the Queen teased. 'Would you like more?'

The girl's head whipped from side to side. Vixia poured, not a drop, but a thin slow stream. A few moments later, the girl screamed, 'Bugger me, someone! Sodomise me! Use my arse. For Sloona's sake, impale me! Ram me with something – anything!'

'Of course,' Vixia promised. She twisted the spiral horn up and out. 'Bring the youth.'

The woman who had been straining to taste the young man's cock sobbed as it was snatched beyond her reach. Guards wheeled the pillar he was shackled to. He was brought to his writhing sweetheart. Vixia took his pulsating member in her own tiny hand, and drew it down. She aimed its head at his darling's twitching rectum, and signalled. Two guards shoved him forward. His glans sank into his lover, opening her eager sphincter. His rigid shaft impaled her deeper, and deeper, until the fronts of his thighs were pressed hard against the backs of hers and his pubic hair tickled the base of her spine. The man threw back his head and crowed. His sweetheart gurgled her delight. She squirmed on her distending invader, rotating her arse in tiny frantic circles.

Their joy was short-lived. At a second signal, the guards tugged the platform slowly back. The boy's shaft emerged from the tight, rubbery, loving clutch. It glistened with a greasy golden dew that was part butter, part nectar. When just the head of his weapon was still gripped in that tiny spasming pucker, he was halted. The thickest part of his bulb distended her sphincter, half within, half without, like an egg in an egg-cup.

He strained his hips forward. His sweetheart pushed her arse back. Both were desperate for unnatural congress. He lusted to drive his cock's glistening head into her butter-slick constriction. She ached to feel that deep distending violation travel the full length of her rectum. Neither could move closer to the other by more than the thickness of a fingernail. The two trembled on the brink of sodomy, avid to perform an act that until that moment both of them would have considered perverse and shameful.

'Bring the other prisoner,' Vixia commanded. 'Fasten her down, flat on her back. Secure her face within a latticed iron mask. Let her gaze up between the bodies of these two "lovers". Be sure that she can clearly see both the girl's sweetly weeping coynte and the youth's rigid seeping cock, but not from directly beneath them. As these two ooze their desire, and its twin nectars drip between them, or trickle down their legs, let her mouth seek the driblets in vain.'

'We'll leave all three of them, posed immobile, in a frozen tableau of lust, for today. We shall return on the morrow, to devise some fresh amusing torment.'

Four

When Queen Vixia had condemned her servant, Rena, to death by erotic frenzy, the Rune Gravers had conspired to save the girl. Parts of the mystic tattooing had been left incomplete. The brother and sister Gravers had then inked-in the rest of the pattern, and added runes that Vixia had not ordered.

Rena's erotic powers had been enhanced beyond the capacity of any normal human female. Those muscles of her body that strive the hardest during carnal congress had been fortified and rendered unnaturally supple. Her lungs' capacity had been enlarged. The power of her heart had been increased. Each of her orifices had been granted the elastic pliability and twice the muscular strength of a ravenous python's throat.

Magically strengthened, Rena had exhausted six virile men while herself remaining capable of draining another dozen, given the chance.

In the course of Rena's frantic couplings with Vixia's brutal guards, body-fluids had erased vital elements of the cryptic patterns, and with them, a portion of her insanity. Thus, she had escaped her fate, in part.

Rena lived. She could walk, talk, eat, and even sleep, though her rest was tormented by carnal dreams. She lived – as Lust incarnate. A hundred orgasms a day only whetted her insatiable appetite. She craved, constantly. Lecherous passions raged through her pale and slender body. Every pore of her silken skin demanded sensation. Her mouth was fierce for male seed, or female spending, it mattered not which. Her nipples were urgent for fingers' touch, cruel or kind. Her coynte was a sucking, swirling maelstrom. Rena's clit throbbed need. Her anus twitched with its wanting. Her rectum coveted the deepest, most distending penetration.

Only mighty Brod, Heir to the Throne of Earth, could give Rena respite, and even so, just for a short moment.

Her friends among the rebels strived to help her.

Marl and Gowan, leaders of the Amazonian brigands who Brod had recruited to the rebel cause, spent a week on the slopes of the volcano, gathering pulseberries. For two days, inside the volcano's honeycomb of tunnels, they cracked the nuts at the berries' centres, and laid aside the shells. For an entire day they pounded those shells with pestles, grinding them to grit and then grinding them again, fine as ashes. Nut dust was mixed with aromatic oils, and stirred into a delicately abrasive paste.

They took two leathern buckets of their mixture to the natural sudorium in the crater's wall. The steam-filled chamber was fed by a hot volcanic spring. The rebels had fitted it with wooden benches. They had hung its walls with ladles and scraping implements.

That humid cave needed no man-made illumination. Its walls were veined with the fiery mineral, orichalcum. The glowing red tracery, the fluid shapes that the lava had formed, and the dew that dripped constantly gave those who visited the oval cavern the illusion that they were within a gigantic lust-moistened coynte. Even the few stalactites and stalagmites were fluid enough in shape to have the appearance of strands of female mucus, stretched from floor to ceiling of wide-gaping vaginal passage.

Marl and Gowan rubbed each other's naked bodies with soap-fruit.

'Who's with her?' Gowan asked.

Marl poured a scoop of hot water over her own head. 'The young Tiblan twins, Pohl and Lahn. It was their turn to tend to poor Rena's needs from midnight to dawn.'

Gowan squatted over the pool and splashed warm water up between her soapy thighs. 'It feels close to sunrise. We'd best go and relieve them before Rena eats them whole.'

Marl laughed. 'She'll have eaten them many times by now, if I know Rena.'

Gowan dabbled her fingers in a bucket, rubbing oily grit between her fingers. 'Do you think this salve will really help her?'

'I pray to Sloona it will. We can but try it. Come.'

They heard Rena's groans long before they reached her chamber. Inside the candle-lit cell, Marl held Gowan back.

'Let them finish their bout,' she said. 'It will make her easier to handle.'

Tiblan men are small, smaller even than Tiblan women. The females of that exotic race are voluptuous, with dramatic bosoms, pliant waists, and luxurious hips. The males grow to similar heights, but are childishly slender.

Both sexes are valued as slaves. The women are prized for their beauty, their long, prehensile tongues, and their self-restoring maidenheads.

The men are mainly bought by boy-lovers. Their hips are narrow. Their rear passages are tight. Even when mature they look young, being smooth of skin, and lacking body hair. Their tongues are just as sinuous as those of their females. While their cocks are no thicker than a finger, they, like their tongues, are incredibly lengthy.

Rena was taking full advantage of her attendants' special attributes. She was laying on her back with her legs spread wide. The twins lay with their heads cushioned on Rena's silky thighs. Their tongues, writhing like snakes, slithered side-by-side into the intricate convolutions of her coynte's inner folds. Their bellies bracketed Rena's head. She had taken one slender cock in each hand, and was pumping them while her mouth sucked at both plummy heads at once.

As Marl and Gowan watched, Pohl's tongue retreated from the dripping depths it had been exploring, flickered briefly over the engorged pearl of Rena's clit, trilled a vibrating path along the crease of her groin, and delved lower, to worm its way into the pulsating clench of her anus' pucker.

Lahn's fingers took the place of Pohl's tongue on Rena's

clit. They strummed. Both youths jerked their hips. Rena released her grasp on their cocks, letting them slide freely between her lips. The Tiblans lunged. Their narrow weapons fed Rena's oral hunger. Marl and Gowan could see that Rena had taken such lengths of man-flesh into her mouth that their heads had to be lodged deep in her throat.

Rena hummed.

The Tiblan twins' tongues stretched to their longest, one squirming the full length of Rena's vagina, even to the mouth of her womb, and the other wriggling its way high into the tight constriction of her rectal passage.

Marl stroked Gowan's buxom rump. Her palm spread her friend's cheeks. One finger found Gowan's sphincter and rimmed it, idly. 'They're going to come soon, I think. Those boys can't stand much more of that.'

Perhaps Rena heard her. She slurped her lips from the two probing cocks and twisted aside. 'This way,' she ordered.

With lust-powered strength, she lifted Pohl bodily and twisted him around, dropping him on his back. She swung Lahn into the position she wanted, also on his back, so that his thighs fitted between his brother's and they were facing in opposite directions, arse to arse, scrotum to scrotum. Two long thin cocks stood straight, side-by-side, like two saplings growing from a single seed.

Rena squatted sideways-on above them, guided the two stalks to her twitching vulva, nestled them within her coynte's lips, and rammed down, impaling herself.

'Sit up,' she demanded, dragging both youths by their necks.

Rena sucked Pohl's tongue into her mouth. She directed Lahn's head to her breast. His tongue lapped out, found her thorny carmine nipple, and wrapped sinuously around it.

Rena's belly undulated. The twins couldn't move their hips, but they had no need. Rena was using the Rune-given abilities of her internal muscles to squeeze on their shafts in an accelerating rippling rhythm.

'Shall we help them?' Gowan asked, wriggling her rear against Marl's probing finger. 'My fig itches.'

'Too late.'

Marl was right. The twin Tiblans' back muscles knotted. Their tongues' frantic flickering, into Rena's mouth and around her nipple, became slithery blurs.

'Now!' Rena crooned.

She, and the two youths, jerked to their climaxes. The Tiblans fell back, groaning. Rena stood, letting their foam-coated shafts slither out of her and flop against the lads' thighs. She stooped over the youths, gathering both cocks into one hand, her mouth agape.

'Quickly!' Gowan said, 'before she starts again.'

Marl and Gowan grabbed Rena by her arms and lifted her bodily from her victims. Rena writhed in their grip, not to escape, but to coil her serpentine body around the statuesque ones of her captors.

'You're going to do something to me,' she gasped exultantly. 'What is it? You want me to eat your coyntes? You want to ram your fingers into me?'

Gowan threw Rena over one muscular shoulder. 'You'll see, in the steam room.'

Rena mumbled at the flesh of Gowan's back, wrapped her thighs around her waist, and humped at her belly, squirming erotically, all the way. Once there, Gowan draped Rena along a bench. Marl produced thongs and started to tie Rena's outstretched arms.

'You're tying me down,' Rena squealed. 'I like that. Make it tight, please, Marl. Stretch me! Make me your helpless captive. Use me as your love-slave.'

They fastened her with her arms extended to their fullest length and her legs folded under the bench, tied ankle-to-ankle, spreading her knees wide apart.

'Do you have dildoes?' Rena demanded. 'Big ones?'

Gowan stroked Rena's cheek. 'You like to be teased first, don't you?'

'Tease? Oh yes! Drive me wild, please, till I'm crazy from it, and then do me good.'

Gowan and Marl each dipped their broad hands into the buckets. 'This will feel good,' Gowan promised. She smeared the abrasive ointment over Rena's breasts.

'You'll like this as well,' Marl added, covering Rena's belly and thighs.

'On my mound, please?' Rena asked. The lust-glaze in her eyes cleared for a moment. 'This is to remove the magic of the runes, isn't it?'

'Lessen it, perhaps,' Gowan said. 'If any of the Rune Gravers' ink remains on your skin, this should grind it off. What is tattooed under your skin, well, that will likely remain.'

'Thank you for trying,' Rena said. 'Now rub me, damn you, rub me hard.'

Gowan ground oily grit into Rena's breasts. Marl scrubbed up the girl's thighs, and bore down hard on her hairless mound with the heel of her hand.

'Scour me! For Sloona's sake, scour me!' Rena shouted. 'But love me at the same time, I beg you.'

Gowan looked at Marl and shrugged. The two warrior-women straddled Rena, Gowan over her face, and Marl across her hips. Marl took another fistful of the mixture. She smeared it over Rena's bald pubes, and squatted. Her vulva, its pendulous lips already spread, engulfed Rena's smaller mound. Marl rotated her hips, bearing down hard. Sex to sex, she humped Rena. The ointment oozed from between them, and was forced into them. It abraded soft inner skin, grinding the top layer away, exposing the new skin beneath. What had been sensitive, became even more tender, more delicate.

Rena squirmed her pubes. Her clit's head found Marl's oversized one, and fenced with it. Marl's thumb pressed on both.

Gowan pulled back on the skin that sheathed her clit and directed it, large as a small boy's cock, between Rena's pursed lips. Rena, sucking and humping, pumped out an orgasm, and another, and a third.

When Gowan and Marl reached their first spendings they dismounted. Rena arched up against her bonds, babbling her demands for more. The two female titans scooped warm water and splashed it over Rena, washing away the smears of ointment. Rena's alabaster skin had turned pink and new, so fine as to be almost translucent.

Marl filled her mouth with water, put her lips to Rena's coynte-lips, and squirted. Again and again she rinsed, until not a trace of the salve remained.

'They graved me inside, as well,' Rena gasped. 'Deep inside.'

Marl lifted one brow, dipped into the bucket once more, and ramed three salve-coated fingers deep into Rena.

'Yes!' Rena squealed. 'I think that helps. Rinse me some more, Gowan, but not with water from the pool. Use your spending, my love. Come all over my body. Give my mouth your clit once more, and I'll coax from your coynte such a sweet flood as will drown me.'

'I think she could,' Marl said. 'Horny as I am, at all times, there is something about Rena's frenzy that makes me ten times as lustful. She is like a fever, that spreads to those who come close. My skin burns, Gowan. I am delirious with my need. My fig trembles. Think, you bitch! What new way can we devise to apply this salve?'

In reply, Gowan spread more ointment, great fistfuls of it, over Rena's left breast. She lifted one foot up to the bench, and hunkered down, bringing her coynte low, and fitted Rena's breast into it. Her hips swivelled as she pushed down, grinding abrasive between her sex's inner lips and Rena's vibrant breast-flesh.

Marl followed Gowan's example. Face to face, they rotated their cores. Each young giantess reached for the other's clitoral shaft, and frigged.

'We'll come on her breasts,' Marl gasped.

'We'll flood her,' Gowan panted.

'My mouth, my coynte, my arse!' Rena demanded.

Both riders reached to the juncture of Rena's thighs. Two fingers from each hand curled into hot wet folds. Two thumbs' balls found the head of Rena's vibrant clit and pressed it between them.

'My mouth!' Rena insisted.

A voice, deep as if it had echoed up from some subterranean cavern, said, 'Let me.'

'Brod!' Rena squealed. 'Bring me your cock, my love. Thrust it deep, please. Show your love-toy no mercy.'

Brod strode to the bench. He ripped his loincloth away and sprang free, long and strong and thick as an oaken club. He sat himself on the end, his cock's bulb against Rena's cheek. Her head twisted. Her lips found the glistening purple orange of his glans. They kissed his weeping eye, and then spread. Slowly they stretched, wider and wider. Impossibly, incredibly, they widened until they engulfed the entire gigantic helmet.

Both Marl and Gowan reached incredulous fingers sideways, to stroke Brod's massive shaft. Brod humped forward. Rena's cheeks bulged. The shape of her face became unnatural. Her lips, stretched beyond any normal capacity, were still able to mumble on his stem, urging it deeper.

Brod humped once more. His glans nudged the back of Rena's throat. It opened. She swallowed. The muscles in her gullet writhed, drawing Brod in, deeper and deeper.

She snorted air in through her nostrils, paused, and sucked even harder. Brod had no need to thrust. His entire length was drawn in. His bush of curly pubic hair was pressed to Rena's face. No other woman could have achieved the sexual miracle, but Rena had taken a thick column of flesh, as long as a forearm, entirely into her throat. No bazaar sword-swallower would have attempted the same feat.

Nor did the marvel end, for even distended beyond the possible, Rena's throat still retained its powers. It squeezed. It pulsed. Its muscles undulated. The compression at the thick base of Brod's weapon travelled the length of his shaft, slowly and coaxingly at first, but then with greater urgency, and greater, until it became a rhythmic pumping.

Excited beyond endurance, Brod drew Marl and Gowan into his arms. Three mouths nuzzled together. Three tongues tangled, wet and luscious.

Rena was small. The three who rode her were mighty. Either of the women were capable of lifting her bodily with one hand, and Brod had grown to be ten times as strong as they were, combined, and yet it was the supernatural energy of Rena's lust that controlled them, enslaved them, drove first the two women, and finally Brod, to cataclysmic orgasms.

And Rena? True, she also had reached her climax, thrice, and yet her need was in no way diminished. Her three lovers dismounted. Still Rena writhed against her bonds, sobbing and demanding more lascivious attention.

'Fetch dildos,' Brod ordered. 'Meanwhile, I shall comfort her as best I may.' He kneeled between Rena's thighs, took aim, and then, just as he was about to impale the avid slut, Dendri, the rebel's leader, entered the cavern.

'Brod, there is news of Raven,' he said.

'News?' Brod nudged his globe between the slick softness of Rena's coynte-lips. 'What news?'

'An innkeeper, one who supports the rebellion, saw her just eight days ago.'

Brod eased into Rena slowly, to the depth of a hand's width. 'Saw her? Where?'

'At the port, boarding a ship.'

Rena humped impatiently, mewing mindless mouth-sounds. Brod slid, advancing a fraction, and pulled slowly back. The lips of Rena's sex clung to his cock, following Brod's teasing retreat like the silken lining of a sleeve's jacket dragged out by the withdrawal of an overlarge arm.

'What ship?' Brod asked. 'Did she go aboard willingly, or as a captive?'

'The *Blue Swan*. She went willingly enough, as a passenger, but ...'

Brod pumped half his length into Rena, thickening her slender waist. She grunted her approval, but still squirmed, desperate for yet greater impalement.

'But?' Brod asked. His thumb pressed on the head of Rena's clit, pinching it down against his shaft.

'The *Blue Swan* has an evil reputation. She is known to turn to piracy, and to the slave trade. The innkeeper warns that by the time the craft was a league from shore, it is likely Raven was taken, robbed, stripped, and now serves as a harlot for the crew until such time as they find a buyer for her.'

Brod took Rena's narrow hips in his two hands, and drew her further onto him. 'A captive? A slave? It may be that they'll find her more than they can handle. If Raven sings her Chaos song, they'll regret their abuses.' He rocked deeper into Rena. 'Nevertheless, she is the Heir to the Throne of Air, and my first love.' His palm stroked Rena's belly. He could feel the ridge of his own shaft through her flesh, as if it was a child, growing in her womb. 'I leave by noon. If Raven's voice fails to defeat that scum, then this will.' The fist that he shook was a small boulder, and yet Rena strained up her head to reach it, and would no doubt have swallowed it whole, had not Brod then dismounted her, leaving her hunger still screaming through her body. 'Take my place till Marl and Gowan return, please Dendri. Rena's need is great. Be not gentle, for that would be a cruelty.' He picked up his loincloth.

'Go in stealth,' Dendri called after Brod's broad back. 'Be wary that Vixia's minions not trail you to Raven. Even united, the two of you would be no match for her sorcery.'

In a candle-lit chamber, in a tower of her palace, Vixia put aside the great iron ring through which she was able to see all that took place within the scope of Brod's iron armband.

'Find her,' she hissed. 'Bring her back safely, dear Brod. Gather them all in, Fire and Water as well. Once all four of you Heirs are within the cup of that volcano, I shall light such a fire beneath it as will toast you to a crisp.'

She tousled Laylanda's cinnamon hair. 'There, my child. Your Queen is happy. We must celebrate. Leave your tonguing, for the moment. Run, little one. Fetch me fine cords. Bring me a big-breasted slave, one with fine plump nipples. I will instruct you in the tying of a few simple knots. I have a torment or two in mind, that I have not yet tested. Bring me a soft sweet victim, and it will be your honour to inflict on her the first of her six agonies.'

Laylanda scurried away, already salivating in anticipation.

Five

Hibiscus blushed as she braided the fifth orchid into her long black hair. Was she being too forward? Was she asking too much? Would three blooms, or just one, have been more seemly?

No! She settled her mind to it. If she was to achieve her dearest desire and lay with Lake that night, boldness was her best ally. After all, Lake was not as other young men. He was taller, and fairer of skin. He had those unnatural round eyes for which he had been named, for they were the same clear and sparkling blue as the limpid depths of Sweet Water Lake.

And, best of all, he was reputed thrice as virile as any of the other divers.

Hibiscus still remembered the day that her elder sister, Jasmine, had explained to her the meaning of the six orchid blossoms that had been woven into the thatch above the door to Lake's hut, beneath the crossed killing-sticks that he used to hunt wild boar.

'They are tokens of the joy that Lake has given in the night,' she said. 'You know what it means when we women attend the counting of the pearls?'

'Of course. I'm not a child. Each youth presents his day's harvest to the Elders. The pearls are tallied by worth, a normal sized and coloured one counting as "one", a pink as "two", and a black as "five". Likewise, the value is weighted by size, smoothness and lustre. The Elder scores each man's catch. When he is done, each youth is given his award, in betel nuts.'

'And the nuts?'

'The young men then trade them for the company of the girls of their choice. The best pearl-diver of the day is given first chance to select from among the unmarried girls and those widows who choose to offer themselves, and so on.'

'Trade them? In which wise?'

'Each, er, each nut is equal to one of the orchids that the girls wear in their hair, so that a man who brings in three ordinary pearls may choose one three-orchid girl, or one with a single orchid and one with a pair, and so on.'

'Choose, for what purpose?'

'Why, to be his companion, his playmate, I suppose.'

Jasmine had giggled. 'His "companion"? His "playmate"? Hibiscus, my dear little sister, you will soon become a woman. Your breasts are already budding. Your hips are grown more shapely, of late. There is down upon your mound. Tell me, tiny one, what do you know of the night-games that youths play with girls?'

'You mean . . .?'

Jasmine nodded encouragement.

Hibiscus took a deep breath and said, 'Well, they kiss, on their mouths, and with tongues. They stroke each other's bodies. The youths suckle on the girls' breasts. And then they, the boys, put their man-things into the girls' woman-things. That's the way babies are made. Then, if a baby comes, the girl gets to choose a husband out of all the boys she's done it with.'

'Go on.'

'And that's all I know.'

'There is more, much more,' Jasmine had explained. 'There is pleasure, beyond any you have dreamed of. That pleasure grows and grows, until at its end, there is a special feeling, as if you die, or are born, or as if Father Sun himself bursts with heavenly fire, deep inside you.'

'But what of the orchids?'

'They are our tokens. If we wear just a single bloom, we are telling the pearl divers that if they give us that special joy just once, we are content. If we wear two, we challenge the man who chooses us to perform the sweet miracle, giving our bodies their choicest delight, twice. If three, thrice.

If he succeeds, when dawn comes we weave our orchid-pledges above his lintel, to show the world that he has fulfilled his manly pledge.'

Hibiscus had gasped. 'And there are six blossoms above Lake's door this morn!'

'Only six? I saw a score and two knotted there once, when he had taken three girls and a lusty widow to his hut the night before, but that is not all.'

'Not all? How do you mean?'

'The widow Forsythia told me once, when Lake had chosen her, that even though she had woven seven blossoms into her hair, by the time the stars were full out her hair was loose and flowerless. She told me that Lake had still not rested, but had continued giving her pleasure without pause, throughout the night, even unto Father Sun's rising. She said that if she had paid the full price by custom there would have been not a single orchid left unpicked, for a hard day's march.'

'Lake is a God!' Hibiscus squealed, covering her blushes with trembling fingers.

'Perhaps. Who knows? He was raised by Durcas and Anemone, but he is not their child, as you know. Perhaps it was Father Sun who set Lake adrift on Mother Ocean's surging bosom, and directed him to the beach of our Island, when but a sucking-babe? Surely none but the son of a God could dive so deep, or for so long, and bring up so bountiful a harvest. And the pleasure that he gives to girls, as I am told, is a divine rapture.'

From that day on, Hibiscus had pestered her sister constantly, for more detailed instruction on the way of a youth with a girl, and for more news of Lake's prodigious prowess. Her curiosity had peaked on the morn after Lake had finally chosen Jasmine for his night-mate.

Hibiscus had needed to curb her inquisitiveness for a full day, for Jasmine had spent it abed, in a deep swoon. On the following day, her questions had still gone unanswered, for Jasmine had been as one in a trance, smiling constantly, glazed-eyed, and moving with a delicious languor.

When Jasmine had finally regained her full senses, still Hibiscus had learned little.

'You will know soon enough, little sister,' she had crooned. 'There are no words to tell what bliss I encountered, with Lake. Wait, my pretty. Once you are bloomed and our mother declares you a woman, then I will do my best to see that Lake takes us two, together. Be patient.'

Now the day of womanhood had come. Hibiscus' mother had made the test, and hung a third pink conch on the family totem, proclaiming the household as one of three nubile women.

Hibiscus had been sent alone to Women's Cove, with whispered instructions and the smooth teak rod that her father had carved and sanded to satin smoothness for her. Hibiscus had taken the rod into the secret soft labyrinth of her body, in honour of Father Sun, rinsed it in Mother Ocean, to ensure Her continued fertility, and returned, ready to perform womanly duties, eager to enjoy womanly pleasures.

On impulse, she knotted a sixth flower into her tresses, and prepared to garb herself, for the first time, in the manner of a woman.

Hibiscus laid a square of plain green silk on the table, and folded it into a triangle. She knotted it low around her hips, tying two corners just beneath her navel, and pulled the free corners up between her thighs, to tuck into the first knot.

Satisfied that her garment was secure, and close-fitting, she took a second piece of rectangular silk, patterned in green and blue, and tied that too, in the form of a skirt, knotted above her left hip. Finally, to signify that although her maidenhead was self-riven, and she was ready to receive a man into her body, she had not yet enjoyed her first congress, she hung a lei of sweet smelling blossoms around her young neck.

Her new-grown breasts were full enough, she was happy to discover, that they held the floral loop open to frame their pomegranate-tipped loveliness. Hibiscus took the comb that her father had carved for her from the tusk of a narwhal and drew it through the trailing ends of her hair, combing them forward into a glossy black veil that draped over the pertness of her bosom. Delicate fingers arranged her tresses, parting them slightly, to allow her nipples' saucy peaks to poke through ebon gossamer.

The sight of her own half-concealed breasts in the trade-goods mirror thrilled her. As a child, she had gone naked except for those ceremonial occasions when she had been allowed a brief apron. As a true woman, once she had laid with a man, she would dress as custom dictated, in the two knotted silks, bare from her waist up. Only today, she hoped, would she hover between childhood and womanhood, with her breasts teasingly half-hidden.

Of all the unmarried girls and young widows who would line up to be selected by the pearl-divers, she would be the only one so covered. Surely that alone, would draw Lake's eye? And then, when he saw the profusion of orchids in her hair, would not such brazenness, in a half-woman, intrigue him? What man or youth could resist laying with a girl for her first time, knowing that she, though yet unpierced by man-flesh, proclaimed the voracity of her hunger so wantonly?

A conch-horn signalled that Father Sun was kissing Mother Ocean's horizon. Hibiscus bit her own lips to redden them, pinched her own nipples to stiffen them, and hurried to the beach.

The lines were already forming. Giggling young girls and sway-hipped sultry widows vied for the prime positions, nearest the top of the path, where they would be able to see the reckoning and be close to the victors as they were proclaimed. The widows outnumbered the girls two to one. Mother Ocean takes many men to be Her own lovers.

Hibiscus, as the newest to the ritual, was ceded first place. Jasmine, as Hibiscus' chosen companion and mentor, and also wearing six flowers, was allowed the second. They squeezed hands, in trembling anticipation.

The long-boats and coracles ground their keels and hulls on the beach. The drummers took up their clubs. Beat, beat-beat beat. Beat, beat-beat beat. The slow insistent rhythm seeped into the waiting women, carried on evening air that was warm as milk fresh-sucked from a mother's breast. The cadence tingled through the sand under their bare feet, vibrated up through their legs, and sent tiny quivering thrills into their loins.

Opposite Hibiscus, Widow Rafflesia's left thigh twitched. Her foot lifted, and stamped. Her ample hips swayed. Her right foot slapped sand. Drusinia, next to her, took up the motion. Hibiscus found that her own hips were rotating. Soon, every woman and girl was swaying sensuously to the drums' hypnotic pulse.

'Lower your eyes,' Jasmine hissed. 'Pout, to make a pretty lip, and move like this. Make your dance a promise.' Her hips rotated, slowly on the first three beats, and double-twitching her loins forward on the last.

The first youth arrived, with his harvest in a manatee-skin pouch. The Elders counted, and tallied. Three. The youth stood aside to make way for the second diver. Two. The third, squint-eyed Darmo, earned a six, the same number as that of the blossoms in Hibiscus' hair.

'Mother Ocean, let his not be the highest score,' Hibiscus muttered under her breath. 'If his is, let him chose any but me.'

Darmo's cousin and crony, Flist, earned but a single nut.

'You are safe from that worm, at least,' Jasmine whispered. 'Thank Father Sun the two did not tally six pearls between them. If they had, they might have pooled their tokens, and taken you to share between them. Neither is a gentle lover, nor skilled. I'd as soon spend my nights in solitude as lay with Darmo or Flist.'

Hibiscus sucked her breath. That possibility, of her six orchids, her six peaks of pleasure, being divided between two youths, had not occurred to her. Now she thought of it, there were pairs of youths she would have accepted, should she not attain her first goal, Lake, but Darmo and Flist did not number among them.

The seventh diver was Lake. Hibiscus thought that his flat rippled belly was like the sand of the beach, sculpted by the retreating tide's parting caress. His thighs were the smoothed boles of young iron-wood trees. The bold outline that drew her eyes to his damply clinging loincloth, that was a treasure for which there could be no comparison.

He spilled his sea-harvest onto the flat counting rock. Hibiscus craned, but could not see how many pearls, or of what quality.

Jasmine took a half-step back. 'Shield me,' she whispered into Hibiscus' ear.

Hibiscus did not understand but she swayed to cover her sister.

The Elder pronounced, 'Fourteen.'

Hibiscus bit her lip. Some youths, with so high a tally, would spend their tokens over two nights, or three. Lake though, was known to use up his entire harvest every night.

Fourteen? She was wearing six orchids, and her sister another six, for twelve. If Lake chose the two, it would mean he would likely select a third girl or woman, one who wore but two orchids, to complete his pledge. Hibiscus wanted her first night of love to be in the company of her sister. She would need instruction in the ways of pleasure, but a third female, just anyone?

Something touched her hair, rearranging it. Jasmine! Her sweet sister had come prepared!

The tallying finished. As usual, no diver had brought up as many pearls from Mother Ocean's bed as Lake. He turned, eyes narrowed. Hibiscus bit her lip. His eyes fell on her.

'Turn,' he said.

She turned, and so did Jasmine, though unbidden.

'. . . six, seven. And seven here also! Two sweet sisters, and by chance, between them they wear my exact count.'

Rafflesia's voice purred, 'I also, wear fourteen orchids, Lake. Do you remember the night . . .'

Before she could continue, Lake asked, 'Will you two sisters accept my poor tokens in exchange for your lush blossoms?'

By custom no woman could refuse, but the twin sigh-laden 'yesses' that blurted from the sisters' lips brought giggles from a number of the others.

Rafflesia said, 'When you've exhausted those two puny children, Lake, and I've drained whoever is bold enough to pick me, we should get together on the beach, by Riven

Rock. Then I'll remind you what a real woman can do for a man.'

There was a moment of hushed silence. It was known that men and women who were not married sometimes had private trysts, unsanctioned by the exchange of nuts; but only the most wanton trollop would offer herself so boldly in public.

Jasmine retorted, 'If you wait on the beach until my sister and I have done with Lake all that we plan to do, then best take ample provisions, Rafflesia. We've prayed to Father Sun to hold back the dawn while three moons are born and die, as He did for the first night that Typhoon laid with his half-sister, Maelstrom, and begat the Island.'

In response, the widow hefted up her bountiful breasts, one on each palm, bent her head low, and suckled at both of her own nipples at once, all the while staring straight and hard at Hibiscus and Jasmine.

'What did she mean by that?' Hibiscus asked as the sisters followed behind Lake, towards his hut.

'It is a challenge, usually between lonely widows. She dares us, both of us, to a night of playing the finger-and-tongue game.'

Hibiscus giggled. 'I've liked that game ever since you taught me how to play it, dear sister, but where's the challenge? Unlike most games, all who play win and none lose.'

'You lose when you cry, "enough!". Rafflesia has never lost, for she is insatiable. I've been told that in one night with her a girl's woman-flower will be sucked so dry that her petals will not unfold, nor her stamen stiffen, for a moon and two days.'

'Oh!'

'I must answer her challenge tomorrow. I will refuse. You are too young, little one, to play such games with one so adept.'

'Refuse the challenge? No, please, sweet Jasmine. If you are willing, then so am I. I will be brave, I promise. I will force myself to endure the ordeal.'

Outside Lake's hut a small fire burned, holding back the dusk. His table was already set. He was a favourite with the old women. It was piled with fresh sea urchins and ripe black pulseberries, as well as the more common fare, boiled roots, baked plantains and ready-shucked oysters. There was also a jug of foamy tarot-root beer, chill from a sea-cave.

Lake and Jasmine set to with a will. Hibiscus nibbled and blushed. Her mind was swimming with eager dread at what would follow their meal.

Jasmine cracked a sea urchin's shell, pulled the brittle coat apart in a broad slit and passed it to Lake. Grinning, he put it to his mouth. His tongue slid into the crack to tease at the glistening carmine flesh within.

'Lucky sea urchin,' Jasmine said.

Lake slurped the sweet meat out. 'Have a baked plantain, Jasmine,' he offered. 'Don't they deserve some fun, also?'

Jasmine stroked Lake's cheek. 'I have a special plantain in mind, to suck on, an extra large and juicy one. I'll save my appetite for that.'

'Then, if that is the nature of your appetite, let us continue our meal inside. There are delicacies that I too, thirst after.'

He touched a twig to the fire and carried the flame in to light his lamps. He had three, all well-charged with coconut oil, so the hut was soon bright.

It was larger than most, and well-furnished. Lake had a second table, though smaller than the one outside, and a bench to sit on. Three hammocks were strung between two sturdy posts, each above the other, and quite close together. This puzzled Hibiscus, but she curbed her curiosity. It was likely some 'man thing', and perhaps it would not be seemly for a girl-woman to ask questions.

Jasmine threw her skirt aside and sat herself on Lake's table in just her skimpy undergarment. She opened her arms and spread her legs. Lake went to her, to be enwrapped by four eager young limbs. Jasmine caressed Lake's back with her hands and stroked the backs of his thighs with the soles of her feet.

Hibiscus watched, hesitant. Should she discard her skirt, like Jasmine, or should she await some sign?

She watched, fingering her skirt's knot, as Jasmine feasted on Lake's mouth, devouring it, sucking on his lips and plunging her tongue into its damp sweetness. What was expected of her? Was she to watch until Lake had taken his fill of Jasmine, or was she supposed to join in their embrace? And if so, how? Not even an eel could have found a way between their tight-pressed bodies, particularly now that Jasmine's legs had lifted higher, to hook her knees over his lean hips. Her ankles were crossed behind him. Her heels were digging into his buttocks, urging him yet closer with rhythmic little kicks.

Hibiscus laid a finger on Lake's shoulder to remind him of her presence. He turned his head away from Jasmine's mouth, and sucked on that finger. The soft wet heat was surely magic, for thrills coursed up Hibiscus' arm and shuddered through her body.

'In just a moment,' he told Hibiscus. 'First I must take the edge off your greedy sister's appetite.'

Hibiscus expected to see Lake do the man-thing with her sister, but he simply lowered her back until she lay splayed on the table before him and ran gentle fingers up the insides of her thighs. Jasmine's hands were frantic at her loin-cloth's knots, for it was taboo for any male to loosen a knot that had been tied by a woman. Should any diver break this sacred proscription he was sure to drown on his very next dive.

Jasmine's fumbling ceased with the knot still half-tied. She seemed to be overcome by some terrible ague, for she shivered uncontrollably, twitched her belly twice, let out a great sigh, and slumped.

'Now make her swear,' Lake said to Jasmine.

Jasmine rolled wearily to one elbow. Sweat shone on her brow, though Hibiscus had seen her expend no great effort.

'Hibiscus,' Jasmine said, 'you must swear an oath, on our sisterhood, that all that passes this night shall be an utter secret between us. Do you so swear?'

'Of course, but why? Does not everyone who is full-grown know the ways of love?'

'It is a secret that must be kept from the men. Lake is

unlike the rest. He has powers to give women pleasure, far beyond those of other men. We women keep this concealed, for Lake is already envied by the other divers. There are those who hate him for his manly beauty, and for his skill in diving. If they knew he also possessed this special magic they might proclaim him a demon, and stone him.'

'What – what "special" magic?'

'Did you not observe? He has an enchanted touch. When another youth strokes your thighs, Hibiscus, it will be pleasurable if you like him, but none but Lake has the power to bring a girl to her gushing glory with but a finger's caress. Now loosen your knots, sister. It is your turn to find bliss.'

Hibiscus dropped her skirt boldly and her loin-cloth coyly, as her sister tossed her own small garment aside.

'Show her, Lake,' Jasmine said.

Lake sat himself on the table's edge between the splay of Jasmine's thighs. She sat up and wrapped her arms around his broad shoulders. Her fingers stroked his chest.

Hibiscus stood swaying, awaiting a kiss, her hands cupped modestly over her sex. Lake lifted the lei from Hibiscus' neck but he didn't gather her into his arms. Instead, his hands hovered before her, one close to each of her breasts, not touching. His fingers stroked air.

Hibiscus gave a little jump. She'd felt his touch! Her nipples – they'd twitched! As his fingers moved, so did her tiny pink buds, following, straining towards his hands. She felt pulses in them, stronger than any she had ever felt. Gazing down at her own flesh she watched in awed fascination as her nipples uncrinkled, throbbed, and grew large.

Lake's palms flattened and moved in circles. Hibiscus felt a tugging. Her breasts lifted towards Lake's hands. As his hands separated her breasts strained apart, one moving left and the other right. He raised his hands, and her breasts were pulled upwards. His hands moved together, and her breasts squeezed against each other, leaving just a cushiony slot between their twin roundnesses. It occurred to Hibiscus that a man might slide his man-thing into that soft groove and use it as though it were her coynte. If he did, its head would emerge on each stroke, so very close to her lips that her mouth might be tempted to form an 'o', and thus make of themselves a target.

The thought made her throat dry up.

Jasmine hugged Lake from behind. 'Now make her "blossom", Lake.'

The young man took Hibiscus by the wrists and drew her hands apart, away from her delicate mound, exposing the tender sweetmeat that her fingers had concealed. She blushed and shivered. Most of her young life she had gone naked and unashamed, but now, in the flickering lamplight, her plump little portal's nudity took on a fresh meaning that embarrassed her at the same time as it thrilled her.

'You are beautiful,' Lake husked. 'My mouth thirsts for the honey-dew that is hidden within this gentle bud. Let me coax it forth my lovely one.'

So saying, his hands fondled air once more. His fingers danced an intricate pattern and once again Hibiscus felt that magic caress, deep inside her body.

Jasmine tweaked Lake's nipples and nuzzled his ear. 'Make it good for her, Lake,' she urged. 'Make her flower open and stiffen her stamen until she cannot bear it.'

Lake's index finger stroked up and down, up and down. Something convulsed inside Hibiscus. Though he still had not touched her skin the ridge that covered her clit's shaft felt his touch. That sly little polyp grew bold and poked its glossy head out from under its hood. Still Lake petted nothing. The little rod stiffened and throbbed. Its head engorged until the pressure was pleasure-pain. Hibiscus felt her knees weaken. An urgency filled her. Her petals throbbed, and parted. The nectar of her body flowed, slowly at first, but then faster, until it spilled to run slick down the insides of her thighs.

Hibiscus knotted her fists. A low moan escaped her lips.

'Shall I give her release?' Lake asked Jasmine.

'Not yet. You should be inside her the first time, Lake. Let me untie your loin-cloth, man-god.'

Hibiscus waited, quivering with need, as her sister uncovered Lake's loins. She had seen naked boys, often, and had been curious about the way the worms that dangled between their thighs shrunk and grew, for no apparent reason. She expected Lake to be similarly endowed, but perhaps grown a litle larger, in proportion to his more mature physique. She was totally unprepared for the pale and wrinkled eel that flopped from his linen to lay along his thigh from his groin to but a hand's span from his knee. She gasped and fell to her knees in awe.

'Touch it!' Jasmine urged. 'Hold it on your palm and Lake will show you a miracle.'

It was warm to her fingers' touch, and flexible. Hibiscus wondered how it was going to force entry into her soft folds without bending. Then it twitched. It twitched, and thickened, and elongated, and rose.

She clung to it, perhaps in wonder at the mystery of it, perhaps in fear of what it might do to her should she release it.

By the time it stood fully erect it was too thick for her fingers to encompass.

'Am I,' she gulped, 'to take this, inside me?'

'Not all of it, not the first time,' Jasmine reassured her. 'Lake is a gentle man. He will not hurt you. Come, sister, lay yourself beside me on the table. Spread your thighs wide. Lake will prepare the way, so that you will welcome his invasion when it comes.'

Hibiscus, quaking, obeyed. Her sister stroked her forehead and murmured soft soothing nonsense into her ear.

Lake kneeled on the bench and dipped his head. His breath scorched her. The heat of his mouth was like a fire under a pot with one oyster, her sex, in it. Like a scalded oyster, her sex opened. Her petals fluttered. The stamen above them vibrated as it strained to grow larger than its skin would allow. Nectar flowed.

Lake licked that sweet spending from the skin of her thigh. If he sought to dry her, it was to no avail. The more he licked, the faster she flowed. As the tip of his tongue tickled the crease of her groin Hibiscus felt herself opening. It was as if her channel parted before the thrust of some invisible, unfelt probe. What had been tightly pursed became an open passage for just the depth that a finger might explore, at first, then deeper, and deeper, until she felt that she gaped to her very core. Hibiscus was sure that if a breeze had sprung up between her thighs it would have cooled the fiery insides of her womb.

Lake stood. He introduced the glistening head of his ram to its tender target, gripped himself around his thick base, and eased forward. The desperate hunger between Hibiscus' thighs was filled. A hot distending orb stretched her tightness. It forced further. Hibiscus welcomed it. She wanted, needed, it to be deeper. Mewing like a kitten, she grasped her own thighs just above her knees, and pulled on them, spreading herself. She wriggled on the table, skewering her own flesh. She writhed.

Lake froze. His hips did not move, and yet his manthing did. It undulated within her. It pulsed. It twisted. It was a thing apart, with a life of its own, and it was making sinuous love to her.

Jasmine leaned over Hibiscus and kissed her lips. She whispered into Hibiscus' mouth, 'Tell him when you want your first great burst of pleasure, sweet little one. It is part of his power that he can give it to you whenever he wishes and more often than you would believe.'

Hibiscus could no longer move. Her impalement was so complete, so filling, that she could barely twitch. She took a long shuddering breath, and gasped, 'Now!'

The great thing that plugged her rippled. She felt that the massive ball of its head expanded and glowed with a tingling heat. Her passage convulsed on it.

Lake grinned down at her, put the tip of one finger to the pearl of her clit, and said, 'Then so be it. Now!'

Lightning struck her clit. Hibiscus was a coracle in a tornado. She was an eel, impaled on a spear of pleasure. She vibrated like a humming bird that was delirious on the intoxicating nectar of lotus flowers. Fire blossomed in her belly. Her blood turned to lava. That boiling liquid rock spilled. Her entire being flowed out through the spasming mouth of her sex, leaving her empty, and unconscious.

She woke to the sounds of sucking and sobbing. She opened bleary eyes and sat up. Lake was seated on the table now. Jasmine was stooped before him, her face in his lap. Hibiscus peered closer. The sucking sound came from Jasmine's mouth as she slobbered wet kisses over the head of Lake's cock. As she mouthed, she sobbed, whimpering her delirium of joy. Her head thrashed, whipping Lake's thighs with the damp tendrils of hair. Her keening rose to a scream. She juddered and seemed to collapse in on herself.

Her lips were still for a moment. She shook herself and then put her tongue out, flat, as far as it would stretch. Holding Lake's shaft in her two fists, she wagged it, beating its head on the soft wet cushion of her tongue.

'Would you like another of those little ones?' Lake asked her.

Without pausing, Jasmine nodded eagerly.

Lake reached beneath the girl, took her nipples between his thumb and fingers, and pinched. Jasmine jerked and gasped again.

Hibiscus was overcome by curiosity. How many orgasms had her sister enjoyed while she'd lain in a swoon? She slid from the table and crouched behind Jasmine. Jasmine's legs were slick to her knees with her spending. The lips of her sex were swollen and purple. Hibiscus touched one tentatively and then slid a finger into her sister's flaccid sex. Her insides were dripping with hot lust. The walls of her vagina were twitching.

Lake reached for Jasmine's breasts once more. Her coynte clamped tight on Hibiscus' finger, and convulsed. More warm liquid gushed, coating Hibiscus' hand.

'Teach me to do the mouth things on Lake,' Hibiscus begged, hoping that Lake would then reward her in the same manner as he had been repaying Jasmine for her mouth's avid attentions.

Jasmine made muffled sounds in her throat.

Lake said, 'There are many things that we will teach you tonight, Hibiscus. Jasmine, stop for now and let us show your lovely sister how to use a hammock.'

Jasmine stood on legs that shook, and walked to the

three hammocks. She laid herself face down on the top one. Her naked flesh pressed through the net in raised diamonds.

'On the bottom one, sister,' she said. 'On your back. Let yourself go limp. Let your legs hand loose over the sides.'

Hibiscus obeyed. Lake slid himself onto the middle hammock, between the sisters, face down. He guided his pole down through the mesh. 'Lift your pretty bum a little, Hibiscus.'

She braced up. Lake took her hips in his hands and pulled her higher. Hibiscus felt his weapon nudge between the splay of her thighs. At its touch, her petals parted, inviting him in.

'Hold still,' Jasmine ordered. She reached down on either side, gripped the two edges of Lake's hammock, and started to rock him. As she rocked, he slid into and out of Hibiscus. Neither had to move. Their coupling was entirely under Jasmine's control. She swayed them softly, and then hard; fast, and then slow. Hibiscus let herself relax, dangling in the tender grip of Lake's palms. She ceased to exist, except where she sheathed his rigidity.

The rocking stopped. There was a pause. The movements began again, but now Jasmine was making tight circles, revolving Lake's cock inside Hibiscus' coynte. As its head rotated, Lake lifted and lowered with tantalising slowness so that his swollen dome was moving now deep, pivoting against the tight walls of her vagina, and now shallow, swivelling barely within the warm wetness of her sex's lips.

Hibiscus climbed towards her climax and was drawn back. She climbed once more, and again was thwarted by a change in the nature of the wonderful sensations.

Jasmine released Lake's hammock and pushed down on his buttocks. Lake pulled Hibiscus higher, impaling her to depths she hadn't known she possessed.

'Isn't that nice?' Jasmine asked. 'And when you have enjoyed a few climaxes this way, you may rock him into my mouth, and then perhaps Lake and I will teach you yet another sport, when I take the bottom hammock, face down, and you guide his cock into my tight little rear. Once he's deep, he will keep perfectly still while I buck up at him. He likes that, and so do I. Buggery is so nice when you can control every movement. You will enjoy it too, when you do it dear sister, don't you think? I'll show you how to thrust backwards so hard that he bounces on your bum. If you change your rhythm then, sister, you can thrust up as he drops down, so that he stabs so deep and hard that you feel like a suckling pig on a spit. Won't that be nice?'

Hibiscus didn't reply. She was already delirious with joy.

The sisters left Lake in sated sleep. They wove their blooms above Lake's door and staggered back towards their home just as Father Sun's fingers blushed Mother Ocean's horizon.

They didn't see Darmo, with a club, and Flist, with a weighted net, creeping into Lake's hut.

Six

Raven tried to fantasise that it was Brod's mighty cudgel pistoning up inside her, not the Captain's puny little twig. If it had been Brod's great cock she would have been able to reach a climax. That climax would have powered her enchanted voice. She could have sung her terrible triple note, likely killing the Captain and certainly sending his crew into mindless panic.

It might have helped if she could have clamped her thighs together to increase the pressure on the walls of her vagina. She could not. The Captain had strung her up to dangle by her wrists from a hook in his cabin's ceiling and tied her ankles to rings set in the floor, spread wide.

Captain Harl, of the *Blue Swan*, humped three more times, for a total of perhaps a score of trembling thrusts since he'd commenced, and spilled his thin sour seed.

Raven tossed her head, wishing that she had seductively tumbling tresses to flick instead of a glossy blue-black cap like an otter's wet pelt. Long hair can be a nuisance, but there was no denying that it aided in seduction.

'Let me down and I will make you hard again,' she begged. 'I can show you things that I learned in Queen Vixia's court, things that will turn you into a stallion. I am skilled in perversions that you have never even dreamed of.'

He wiped himself, drew up his greasy pantaloons, knotted a ragged sash, and left her alone.

Raven spat a curse. She would have stamped her pretty little foot had she been able. Not only had she been robbed, betrayed and taken as a sex-slave, but her captors didn't even make good use of her helpless body. Being a defenceless prisoner was bad enough, but to also be kept in a state of constant sexual frustration made it ten times worse.

She thought about Brod's beautiful weapon, pounding into her from in front, and perhaps Pasnar, the Queen's Seneschal, reaming her rectum from behind with his enchanted-to-steel cock, and wept.

Perhaps M'ree's long and lithe tongue might have served to complete her pleasure? Or the nimble fingers of the Tiblan's tiny hand, squirming deep, teasing at the mouth of her womb? Having the lips of her sex stretched around M'ree's slender forearm would be almost as distending as being impaled on Brod's massive member.

Raven itched from the lust that her own fantasies brought, but was denied even the simple relief that her own fingers might have given her.

Being hung from a hook was no great discomfort for Raven. Those who served Vixia soon grew used to such minor torments. At least, had she been dangling in one of the Palace's corridors, passers-by would have dallied, from time to time, mainly to tease or torment, but once in a while one would have been kind and given her clit a good hard frigging. Even a wanton child's smallest finger would have filled her aching void better than Captain Harl's tiny member.

Desperate, Raven cleared her throat and tried a few notes. Her voice warbled at first, and then soared, but there was none of that twisted-throat feeling that signalled her approach to the Chord of Chaos. Instead, her longing tainted her voice. It grew stronger, and louder, but in a different way than ever before. Raven concentrated her mind on thoughts of male seed flooding her mouth with its musky savour. She conjured up memories of fingers stroking, pinching, tweaking. She imagined cocks, large and gnarly, stretching her vagina and rectum with their tireless pounding. Lips? Hard and hairy male ones, or soft smooth female ones, mumbling on the head of her clit. Sucking its pearl till it seemed about to be drawn clean out from its sheath.

Lust seeped through her. It vibrated in her abdomen. It throbbed in her chest, and it had only one way to exit – through her voice.

Above, on the deck, sailors paused in their duties. Their hands stilled from sewing canvas. Their fingers laid aside marlin spikes, leaving ropes' ends unravelled. They cocked their heads, listening. One groped his own stem through rags of soiled linen. Another rubbed himself in the bum crease of the kohl-eyed cabin lad who was kneeling to holystone the deck.

Entranced, they turned towards the hatchway that led below to the Captain's quarters. His puny balls recently emptied, and less lusty than most of his crew, Captain Harl drew his cutlass and barred the way. His first mate clubbed him down from behind.

As the Captain slumped it was like a signal. A dozen men fought each other, kicking and gouging, down the companionway. The burst into the cabin, slashed Raven's bonds, and carried her bodily up on deck.

'Lash her to the mast,' one sailor cried. 'We'll have at her in turn for as long as she lasts.'

'There's three ways to do her,' the carpenter said. 'Tie her so we can use them all.'

They bound Raven's wrists high on the mast, and one ankle to it, at its foot. A sailor knotted a line about her other ankle and tossed its end up over a jib. Two more pulled it down, lifting Raven's leg up and out, straining on it until she felt her hip was close to dislocation, before tying it off.

Standing on one foot, with the other so high that its toes pointed to the sky and her knee nudged her breast, Raven's coynte and arse were both tugged wide open. Cruel thumbs parted her sphincter. A cock's bulbous head forced a brutal entry and slithered to the depths of her rectum.

Another sailor, a bearded fellow with a scar from chin to brow, crouched and rammed up into Raven's coynte. Grinning, he took a fistful of the soft flesh of Raven's hip in one hairy hand, her uplifted calf in the other, and humped furiously.

Raven concentrated on her pleasure. If she could just manage a strong enough climax, perhaps her deadly song . . .

Two figures were in the rigging above her. The cabin boy perched on a spar, swung himself backwards to dangle by his knees, and took the toes of Raven's uplifted foot into his mouth.

Raven welcomed every new sensation. Each one lifted her lust higher and closer to her goal, but the carpenter, now naked, scurried down the mast she was bound to, held on with the two remaining fingers of his maimed left hand, squeezed the hinges of her jaw with the fingers of his right, and thrust his cock into her mouth.

She was gagged! Perhaps if she worked her mouth hard and brought the man off quickly, her note would be ready to burst forth when he withdrew. She sucked and lapped, twisting her head from side to side, nodding, desperate to bring him his climax as fast as she could.

The cock in her arse squirted greasy warmth and withdrew to be replaced by another. Sailors crowded round, groping into the huddled mass. Fingers pinched her nipples. Sweaty hands pawed her buttocks. The bearded man came deep in her vagina and was replaced by the one-legged cook's cock before the first dribble of semen had time to run from her coynte.

The cabin boy reversed his position, now hanging by one hand. His free hand pressed the sole of Raven's foot against his thin young cock as he humped, sliding in the saliva that his mouth had left.

Raven concentrated on the carpenter but he was no longer a young man. Though he chortled and drooled, there was no sign that he was nearing his spending.

Damn! She'd found that her voice had a second power, the ability to inspire crazed lust, but it still had not freed her. It was hard enough for her to wring pleasure from this unschooled crude mob of repulsive men, but now anger boiled up inside her, driving out her lust. Raven felt her face flush and a pressure in her chest. Had she been free to speak, she would have cursed these filthy brutes with such a curse as to blast their hairy ears from their ugly heads.

Rage throbbed through her, to her throat, and was blocked there, forced back by the carpenter's thrusting flesh. It mounted. Her throat thrummed with it. Blood lust vibrated from her diaphragm.

The man who was buggering her turned his head and shouted, 'Leave my arse alone, you sodding fat git!' He whirled and gave the man behind him a great clout. At the back of the mob, steel hissed. A man gurgled his life through the ragged rent in his throat. The carpenter reached over to the cabin boy and tugged at him, screaming, 'Leave her foot, damn you. It's mine, once I've done with her mouth.'

The boy fell, bowling the cook over. Someone kicked him. He bit an ankle, but not the one that belonged to the foot that had struck his ear. The second mate clawed the bosun's face.

Within moments, Raven was alone. Even the carpenter had been yanked down from his perch.

Raven's song of rage burst from her throat. The crew paused for a heartbeat, listening to every tortured note. Knives were drawn. Clubs swung. Fists flew. Men died.

The Captain, recovering, staggered to his feet. When he saw the melee, and heard Raven's song, he realised what was happening.

'It's her!' he shouted. 'She's a sea-witch, a siren. She's driving you all mad with her song. Kill her!'

He found his cutlass and charged at Raven, stumbling over the bodies that littered the deck. Raven, terrified, found yet another voice. Her song of rage curdled into one of the direst dread.

Terror poured from her throat.

The Captain fought against his fear but Raven's voice was too strong. He, along with those of his crew who still lived, rushed for the side of the ship and threw themselves over into the endless ocean.

One man, just one, the carpenter, who was deaf in one ear, had the presence of mind to slash through the line that secured the dory they towed. Once in the water, he scrambled into the small boat and paddled away as fast as his arms could drive him, leaving his mates to drown.

Raven's magic voice had freed her from the Captain and his crew. She was no longer a slave. Now she was alone, bound to a creaking mast, with one leg tethered achingly high, on a drifting ship, but free.

Raven was free to die of exposure, thirst or hunger, whichever came first.

It started to rain. A squall whipped white caps onto the waves. A sail cracked as the wind billowed it. A split started in one canvas corner.

Seven

M'ree forced her way up the slope, heedless of the deep bracken that blackened and scratched her legs. There was water ahead and she thirsted. She remembered that there was a bubbling spring just beyond the next ridge, having been in these foothills before. She could recall little else.

The tiny Tiblan had forgotten Pasnar, of the steel member and brass testicles, who had been her master for the five long years since he had found her wandering mindless in these very hills. She had no clear recollection of black-eyed Raven, who Pasnar had rescued from Vixia, and who M'ree had lovingly nursed back from the erotic insanity that Vixia's Essence of Sensation had condemned her to.

There were just shadow pictures in her mind, of a beautiful but faceless woman who she had bathed inside and out with precious oils. Who she had loved.

M'ree's mouth and long prehensile tongue had stronger memories, of the savour of Raven's spending, of which she had drunk deep, and often. It was M'ree's ears, however, that retained the strongest trace of Raven. They still echoed with the gibbering twisted chord that had hurled M'ree's mind back into the chaos it had been in when Pasnar had found her.

She paid little heed to the seamless golden girdle that sheathed her from the cups that cradled her breasts without covering them, down to but a hand's breadth above the puffy cleft of her sex. She did not heed the heavy golden manacles that circled her wrists, thighs, and ankles, nor the broad metal choker about her slender throat. Perhaps everyone went so adorned. Mayhap every waist was so strictly compressed that a pair of small hands could encompass it. Perhaps every navel was visible only as a dimple in a gleaming metal coat. M'ree had no way of knowing.

The spring was where it had always been, sweet and cold. M'ree drank her fill. Thirst slaked, but still hungry, she followed the flow downhill, not just so that she would have water on hand for when she thirsted again, but because she knew that was the way she should go, even if she knew not why.

Coarse bracken gave way to the finer fronds of ferns and to flowering gorse. M'ree stooped to a bright yellow flower. Its scent was strong and strangely exciting. When she strolled on her hips swayed. Her thighs rubbed together. Her breasts were heavy. Her nipples were throbbing thorns.

Bees buzzed, lazy in the haze of noontime heat. Suddenly conscious of the grime that coated her legs, M'ree washed in the stream. It was as if she was coming home after a long absence, and wished to look her best.

One bee hovered about her head, inspecting her. M'ree felt a rush of warmth. It was good to be close to another living being, however lowly. The creature flew closer. M'ree had no fear of its sting, though this bee was larger and brighter than – than other bees? Had she once seen lesser bees, and thought them undersized?

The insect danced before her eyes. She followed its movements. Of course – it was talking to her. M'ree spoke the language of the bees. She understood it well. Was that not as it should be?

The bee told her to – no, begged – her to follow it. M'ree had no place to go, so she did. It led her over a rise to pulse bushes, heavy with glossy black fruit and surrounded by patches of the low-growing aromatic yellow blossoms.

She ate her fill and thanked the bee with flutterings of her fingers. A second bee joined the first. And a third. Their dance wove intricate patterns in the air, a mobile design that told her she should rest, that she was safe, that they would guard and comfort her, and that they loved her with a devotion beyond any human had ever felt. They called her 'Queen'.

M'ree stretched herself on a grassy bank. A dozen bees hovered over her, then a score, and a hundred. Soon the air was thick with their humming. A bold one settled on her left breast. Its wings fluttered, caressing her nipple with a tickling touch that was almost too gentle for her to feel.

She peered at it, so close to her face that she could discern each hair-thin leg, and even the individual bristles on its segmented body. It danced a request that she recognised but could not recall the precise meaning of. M'ree's fingers gave assent. She was sure the creature could mean her no harm.

It turned its back on the dark brown spire of her nipple. It wriggled its abdomen. Its stinger, a black needle, slowly extruded. It was tipped with a drop of clear yellow fluid. Still M'ree felt no fear. Rather, she felt a strange quivering excitement. She had lain thus before, though she knew not when. In another life, she had seen these giant bees extend their stingers, and it had been a promise, not a threat.

The spine stabbed her nipple. The bee's abdominal sac pulsed, pumping venom into her tenderest flesh. No, not venom. There was no pain. The fluid was no poison. It was liquid heat, delicious as its warmth coursed through the pale blue veins that marbled her breast, delightful as it seeped tingling heat into the roots of her nipple.

Her insectile lover flourished its wings and took flight, to be replaced by a second. Yet another landed on M'ree's right breast, stinger already extended. A third and a fourth alit, and then the whole swarm descended, covering her limbs, her face, her neck, and every part of her skin that was not sealed in gold.

A thousand stingers pierced her. M'ree lay very still though her body writhed inside its skin, delirious with yellow ecstasy. They stung her toes, and her calves; her thighs, and the lips of her sex. One bee, the largest of them all, settled on the protruding pink pea of her clitoris. When its stinger stabbed, and the thrilling venom pulsed into her, M'ree climaxed.

She reached her juddering joy ten more times before she slept. She lay there, under the afternoon sun, covered from head to toe by a soothing, droning, loving, crawling brown and yellow blanket.

M'ree, human Queen of the magic bees, from whom Queen Vixia had stolen her aphrodisiac honey, had finally come home.

Eight

Brod wrapped his cloak tighter around his massive body. He pulled his hood forward, to shield his face. His iron-wood staff pounded three times on the oaken door, and then twice more. There was a rattling of chains. The door creaked open to the width of a hand. Chan-sahl, the innkeeper, squinted through the crack.

'Who? Oh – it's Brod, is it not?'

'You know me?'

'Who else, the size of a mountain, would come to my door at noon, when all know I open at dusk? Come on in, before Her Proctors note you, and you bring disaster to us all.'

Chan-sahl served Brod a par-boiled haunch of wild hog and a pewter pitcher of sour green wine. 'There's no use in chasing after the girl,' he said. 'She'll be half way to the market by now.'

'Market?'

'The slave-pens on the Great Island of Lothia. She was a pretty thing from what I saw of her. The *Blue Swan*'ll be clear across the Sea of Lur by now, and on the Ocean, heading for the Ormitian Straights, there to meet up with a filthy slaver or two. The scum are as thick on the Ocean as beans in day-old pottage in them parts, on account of the Lesser Islands' folk being so comely and defenceless. Once the *Swan*'s hold's full of pretty boys and girls it'll be north by north west, to the Great Island. She'll trade her human cargo for furs, and back home again. It's her regular route.'

'Once the girl is in the pens, there'll be no finding her.

She'll be one in ten thousand poor young souls, and then sold off to some petty western potentate as a body slave. They're a cruel lot, those western princes. The girl'll be 'most as hard used as she would be by our own cursed Vixia. If she lasts three years with 'em, she'll have aged fifty and then be good for nought but hound-food.'

Brod laid his flagon down carefully lest he crush it in his hand. 'That won't happen,' he said. 'I won't let it. And tell me, Innkeeper, how will she likely be treated on the *Swan*?'

'If you want the truth, not well. If she's a virgin they might take heed not to rend her maidenhead, and so lower her worth, but they'd still likely take sport with her in sundry other vicious ways. 'Tis well said, "Every woman is a triple road to Paradise, and a man must try them all, to find the surest".'

Chan-sahl scratched at the scabs on the back of his hand, no doubt recalling some of his own travels along those three narrow roads. 'It's an easy sail this time of the year. There'll not be much to keep 'em busy, 'cept for tormenting prisoners, and she'll likely be the only captive on board until they get to the Straights. There's no doubt her mouth and arse'll both be kept busy, four watches out of five. Still, at least she'll neither hunger nor thirst. They'll likely force-feed her man-milk till she fattens on it. It's a healthy diet, or so I tell my wife.'

Brod forced his fist to unclench. 'Could a fast ship catch her before the Straight?'

'Never. Not before. But there might be a way afterwards.'

'How?'

Chan-sahl spilled wine on the table and dipped a stained fingertip in it. 'The *Blue Swan*'s heading west, like this.' He drew a straight horizontal line. 'She's just a few days away from the Straights by now. Likely she'll take a day or two for trading. Then she'll head north by north west, like this.' He drew another line, almost vertical to the first. 'A fast ship, travelling this way,' he drew a third line, making a triangle, 'might, just might, if the wind is fair, reach her before she gets to the Great Island.'

'Then I must have a ship.'

'That'll be hard and cost you dear.'

Brod dropped a clinking sack onto the table. 'I'll pay, with Vixia's gold.'

Chan-sahl licked his cracked lips. 'I'll do what I can. Leave the gold with me and return at dawn.'

'I thought to stay with you.'

'I've nowhere to hide you. If you were found here, it'd be my life, and that of my family, if we were lucky. Go, Brod, and trust me.'

Brod stood towering. 'Of course I trust you, Innkeeper. No man would be so foolish as to cross me for a few coins.'

Vixia laid aside her iron ring of seeing. 'The trap is set, and ready to spring,' she gloated. 'Come, Laylanda, let us take salt and vinegar, that we might sooth those three clumsy serving girls whose breasts we had flayed this morning.

Brod skulked as well as one who stands two heads taller than the tallest of those around him may skulk. He was just about to congratulate himself on his crafty invisibility when he heard the clattering of iron-shod feet on the cobbles. The throng in the marketplace dispersed like dust before a new broom. Vixia's guards poured into the Square from two sides, and then three. Brod's first instinct was to fight. He'd defeated a score of Vixia's men, alone, before. If one score why not ten?

Reason won. Even if he slew the entire force, his identity would be revealed. Vixia herself would come seeking him, and Her he could not prevail over. Who then, would set sail to rescue his sweet Raven? Who then, would lead the rebels to Vixia's ultimate downfall?

He ducked into an alley. It was a dead end. He leaped, caught an overhang, scrambled up onto a flat wooden roof, ran and leaped again, from rooftop to rooftop. Six alleys away from the Square he came to a broad avenue and was forced to drop back to the cobbled ground.

Which way?

A husky contralto called from across the avenue, answering his unvoiced question, 'This way!'

Brod had never suffered from trusting women. Even those who had proclaimed themselves his enemies had somehow always become his allies, eventually. Women confuse lust with love, and Brod was well-skilled in inspiring lust.

He strode across the way and followed the cloaked form through an open door. She led him along a corridor, out the other side of the building, through an unweeded vegetable garden, across the narrow bridge that straddled what had once been a stream and was now a sewer, through three more twisted alleys, to a featureless towering stone wall.

The mysterious woman paused in a doorway. 'This is Holy ground,' she said. 'You must leave your sandals.'

Brod kicked them off. He had no need of them, anyway. The skin on his feet was thicker and harder than their leather.

'No unrestrained male may enter the Sacred Temple of Sloona,' the woman told him. 'Nor may the eyes of any man behold the Holy secrets within. Don't be afraid. We mean you no harm. The Goddess welcomes you, Brod, Earth Heir. She has told us of your quest, and of your need to remain concealed until the morrow.'

She took a strip of black silk from under her robe. Brod, grinning, stooped so that she could cover his eyes.

'I must also bind you,' she said.

Brod felt a similar strip of silk wrap his thick wrists. He didn't laugh, even though it would no more restrict him than a single hair plucked from a maiden's head could tether a bull mastodon in 'must'. He knew that in matters of religion, form is of more import than substance.

'Now that you are helpless, I must lead you.' A tiny hand wrapped one of Brod's fingers and tugged. He followed.

Impah, a novitiate whose duties were mainly confined to the Temple's laundry, heard a deep voice muttering curses at uneven flagstones.

A man! There was a man within the Temple of Sloona,

where no man may tread except he be bound and helpless, his eyes covered, and he be brought in to serve the Goddess in certain arcane erotic rites.

Impah had entered the Temple's service six moons before, eager to serve Sloona in her Aspect as The Slave. She had been avid to be used. Visions of bone-wracking, sinew-straining bondage had heated her fervid imagination. Her body had ached with perverse desire. The need to be abused had been a seething tide in her blood.

True, at her Initiation she had been chained, ritually deflowered, and lightly whipped on her buttocks. Since then, to her deep regret, her only degradation had been that of endless toil, washing the robes of the Priestesses, the other initiates, and of the dozen painted eunuchs who served as guards and gardeners.

She was impatient for more. Such was her frustration that even the sound of a whole man's voice dampened her sex. No more able to resist the temptation than a rabbit can flee a cobra's stare, Impah padded silently, following the voice through dim corridors and into the domed vastness of the Sixth Chamber, known to disrespectful giggling novitiates as 'The Milking Shed'.

There she concealed herself in a shadowed niche and watched.

The nine Priestesses shed their robes. Beneath, they were properly clad as befitted each one's role of service to Sloona. Three wore long gauzy skirts, and nothing else. They were the ones who served Sloona-the-Mate. By their bodies they might have been sisters, for Sloona, in her aspect of companion and playmate, is ample-breasted, narrow-waisted, and voluptuously hipped. Her belly is a billowing wave, indented by a navel that can hold a cup of wine without spilling a drop. Her mound is downy, but not so thickly coated that the ridge of her clitoris and the thick pulpy lips of her cleft do not protrude.

Those who were dedicated to Sloona-the-Mistress were taller, slim of hip and waist, but with blossoming breasts that trembled tightly at each step they took. Their thighs were muscular columns, vibrant with coiled strength. Their feet were narrow, and high arched.

They were clad in high-heeled boots that stretched almost to their naked hairless groins, tight-fitting gloves that were shoulder-length, and broad leather chokers, adorned with sharp spikes of polished copper.

The third trio, those Holy Slaves whose ranks Impah yearned to join, were allowed no raiment at all. There small, svelte, almost bosomless bodies were naked but for the cords that constrained them, cruelly criss-crossing tender white skin and grooving viciously into the soft flesh of arms, waists, and thighs.

A Priestess of Sloona the Mistress tugged loose the bows that bound the three Slaves' wrists behind them and set them to the lighting of flambeaux and candles. Soon there was a circle of flickering light, centred on two stone phalluses, each half as tall again as a tall man.

Two of the Mates were straining up to whisper into the ears of a blindfolded man. Or was he but a man? Impah had never seen the like. Surely he could not be a mere mortal. He towered, almost as high as the twin stone pillars he stood between.

A Mate took the cloak from his shoulders. Impah gasped. Her knees trembled. Something inside her belly melted.

He was beautiful! The muscles on his body were like mobile slabs and scrolls of bronze that had been sculpted by some master artisan and cunningly fitted together to depict an Ideal of Manhood.

A diminutive Slave knelt before this demi-god, though she had no need to stoop. Standing, her head came but a scant way above his tapered waist. With reverent hands, the Slave loosened the man's loincloth.

Impah clutched at her own breasts, awash with a flood of hot desire. The man's scrap of linen was tossed aside. It revealed a manhood so magnificent that a voice in Impah's brain screamed, 'Impale me!' Her mouth flooded with saliva. Her lips slackened, so that she had to wipe the drool of lust from her sharp little chin.

The man's phallus was not erect. Neither was it flaccid. It lolled, self-supported, at a downward angle. Even so, it was as thick and as long as Impah's forearm, with a foreskin-shrouded head that was the size of her fist.

'Engorge!' her mind begged it. 'Show me your full magnificence!'

Two of the Mistresses took the man's wrists. They guided his arms, for they could never have forced those mighty limbs, until he was stretching to both sides. His tree-limb wrists were wrapped in soft leather, and then manacled. Chains from his bonds were stretched to the pillars, and there securely fastened.

Any mortal man would have been held helpless, but Impah was sure that if those titanic muscles had but flexed, either the chains would have snapped or the pillars would have tumbled.

The pretence of bondage was there, as when Impah and her cousins had played their Cruel-Mistress-and-Docile-Slave games, as children. In fact, none but Sloona herself could have restrained so superb a physique as this young giant possessed.

The three Slaves' wrists were rebound behind their backs. They were led to kneel before the man. A Mistress took each by the nape, and guided their faces. They were commanded to extend their tongues. As if each tongue was a brush, and the Mistresses were painters, the Slaves' mouths were steered, one to smooth over the man's slowly emerging glans, one to be smeared along the underside of a lengthy shaft, and the third to lave at a pair of testicles that dangled like two ripe oranges in a wrinkled leather sack.

Impah tucked her short skirt up to her waist, spread her thighs, and tugged gently at the already-loose lips of her sex, deliberately teasing herself. The ritual that was just commencing would not be a short one. If she could remain concealed there would be ample time to savour every delicious moment.

The man's weapon swayed, thickened, and reared up. He spread his thighs. His narrow hips twitched. Two Mistresses pulled their human instruments back before returning them to new, higher, positions. The Slave who was tonguing the man's scrotum was forced down, to kneel between the man's feet, beneath him. As his legs were now spread her target was dangling lower. Craning, and stretching her tongue to its fullest length, she could just reach high enough to tickle the curly hairs that adorned his crinkly bag.

The other two Slaves were pushed closer. One's mouth opened wide. Her lips stretched. They covered the eye of the man's cock, widened even further to engulf half of a glistening purple helmet that had the circumference of an apple. Even from her alcove, twenty paces away, Impah could hear the Slave's delighted slobbering and snorting as she spread her saliva over the throbbing dome and tongued the man's seepings into her avid mouth.

The third Slave distributed wet kisses and nibbled love-bites along the underside of the man's shaft, from root to crown and back again.

These ministrations roused the man's column yet higher, harder, and longer. The Slave who worked so eagerly on its globular head was forced to stand, for now the man's glans was higher than his navel.

The pad of Impah's thumb found the slippery pip of her desire, and tried to crush it against her pubic bone, but it slid aside, to be found, crushed, and slide again.

The Mistresses pulled two of the Slaves back, though they whimpered and writhed in their futile attempts to be granted their oral delight once more. One of the three Mates, likely the senior of the trio, tore off her flimsy skirt. Her lust was plain to see. The lips of her sex had engorged and inflamed. They hung, enpurpled, open, pulsating with woman-want. Her clit had likewise enlarged. Now it protruded from its sheath for the length of one finger-joint. Her sex had been a tight bud. Now it was a full-blown flower.

A Mistress instructed the man. His legs bent yet further, until his thighs were two sloping platforms. The Mate stepped up, clinging around his neck. Her mouth found his lips and devoured them.

One Mistress guided his mighty shaft as another's fingers

parted the Mate's sex even wider. The gloriously solid orb was fitted to the welcoming soft wet socket. Two Mistresses' hands held the man by his hips as they whispered to him coaxingly, as one might calm a boisterous stallion in preparation to its mounting a lusty mare.

The third Mistress took up a silken three-tailed whip. Impah knew the instrument well. Its lashes would sting but not cut. The skin it kissed would blossom and blush, tingle and glow, but would not bleed or be scarred.

The Mistress cracked the whip across the man's crouched buttocks. He jerked forward and up. The Mate who balanced on his thighs stumbled, but did not fall. A full half of the mighty shaft was driven up into her. She screamed an ecstatic cry of erotic delirium.

The whip cut the air once more, whistling its passage. The full length of the man's column disappeared as it thrust into yielding flesh. The Mate tossed back her head, as if to scream again, but the internal impact of that fleshy battering-ram was so strong that the air was driven from her lungs in a long gurgling gasp.

So jolted was she that she lost her footing. She clung to the thickness of the man's neck, her legs dangling. They did not hang together, but in a wide 'v', held apart by the gigantic probe that filled her.

The whip struck again, and again. The man's hips jerked at each blow. The Mate was a glove-puppet. As his cock jerked, so did she. Her body hung like a doll on a spit, twitched and quivered by the massive prong that distended not just her sex, but her entire body.

A hoarse croak signalled her climax. Her hands, locked behind the man's neck, unclasped. Her arms flopped limply beside her. She toppled backwards in a swoon, to be caught in the arms of a Slave and another Mate. They lifted her up and off the man's cock, and laid her down.

The rampant erection stood proud, stiff as ever, ready to destroy its next challenger.

Impah's insides crumpled with her first wrenching orgasm. Her inner thighs were coated with her own spending. She held the wall for a moment, until she recovered her strength, slithered her slippery thighs one against the other, and started to toy with her coynte's tender lips once more. In a moment, her lust reignited. Plucking at a rigid nipple with the fingers of one hand, and slowly fondling her sex with the other, she returned her attention to the lubricious rite.

By the ritual set forth in Chapter Twelve of the Book of Sloona, the next impalement should have been the sodomising of a Slave. That was clearly impossible. The girth of the man's weapon looked to be half that of the Slave's body. Sloona is the Goddess of Love, in its three Holy aspects. She demands physical sacrifices on the part of Her Mate-Priestesses, if it be for the pleasure of their men.

She asks Her Mistress-Priestesses to delight in the infliction of tantalising discomforts, if they be erotic in nature. She requires of Her Slave-Priestesses that they endure certain forms of torment, mainly in the forms of abject grovelling service, strict and severe bondage, and zealous, unflinching prostration before the twin symbols of Domination, the gentle rod and the soft lash.

She does not charge Her Holy Priestesses to endure scarring, maiming, or death. All that it is possible to give, in Her Erotic Service, short of these, she imposes.

A Mistress consulted with a Mate. They nodded agreement. A trembling Slave was set before the man. Impah too, would have quivered, in that plight. She was sure that one thrust of that mighty engine into a kitten-hipped Slave's fragile rectum would have riven her.

They bent the Slave over, spread-legged, until her hair brushed the ground between her feet. They bound her wrists to her ankles. She was admonished not to let her knees bend. A second Slave was sent for a pitcher of aromatic oil.

Lavish quantities were poured over the cheeks of the Slave's uplifted arse. Oil trickled through her crease, saturated the backwards-pouting lips of her swollen sex, and ran down the backs of her legs. The man's cock was similarly anointed.

Impah's fingers froze on her clit and in her coynte. Surely they didn't mean to . . . ?

A Mate measured the distance that separated the Slave's cheeks from the man's pubic muscle. A Mistress adjusted the Slave's position. Two Mistresses braced her. The first took the man's mighty cock in both of her hands, gripping it just beneath the bulge of its head. She forced it lower. It tapped the small of the Slave's back. She shuddered in expectation. The Mistress signalled for the Slave to be moved further away by a finger's length.

She forced the bulb down between the Slave's cheeks. The two other Slaves were commanded to spread their Sister's trembling buttocks wide for her, fully exposing the wrinkled pink slot of her delicate anus.

As she was a Slave, Tried and Accepted, her arse was no virgin. She would have passed through her Second and Third Deflorations, and have partaken in numerous rituals that had required various Holy Objects to be introduced into her rectum. She would have been taught the Five Stages of Anal Welcoming, the relaxing ritual that dissolves the tight clench of a terrified sphincter into the relaxed yielding softness of warm butter.

Nevertheless, that cock could no more enter her arse than a bull's pizzle could spear the anus of a mouse.

Despite her horror, Impah found her fingers dancing a wild saraband, stroking and thrusting.

The Mistress wagged the man's cock lower, sliding it over the eye of her sphincter, lower yet, between her thighs, and then urging it to thrust between them.

One slippery thrust through those slender legs' embrace, and it was dragged up again to gloss over its tiny target, and then down again.

Impah let out her breath. It was not true sodomy, as the Rite prescribed, but it was as close as it could be, without destroying the girl.

What would it feel like, to have that great oily sphere slide over one's tight pucker, threatening, but not actually penetrating? The fear would be delicious, for one small involuntary jerk of those inexorable hips would mutilate the girl beyond healing. Was that tiny rosebud tensing tightly, from the danger, and then perhaps unpursing, as the tempting pleasure grew stronger? Was the minute mouth twitching, hungry for sensation, yet afraid of the dreadful consequences of that yearning being satisfied?

And when the pillar of flesh probed lower, sliding over the sensitive inner lips of the girl's engorged vulva, stroking the tip of her protruding clitoris? What a delightful thrill that must be! Impah could conceive of no greater delight than to feel infinitely small, and vulnerable, while lovingly menaced by so titanic a power. She quivered from the mere thought, like an aspen in the path of an avalanche.

Impah's fingers slithered in the froth that they had whipped up from her own spending. She groped her own arse, parting her cheeks and rubbing the slippery ball of her thumb over her twitching sphincter, rimming it, trying desperately to evoke some small echo of the lubricious ecstasy that the Slave's anus was enjoying.

Tightly bound, in dire peril of excruciating agony, and experiencing intense erotic stimulation, the folded Slave did not last long. She collapsed as she gurgled her climactic surrender.

The man was still erect, and hard, though the Ritual called for a period of stimulation for him, in the expectation that he would have foamed his man-cream twice, at least, by this stage in the sacred Ceremony.

It was the turn of the three Mistresses. Under their direction, the two Slaves who were still able anointed the man's body with precious aromatic oils, and rubbed his skin with pumice, sensitizing it. A balm compounded of eucalyptus, mint, and myrrh was massaged into his shaft, and palmed over its head.

One Mistress teasingly threatened his scrotum with nails like talons. One knelt behind him and probed his anus with two long oily fingers. Their pads found the solid walnut of his prostate and massaged it. The third Mistress bent to his belly and took hard little nips at his skin with her tiny sharp teeth.

When enough time had passed for the Ritual to assume the man had been aroused once more, then came the prescribed enslavement of his sex, to maintain that arousal.

A leather collar was wrapped around his shaft, two finger-widths from its base. The strap was supposed to be tightened afterward, but as it barely stretched around his weapon's circumference, no further tightening was possible. A springy double-helix of smooth whalebone was coiled around the man's cock, and then a second collar, immediately behind the bulge of his glans.

Any other man's cock would have been gently but firmly stretched, able to extend, but not retreat. With this man, the device did nothing but obscenely adorn his vibrant shaft, but the Ritual demanded it, and so it was done.

It is part of the function of the Priestesses of Sloona for the Mistress to excite a man to unbearable lust, yet to deny him completion until the need alone brings forth his seed. This is achieved by the use of restraints, small pains, and subtle stimulation. The three Mistresses prickled the man's skin with the filed points of their nails and stung it with flicks of their soft whips. They bade the two remaining Mates, and the two Slaves, to clamber over his body, rubbing their open quims along his limbs and over his torso in wild abandon, smearing his body with their seepings, for lust is a contagion. The rich savory aroma of a woman in urgent erotic need and the liquid proof of her lubricity slick on his skin, are both powerful aphrodisiacs that few men may resist.

To add to the man's excitement, one Mistress took a palm of the tingling salve, and polished his glans with it rhythmically, too gently to bring his completion, but strongly enough to drive him close to it.

Perhaps that Mistress, in her glee, grew careless, for there was a loud crack, and a second, as the two collars that constricted the man's penis both burst from the pressure of his expansion. The Mistress, in worshipful awe at what the man had wrought under her ministrations, fell to her knees before him and rubbed his glans vigorously between her damp palms in much the same manner that a primitive might twirl a fire-stick.

That final avid caress, perhaps because it betrayed the Mistress's own uncontrollable passion, finally brought forth what all nine women had been striving for. The man fountained. His liquid seed splattered the kneeling Mistress's open mouth, face and body. She gulped down what she could, and scooped the spillings off her breasts into her cupped hands, to lap. Her Sisters, Mistresses, Mates, and Slaves, rushed to her, not to be denied their own share of the Sacred Spending.

Impah shuddered her own climax once more, the fifth since the ritual had commenced. It was at that moment that she realised she was in love. Her short life had been dedicated to serving, through Sloona, the abstract concept of Manhood. Here, naked before her, was that Ideal, personified. This was not *a* man, but *the* Man.

And then it was the second Mate's privilege to give pleasure to their captive, and milk him of his fertile essence once more, to the greater glory of Sloona, Goddess of Lust.

Nine

Lake panicked. He had woken lying on Mother Ocean's sandy bed. He was bound up in a weighted net. He ought to have drowned, for not even he could hold his breath indefinitely.

But he was alive, and breathing.

He was breathing water!

Fear drained. Lake had no way to understand what had happened to him, but not only had he survived, he felt better than he had ever done. It was as if he had lived his whole life with some weakening illness, and had just been cured. Now, for the first time, he knew what it felt like to be whole and well.

Except for the back of his head. There was a throbbing lump there that he dared not even think of touching.

When he had woken, the surface, far above him, had been a sheet of rippling light. By the time he gnawed through enough strands of the net to escape it, the only illumination was the weak glow of fire-coral. Once free, he found oysters and clams, ate them raw, curled himself into a ball, snuggled down in a patch of waving weed, and slept.

A sturgeon nudged him awake. Lake yawned water, stretched, and kicked himself upwards. It seemed he now had little buoyancy, even when he expelled the water from his lungs. It took more energy to swim towards the surface than he was used to using, but it mattered not. Lake had more vigour than he could burn.

Half way to the air, he was overcome by the joy of his newfound strength. He dove again, rolled, zoomed and flipped. Spying a passing porpoise, he gave chase. The beast grinned at Lake and flipped its muscular tail at him, as if deriding his temerity. Its expression turned to wide-eyed awe, however, when Lake slowly drew level with it and finally overtook the sea creature, even though it swam at its fastest.

Lake knew that his body alone could never propel him through the waters at such a rate. His strange power, that he had only ever exercised over the bodies of women and girls, was augmenting his swimming ability. Blood is salty, and liquid, like Mother Ocean, sure proof of Her Holy Maternity. It had to be salt water that he influenced, not just his own sexual parts and those of the women he laid with.

When he had commanded his own cock to rise and expand, it had been the blood he had controlled, not the flesh. When he had engorged the coynte-lips of his lovers, and pumped their pink pearls close to bursting, that too had been just another aspect of his mastery over brine.

Now he was directing the waters of Mother Ocean Herself, that they part before him, and carry him forward. Lake let his arms and legs relax. Still he surged ahead, until he willed it otherwise.

Was he, as some of his lovers had gasped in the throes of passion, the Son of Mother Ocean? If so, who could be his true Sire? Typhoon? A merman? Some spirit of a waterspout?

Malignant or benign? Benign, he decided, for he had never harmed a living soul to his knowledge, though for sure someone felt he had cause to hate Lake. Someone had clubbed him as he slept, and consigned him to the deep.

That was of no import now. The petty jealousies of mere humans held no interest. That was in a past life, before he had awoken to his true self. Now, he had a mission. Lake sped through the waters, intent on finding his destiny.

Two days passed in underwater frolic before a stirring at his groin reminded him that he still possessed human appetites. Not since his voice had changed had he gone so long without the solace of female companionship.

Lake broke the surface and looked around him. Mother

Ocean's bosom was indeed vast. North, South, East and West, all he saw was waves.

As soon as air tickled his nostrils Lake's chest contracted. Water spouted from his mouth. He breathed in, and found that air, though not as rich as water, still served him well enough. He chose a direction at random, and swam.

Father Sun was stooping towards His Love, Mother Ocean, when Lake heard a distant song. Curious, he turned towards its source. As he got nearer, he found that he was moved by the plaintive crooning. It called to him, sad and helpless, whispering of a lovely girl in dire distress who desperately needed his succour.

Could it be the song of a Siren? By legend, they called sailors to their doom, but always with promises of sweet kisses, and supple limbs. Perhaps the tales lied? Some Sirens might lure in that wise, but others might appeal to the seafarers' better natures. Lake decided to proceed but with caution. It would be bitter indeed, to find his true self, and straightaway lose his life, though any Siren or Sea Maid who tried to drown him might find the task more gristle than meat.

He saw a mast's tip, and then ragged sails that hung limp. Soon there was a dark hull, wallowing. Its prow bore a figurehead, a Swan with a maiden's proud bosom, carved as if the bird-woman was about to take flight. Flakes of blue paint clung to one pert breast, and flecked an outstretched wing.

The song was stronger now, coming from the deck above him. Lake found a dangling rope and swarmed up it.

The ship was deserted, except for one girl, cruelly bound, her head dangling on her shoulder as if she was exhausted. Her song trailed off into a mumble.

'Who are you?' Lake demanded from the scuppers, too cautious to approach.

The head lifted wearily. She was a comely lass, even bedraggled and bleary-eyed. With her hands tied above her head, her ripe pink-nippled breasts were lifted, enticingly. Her waist was slender, though distorted and folded by having one hip cocked so high. Both of her legs, the one that had been cruelly wrenched to point to the sky, and the one she stood upon, were shapely. Her sex would have been a small plump pillow, fit for any man to rest his cheek upon, had not its livid slit been so widely and invitingly parted.

'Are you real?' she asked. 'Water? For the love of all the good Gods and Goddesses, water!'

Lake, a child of Mother Ocean, could deny no one water. He found a barrel, and a ladle.

When she had drunk her fill, she pleaded, 'Release me, kind sir. Have pity.'

'Are you a Siren?' Lake asked.

She looked puzzled. 'A Siren? No. I am but a poor unfortunate traveller, betrayed by the crew of this ship, and abused by them, for their cruel libidinous pleasure.'

Lake looked around him. 'If so, where then is this vile crew? I have heard tell of ships abandoned, left to drift on Mother Ocean's breast. Always it is the foul work of Sirens, whose songs have lured the sailors to watery graves. Tell me, whatever you are, what enchantment rid this craft of her crew?'

'Do I look like a Siren?' Raven asked. 'Would a Siren suffer herself to be bound thus?'

'I know not what a Siren might look like. By the tales, they are unnaturally beautiful, and so you might well be of their alluring number. As to your being bound, on the Island the old men set traps for lobsters, baiting them with dead fish. You might be pretty bait, and this ship might well be such a trap, but I am no lobster to creep too close, unwary, and be caught and boiled for your supper.'

Raven tossed her head. 'Am I a dead fish? If I smell as such, wash me, my saviour, that I might smell sweeter.'

Lake looked at the deck between his feet. 'I did not mean . . .'

'Of course you didn't,' Raven said. 'I know I am clean, for I have hung here in these cruel bonds for two days, rained upon for all but the last short while. The blessed rain sustained me, but what I could catch in my mouth was only enough to maintain my life, not slake my thirst.'

'Two full days? How is it then, if you be not supernatural,

that your limbs are not racked with agonising cramps? Those women I have known would be screaming for mercy after but a brief moment, if tied into positions but half as unnatural as yours.'

Raven looked up at him from under her lashes, slyly. 'And, handsome stranger, have you often dallied with women who were bound into unnatural positions?'

Lake blushed, remembering the Widow Silesia and the peculiar ways she found her pleasure. But still, even the supple-limbed young widow could not have born such a vicious distortion of her limbs for so long a time.

Raven tried to look as coy as one whose two clefts are stretched wide open can look. 'I,' she began, 'I have certain skills, sea-man. Where I come from, if a girl is considered pretty, she oft-times finds herself taken as a slave, by the Queen, Vixia the Maleficent. Perhaps you have heard of Her Depraved and Insatiable Majesty?'

Lake shook his head.

'Then you are fortunate indeed. If She but laid her evil eyes on you, you would surely be taken into Her service, whether you willed it or not. Then, you, like I was, would be subjected to strict training. Your limbs would be taught to be pliable. In her service, you would find yourself bound, and left hanging in your chains or straps for days, your most intimate parts available to the debauchery of Her Court. I have been displayed thus, for as long as three full days. My body has learned to endure, by force of necessity.'

'Then,' Lake said, 'you will come to no great harm if I leave you as you are for another day, provided I give you food to eat and water to drink.'

Raven let her eyelids droop and her mouth go slack. 'Feed me and water me? Am I a beast of the field? But what of my other appetites? Even in Vixia's Court I was not denied the comfort of a man's arms.' When Lake seemed not to understand, Raven added, 'And a man's lips? His tongue? His cock?'

Lake mumbled, 'Sirens are said to be insatiable in their need for love, and shameless.'

86

'And Sirens are known to be cold-blooded. Touch my skin, and test it for warmth.'

Despite himself, Lake stroked the tautly curved underside of Raven's upraised thigh. 'You are chill,' he said.

'Of course I am, fool,' Raven snapped. 'I've been two days exposed to wind and rain.' Her voice softened. 'Your pardon, handsome one. I forgot myself, as a mere human will. Try my heat elsewhere, where I have not been chilled by the elements, if it please you. If my teeth afright you, there are other entrances where you might test the true human warmth of my body.'

As best she could, she flexed towards him, though, if the sight of her gaping naked coynte and the tugged-apart cheeks of her bottom did not move him to touch her, she doubted a mere wriggled invitation would.

Still wary, Lake held the flat of his palm before her mouth, but beyond her teeth's reach. 'Breathe on me,' he invited.

Raven took a deep breath and then exhaled, being sure to exaggerate the rise and fall of her bosom.

'Your breath is warm,' Lake allowed.

'But my skin is cold. Warm me, I beg you. If you will not release me, then press me close to your manly heat, for my body's comfort.'

Lake shuddered in his battle to overcome his sudden desire. 'You need food,' he said. 'I will seek below, and think on what I am to do with you.'

In the *Blue Swan*'s galley, as he laid a platter with hard biscuit and harder cheese, Lake heard a crooning from the deck above. It was wordless. His ears made no sense of it, but his body knew its import. Raven's song called to his manhood. His mouth watered. A chill shivered between the blades of his shoulders. Goosebumps prickled his bare buttocks. His belly felt as if it had turned to liquid.

His cock rose.

Lake was a man, as other men. When lust is strong, reason weakens. He picked up a bottle of some dark red liquid, and hurried back on deck.

'You must needs feed me, if you will not untie my hands,' Raven told him, licking her lips.

Lake laid his provisions down, broke off a morsel of cheese, and held it to Raven's mouth. Though the piece was small, she nibbled at it with her tiny sharp teeth, drawing it closer with each little bite, until her lips touched Lake's fingertips. The point of her tongue lapped out, licking off an imaginary crumb. Lake shivered.

'Some wine?' she asked.

'Wine? What is wine?'

'You know not wine? The bottle. It contains a potion that will strengthen me and bring me warmth. I would drink, if you would be so kind.'

Lake held the bottle to her mouth. She deliberately let some spill, so that she might have reason to display her tongue once more, licking red dribbles from her lower lip and chin. Raven was rewarded by the sight of Lake's Adam's apple bobbing as he swallowed back his own lust.

'That was good,' Raven sighed. 'Try some. There is ample for two.'

Lake had no fear of any liquid, no matter that it was the colour of fresh-spilled blood. He drank, and found that it tasted strangely, almost as rotting fruit smells, but it was warming to his stomach, and, as Raven had said, it seemed to strengthen him.

Emboldened, he broke off another piece of cheese to feed to Raven. This time, when she sucked the last traces from his fingers, he did not flinch. Her mouth was not warm, but hot. Lake was almost sure she was no Siren. He considered releasing her. His cock had other ideas. If he cut her free from her bondage, he had no doubts that he could seduce her, but while she was constrained by the cords, she was the seductress. There was a pleasure in that, to be persuaded, and to let himself slowly yield.

His heart was moved to pity Raven her discomfort. His cock, though, cared not a fig's seed for the strain on her sinews. It only knew that while she was thus bound her coynte and arse were infinitely available. It knew that the way her hips were twisted by the unnatural elevation of her leg, her vagina would be folded and constricted. Cocks are universal in their approval of tight.

'More wine?' Raven asked.

Lake gave her a drink, and took some himself. The taste was growing on him.

'It is better served warm,' Raven purred.

'Warm? There is no fire in the galley.'

'Not heated by a fire, unless you count my mouth as a cook-pot,' Raven said. 'Give me a drink, and then take yours from my lips. You will find its savour much improved, I promise you.'

Lake's mind urged caution. His cock reasoned that if Lake stood mouth-to-mouth with the girl, it would likely be pressed to her flesh. His cock's argument was the more potent. Lake tilted the bottle to Raven's mouth, removed it, and replaced it with his lips, sealing himself to her.

Warm wine flowed from between her full lips and over his thirsty tongue. Lake drank, and sucked. Raven's tongue was drawn out, between his lips, and into his mouth. There it darted and squirmed, retrieving the tiny droplets of wine that remained. When it eventually retreated, Lake's tongue followed, to similarly explore the warm spicy wetness within Raven's mouth.

Lake swayed. His cock's exposed head slid across the soft undercurve of Raven's belly, leaving a slippery trail to mark its passage.

'Lower,' she breathed into his mouth. 'I cannot guide you to my core, for I am constrained. You must do it yourself. Let your hard flesh force a passage into my softness, I beg you.'

Lake's palm cupped Raven's mound. He willed her to flow, for though his cock would have willingly pressed a dry entry, Lake was a kind man.

Raven shivered to his touch. Her eyes opened wide, for she knew that even though her lust was building, her lubrication was flowing before its natural time.

Lake had no need to steer his weapon. The first part of the way was an open funnel. His mace nudged between the lips of Raven's sex. His hips twitched, and thrust. Yes! The way was tight, and convoluted, but his rigidity was adamant. It penetrated deep into the warped channel, straightening it. The sensations, as his naked glans slithered over the oiliness of her narrow passage's walls was pure bliss.

Raven craned to nibble at Lake's ear. 'I'm tight, aren't I?' she whispered. 'I'd be tighter yet if something was worked up into my arse.'

'Something?'

'Your finger, damn you! Ram a finger into me, and swive me with a will, my Sea-god! I've had nothing in me for two days, and hunger for it! Open me to your pleasure, fore and aft. Use me, my mystic lover.'

If she hungered for penetration in both coynte and arse, Lake would willingly feed her. His finger found her rear, probed, and entered. She was right. As her rectum was distended, so was her vagina further constricted. Lake's fingertip massaged the underside of his own shaft through thin muscular elasticity. Raven panted her joy at the double penetration. Lake's free hand stroked the long curve of her raised thigh, savouring the silk-on-marble strength of it. He summoned up his powers as he slowly pumped into her heat. He commanded her nipples to engorge and elongate until they were drawn out into quivering spikes, tip-brushed by the hairs on his naked chest. He ordered her juices to flow yet more copiously, until she squelched with each thrust and dribbled her nectar over his piston and down both his thighs. He directed the blood in her veins to flow faster and to engorge her clit to its fullest, and then more, so that it enpurpled and became glossy from the tautness of its skin. As he pierced, he rotated his hips, so that the wiry curls on his pubes teased the head of her clitoris with each circular grinding motion.

Lake had possessed the ability to command a girl to her climax since the first time he had laid with one. Now, now that his powers were Ocean-enhanced, his strength over woman-flesh had multiplied ten-fold. He willed Raven to judder and spasm once, twice, thrice, before allowing himself that sweet flood of joy, and then re-engorged himself without pause or withdrawal, to pound her into three more gut-wrenching orgasms.

When Raven was limp and moaning, he snapped her bonds between his hands. She fell to the deck, writhing with the agony of returning blood. Lake bathed her face, and her body, and used his power as best he could to ease her pain.

Raven recovered. She crawled a space, and then dragged herself to her feet by the ship's rail. Gazing out over the waves, she asked, 'But where is your craft, my lover?'

'I have no craft. I swam to you.'

She turned and looked at him. 'No mortal man could swim so far. There is no land, not even on the horizon. Tell me true, my sea-stallion, what manner of being are you?'

'I came to your call,' Lake said. 'No mere mortal woman could have summoned aid from such a distance. Tell me first, what sort of a being are you?'

Raven looked puzzled. 'I – I thought myself but human, I promise you. My voice was enchanted, when the Runegravers gave me this.' She pointed to the small black bird that was tattooed on the side of her throat. 'Now, now I am not sure. The magic was to give me the power to strike death and madness with my voice. I can do that, under special circumstances, but of late I seem able to do more. The crew of this craft died when I sang rage, and then fear. Those powers were not engraved on me. I tell you truly, I know not what I am, but I suspect.'

'You suspect what?'

'There were once four Royal babes, spirited away from the grasp of wicked Queen Vixia. They would be full grown by now. Once, in another life, when I was someone else, I was set to find one, and slay him. He, I now know, was the true Heir to the Throne of Earth. By his might, he escaped me. Praise be to the Powers of Order that he did.

'Each of those babes were sworn to an Element. He was Earth. I suspect, now, that I might be Air, for is not a voice but air, influenced by Order?'

'And the other two children?' Lake asked, suddenly excited.

'They are Fire, and Water. Could it be . . .?

'That I am Water, as you are Air? Perhaps it is so. You

bear the mark of a bird, and could be the Heir of Air. I too bear a strange mark. On the sole of my foot there is a design, three wavy blue lines. I thought it but a birth mark, as that on the rear of a girl I once knew. Mayhap it was not Chance that brought us together. Should we then, seek out Earth, and also the fourth babe, Fire? Will we know them by special signs marked upon their skin?'

Raven's shoulders slumped. 'Likely, for I know that Brod, Heir of Earth, is so signed. Be that as it may, I am helpless. You, Water, may be able to swim to land, but I cannot. Even if you carried me, I would surely drown, or else die from thirst. You must leave me here, on this drifting ship. Perhaps you will find aid before the craft founders and I perish.'

'Leave you? Now that I've found you? Never. We shall sail together.'

'But the ship is adrift. Her sails are rags. What use would it be for you to stay and die with me?'

Lake looked down at the waves. 'I am just coming to know my full powers,' he said. 'How great they are, I know not, but this I know. The Ocean is my Mother. On her billowy breast, I am safe. It is time to put myself to the test. Be quiet, for now, for I must try myself to my limits.' He looked down upon the waves once more, his face betraying some great effort, though he didn't move.

Raven looked on in wonder as the ship shuddered, and then seemed to lift. She ran to the prow. There, where the waves had idly lapped, they now parted and foamed. The *Blue Swan*, driven by the power of Lake, Heir to the Throne of Water, surged forward.

Grinning, Lake turned to her. 'Before now, my powers have only been used to give pleasure to women. Your song, the one you sang when I was in the galley, had a like effect on me. What would happen, I wonder, if I was to use my power to arouse you, and at the same time you used your song to excited me? Would our powers of love, united in common cause, multiply?'

Raven ran her fingers down her own body, caressingly. 'Well,' she said, 'we shall have to find out, shall we not?'

Ten

M'ree woke when her living blanket took flight. She gazed up at the swarm hovering above her head in a dark cloud, buzzing an angry warning.

She blinked about and saw that she was surrounded by men, perhaps a dozen of them. Each was down on one knee, as if in worship. One, dark-eyed and handsome, lifted his head to meet her gaze. 'Welcome home, My Queen,' he said. 'I am Xonorius, leader of this patrol.'

His language was strange, but, like the dance of the bees, M'ree discovered that she understood it well.

'Will you speak to your flying subjects,' the man continued, 'and tell them that we mean you no harm? We are as loyal to Your Majesty as they are. Indeed, it was through us that You became their Queen, many years ago. Does Your Majesty not remember?'

The dam that blocked that portion of M'ree's memory broke. She recalled being stolen away from her people when but a young maid. Styxian Slavers had taken her by force and carried her to this land. She had been sold. The price had been paid in pots of yellow honey, which the Slavers seemed to have valued more than gold.

Her new owners had treated her kindly, almost reverently. It seemed they had need of a virgin. Tiblan females are eternally so, for within a day of their maidenheads being riven, they mend.

These people called themselves simply, The Bee People. They adored the colour yellow. They had no mines, but had amassed a great quantity of gold through trade.

M'ree had been given a draught that had put her into a

deep swoon. When she had woken, her body had been adorned as it was now, in a seamless golden girdle. They had explained to her that she was to be given to the bees, to be their Queen. If the bees accepted her, then she would be Queen to the Bee People, also.

They anointed her 'The Chosen One'. None but a Tiblan would have served their purpose so well. A girl who was completely innocent would die from the shocking ecstasy brought by the stings with which the bees would greet her. A girl who was not a virgin would be rejected by the bees. A Tiblan could fulfil both needs. A Tiblan girl could be well used to the joys of lust, and thus cushioned against traumatic ecstasy, and yet would still be a maiden. What the Bee People had sought, and thought they had purchased, was a 'virgin-whore'.

M'ree had tried to explain that she was young, and although she had lain with a youth it had been but the once. They had not understood. The tales they had heard of Tiblans were of a lusty people who coupled wantonly and often, from puberty. The tales, unfortunately for M'ree, were not true. The land of the Tiblans was far away. Distance does strange things to tales.

She had been given to the bees. They had accepted her. They had covered her then, in the same manner as they had just greeted her. From that moment, to the time she had found herself wandering in these hills, her memory was a blank. The supernal joy the bees had given to her had not killed her, but it had rendered her mindless.

M'ree could only suppose that in that shrouded life she had become the practised harlot that the Bee People had first taken her for.

'Will you come with us, to your human people?' Xonorius asked. 'We would celebrate Your Majesty's safe return.'

M'ree signed to her insectile subjects that she was safe and would return. They danced back their regrets at losing her, even if briefly, but they would watch over her, for they were everywhere. The bees, it seemed had no concept of a world beyond their own territory.

Xonorius helped M'ree to her feet. When she was erect beside them, M'ree found that the men were less tall than she had thought, standing but a head above her own modest height. Nor were they so uncivilised as she had judged them.

The brief skirts that the men wore wrapped around their loins were made from well-tanned soft deer-skin, intricately embroidered with bright yellow threads. Their feet were shod in boots made from the same material. Each one wore a leaf-shaped obsidian blade at his hip and carried a quiver of stone-tipped javelins over his shoulder. From the uniformity of their dress and arms she took them to be soldiers, of a sort.

They took M'ree south, upslope. The land became more rugged. Lichen-tinted outcrops of grey stone broke through the greensward. The land to left and right rose. By noon they were between vertical walls, walking into the mouth of a broad ravine.

Clumps of cut-thorn bushes appeared. The party circled the vicious plants with greater and greater frequency until there was only a narrow winding path that they were forced to travel in single file. Then the way was blocked, or so it appeared to M'ree. By that point, the ravine was just a bow-shot wide. A solid stand of trees grew from side to side. Closer, though, M'ree made two discoveries. There was a way between the crowded trunks, and it was not a forest of many trees, but just one many-trunked mighty growth. She recognised it as a naynab, which first spreads broad branches and then drops shoots from their tips, which root, and become trunks themselves. So spreading, a single naynab might cover an area larger than a city.

This giant had been cultivated, so that its northern edge formed an almost impenetrable barrier. Above, at twice the height of a tall building, the leafy branches interwove, making a living ceiling.

The ground was soft and loamy underfoot and strangely warm. When M'ree remarked on this, Xonorius told her that they walked on a thin skin, beneath which the volcano's blood boiled. For this reason, the Bee People were able to raise three crops a year, independent of the seasons.

The party came to a clearing. Briefly skirted youths and maidens ran gleefully to M'ree, laden with wreaths of the seductive yellow flowers. By the time a dozen had been hung around her neck, she was quite drunk on their musky aroma.

A quartet of sturdy matrons took M'ree into their charge. She was taken into a cave in the ravine's wall, where a hot spring bubbled. There they bathed her and groomed her, thoroughly and intimately. With the yellow flowers' scent still in her nostrils, M'ree found that their ministrations roused a strange urgency in her.

It was hard for her to control her hips when one plump woman followed her soaping of M'ree's sex with a rinsing, applied by squirting warm water from her mouth in a jet that was directed between the thumb-parted lips of M'ree's coynte. Likewise, when the same form of cleansing was applied between the cheeks of M'ree's plump little arse, she bent forward instinctively and her sphincter relaxed, welcoming the liquid invasion.

When she was clean, they dried her with soft cloths and braided yellow blossoms into her hair. The women proclaimed M'ree ready for the revels, though she was offered no clothing.

Naked but for her golden girdle and her chainless manacles, M'ree was led to a grassy terrace and sat upon a protruding naynab root that had been trained into the shape of a couch.

Xonorius asked, 'By Your permission, Your Majesty, the celebration of Your safe return is ready to begin.'

M'ree nodded. Music started – claybours for rhythm and a reedy fyrinx for melody. A whole roast eland was carried out. Platters of fruits and berries appeared. A pretty girl-child of perhaps thirteen summers presented a dish to M'ree. It bore small pieces of dripping honeycomb. M'ree took one between thumb and finger. Her simple action was greeted by an enthusiastic cheer. More dishes of honeycomb appeared and were passed from hand to eager hand.

M'ree noted that though all were eager for the sugary

treat, none took more than a single morsel. She tasted the piece she held. Not only was it sweet, but its savour was like that of the yellow flower, yet tenfold as potent. As it melted on her tongue her mouth was consumed by thirst, but not for water, nor wine. She knew that only kisses could slake that peculiarly pleasant dryness.

She was not alone. Between bites of meat and sips of some drink that M'ree had not yet been offered, every mouth in the company sought another's lips. There were biting kisses, and slow languorous ones; kisses that but pecked, and kisses that devoured. Tongues played with tongues. Lips mumbled on lips. Of all the women present, only M'ree, cause and Queen of this revel, was left unkissed.

She turned to Xonorius. 'Is my mouth the only one to be left athirst?'

'It would not be seemly for any here to offer, Your Majesty, but there is no one who would not feel honoured to taste the honey in your mouth.'

'Then kiss me, damn you!'

He bent over her. His lips brushed hers. Impatient, her mouth opened. Xonorius's tongue explored, gently and tentatively at first, but then fierce and demanding.

'Sit by me,' M'ree ordered.

He smiled. 'Willingly, My Queen, but would you bring these celebrations to a close before they are rightly begun?'

'Explain yourself.'

'You are our Queen, Your Majesty. We are ruled by you and by your actions. When you accepted the honeycomb, it gave leave for all to do the same. Were we to sit close, with the sacred sweetness in our mouths, we would kiss again. Kisses would lead to fondling. Fondling would inflame us. I would no longer be able to resist your Majesty's loveliness. I would find myself parting your glorious thighs, perhaps, and sipping the nectar of the flower that blooms there. From that, coupling would surely follow, and once your Majesty reached her peak of happiness, that would signal the revel's ending.'

M'ree brushed her fingers over the front of Xonorius's

skirt. She felt the hard throb that pulsed beneath it. 'And?' she asked. 'Would not all be likewise engaged? And if all must await my lead, why do I see lovers fondling already?'

Xonorius followed M'ree's eyes, to where a youth was suckling at a young girl's breast, his hand busy beneath her brief skirt.

Xonorius grinned. 'Young blood runs hot, Your Majesty. See them not, if it please you.'

'I am not old, Xonorius. My blood too, is hot. When, I ask you, would it be seemly for me to see the weapon that your skirt conceals, and stroke it, and perhaps . . .' She extended her long slender Tiblan tongue, let it curl, uncurl, and ripple, demonstrating its exceptional mobility. '. . . and perhaps,' she continued, 'teach my loyal subject that his Queen is a woman of rare talents.'

Xonorius swallowed. 'There – there is to be an entertainment. I would not disappoint the performers, but once it is done, if Your Majesty commands her abject subject?'

'Let the entertainment begin then,' M'ree commanded, 'and, if a Queen can pretend not to see Her subjects caressing, then so can Her Subjects be blind to Her small pleasures. Give the signal and then you may seat yourself at my feet, as is befitting. I will further instruct you once all eyes are on the performers.'

Xonorius clapped his hands. Six naked youngsters, three girls and three youths, ran to the middle of the clearing, and bowed low.

'Are they going to dance?' M'ree whispered.

'A dance of love, Your Majesty.'

M'ree sat forward. The honey had reached her veins. Any mention of love was interesting.

The claybours thumped. The fyrinx skirled. A girl with breasts that were widely separated, and each as mobile as a frantic kitten confined in a boar's bladder, cartwheeled into the open space, landed in a splits, and rolled onto her back. A youth whose cock was as long, slender, and pale as white asparagus, back-flipped to land flat, face up, a body's length to the girl's right.

They were joined by another pair, he stocky and dark,

she fair-skinned, with hair the colour of autumn leaves. The second boy knelt down, astride the first girl's head. The second girl took a similar position, over the first boy's face.

To the music's insistent beat, each jerked their hips lower. The boy's fingers found the stem of his own cock, and aimed it downwards, into the gaping mouth of the girl beneath him. The kneeling girl spread wide, and opened herself. Her coynte's lips splayed over her partner's impatiently waiting mouth.

'Lean back between my thighs!' M'ree hissed at Xonorius. She wrapped her hands around his forehead and tugged the back of his neck snug into her groin. Her hips humped her closer until her coynte's humidity was pressed hard against his nape. 'Just keep still, for now,' she ordered, grinding herself on the knob of his spine.

As one, the two kneeling lovers reached out over the bodies beneath them. The pair who were on their backs lifted their legs. Hands grasped behind raised knees, and tugged. A boy and a girl were drawn up and folded, until their weight was on their shoulders. Their legs spread wide. The two who were above leaned over. The girl took her lover's long white cock into her mouth. The boy extended his tongue, and gave his lover a long lap, from anus to clitoris, before pursing his lips on her polyp, and sucking on it in an urgent rhythm, like a thirsty baby suckling at its mother's nipple.

M'ree squeezed Xonorius's head between her thighs. He squirmed back, relishing the wet heat of her sex on the back of his neck. His fingers idly stroked her calves, sending shivers up her legs.

The third pair of youngsters joined the first two. The boy turned his back on the girl who's clit was being sucked. Its sucker sat back, making room. The third boy sat down on the girl's upended arse, pointing his cock down with his fingers as he descended. His aim was true. He sank into her pulpiness, to the hilt.

In a similar manner, the last girl lowered herself onto the bum of the curled boy. The other girl, the one who had been fellating him, held his cock upright and steady. The newcomer skewered herself onto it.

The two new riders squirmed, grinding down on their mates. The kneeling boy continued to enjoy the oral attentions of the girl he bestrode, and occupied his fingers with teasing her nipples. The girl who was being given cunnilingus from beneath leaned forward, parted the arse of the girl who was riding her oral lover, and put her mouth close to her anus. Her tongue extended. It lapped, from her friend's pucker, to that of the boy, and back.

M'ree imagined herself in each of the girls' positions. It was the one who was wriggling on her boy-love while being treated to anilingus by her girl-love who she envied the most.

Being impaled in that unnatural straining position, the head of the boy's cock must have been pressed hard against the supple back wall of the girl's vagina. At the same time, leaning forward, the girl was able to stroke her clit's head against the ridge that ran up the underside of the boy's column, and tickle it on the hairs of his scrotum. Those sensations, with the additional pleasure of having a hot wet tongue working its sinuous way into her sphincter, must have been bliss indeed!

The audience was also not unmoved. Everywhere that M'ree looked, skirts had been cast aside. Cocks and fingers were probing mouths, arses, and coyntes. Nipples were being pinched and plucked. Sharp nails were clawing at vibrantly flexing bums. Stooping girls and women gobbled voraciously at straining cocks. Couples writhed together as they shouted words of encouragement to the two triple sets of lovers who occupied the centre of the glade.

M'ree threw her thighs wide, releasing Xonorius from their soft firm grip. She grabbed his ears and yanked his head round to face her. Her hips thrust, squelching her dripping coynte onto his mouth. She was already close. His strong tongue flickered its dance on her clit. In a few moments she spilled her juices, to pour over his chin and trickle down his naked chest.

'You want entertainment?' she growled at him. 'Stand up, and I'll show you what a Tiblan woman can do.'

He jumped to his feet.

'Keep perfectly still,' his Queen ordered. She pulled his leather skirt from his loins. His cock was hard and eager, already seeping from its eye. M'ree's hands gripped his buttocks. She took careful aim. Her mouth opened to its widest. When she swooped, his cock passed between her lips without touching them. Nor did his glans feel her tongue. Straight to her throat it went, making no contact until it butted the back of her mouth, and was forced by her lunge into the constrictive, swallowing channel of her convulsing throat.

Once it was securely lodged, M'ree started to hum. Her deep trill vibrated through his solid orb. Her tongue curled back on itself, flickered along the underside of his straining stem, undulated out between her gaping lips, tickled around his swaying balls, and past them, to his anus. Its tip insinuated itself, threading the knot of his sphincter, and did not stop until a finger-joint's length was embedded in his rectum.

Xonorius stood in erotic shock. Never had he dreamt that it could be possible for a woman to perform deep fellatio on him, and at the same time engage in probing, squirmy anilingus. For a moment he was unable to move, but then M'ree's hands kneaded on his buttocks, dragging him closer, and moving him back, until he recovered his senses and did as she wished him to do – fuck her throat.

When the revel was finally over, when lovers swayed away from the glade, arm in arm, hip to hip, M'ree yawned a deep sated yawn. She lifted her head from Xonorius' belly and asked him, 'Tell me, Xonorius, our people seem content and well provided. Why is it that you need me to be your Queen?'

Stroking his own limp flesh in case there might be some life left in it, he answered, 'My Queen, without you, we cannot speak to the bees. We need their aid. Their stings are a powerful weapon. Since your predecessor died we have been helpless against the depredations of foul invaders, who steal our bees' honey, and our sacred flowers' pollen. We need you, O Queen, to unite your armies. Before this new moon grows fat, My Lady, you must lead us to bloody war.'

Eleven

At dawn, Seneschal Krotor's personal slaves were already preparing the Great Hall for the coming night's debauchery. The Hall's Grand Entrance was fifty paces wide by seventy long, though its ceiling of plain stone slabs was but one and a half times as high as a tall man above its marble floor. The disproportion was not accidental. Queen Vixia had planned it thus, when she'd had portions of the old building restructured. Those who entered were at once awed by the vastness around them, and cowed by the lowering oppression above. Their shoulders hunched. Their necks shrunk. Vixia encouraged timidity in those around her.

Krotor's slaves were decorating the Entrance's copper-sheathed walls. Two horizontal rows of iron stanchions had been hammered into each long wall. Polished wooden rails had been bolted to those strong posts. Ring bolts had been set into the floor below and into the ceiling above. Buckled straps and gleaming chains lay ready.

Krotor's senior slave, Dismus-one-tooth, manacled the wrists of the first naked young victim, a youth. Two brawny slaves lifted the boy to the ceiling. His wrists were fastened to an iron ring. Dangling thus, his buttocks were at a level with the higher rail.

Dismus lifted up the youth's right leg. A slave wrapped the boy's thigh, next to his groin, with a strap that also circled the rail. Another slave restrained the lad's ankle, in like fashion, so that his leg was firmly fastened, held rigidly straight, parallel with the floor.

The handsome youth bore that mild discomfort well

enough, but when he felt his left leg being grasped in an iron grip, and raised, a whimper escaped his lips. The two slaves forced the boy's leg higher. The tendons that ran inside their victim's thighs creaked. He swallowed a groan. One vicious strap, and then another, were tightly fastened. He slumped, half his weight taken by his upstretched arms, half pressing down on legs that now formed a perfectly straight, straining, line. His testes hung, vulnerably draped over the rail. His cock, however, despite the painful tension that wrenched his limbs, stood as hard and proud as if it were contemplating its wedding eve.

Slaves with paints and brushes stepped forward. The ridge that ran along the underside of the boy's cock was tinted red and highlighted with white. Each proud vein that decorated his shaft was limned with pale blue. Dismus pulled the boy's foreskin back. Purple dye was dripped onto his glans, staining its skin even darker than its engorgement had already tinted.

A girl was next. She was commanded to execute a handstand directly beneath the boy. Her legs were stretched out, as his were, and buckled to the lower rail, a forearm's length beneath him. When her legs were secure, and so wide-parted that the delicate petals of her sex were tugged into a gaping oval, her hands were pulled together beneath her, and chained to the floor. Like the boy, even though her body had been forced into an unnatural pose, the girl's sex exhibited sure signs of arousal. The other lips of her coynte were engorged and slack. Her inner lips glistened and throbbed. The shaft of her clitoris was thick. Its glossy pink head peeked inquisitively from within the wrinkled folds of its cowl.

A slave took a soft hairbrush. With a few deft and delicate strokes, he parted the pale fuzz on her mound along the line of her clitoral ridge. Yet another slave arranged her coynte's lips, everting them into an even greater semblance to some exotic tropical blossom. Another slave applied cosmetics, powder for pallor, and rouge to emphasise the dramatic pinks of her secret folds. Finally, a fine brush stained the very edges of the girl's coynte-lips with a vermilion so deep that it was almost black.

Then it was the turn of another girl, to dangle next to the boy, and another boy, to be upended and spread beneath that girl, and so on, until both walls were lined with naked young bodies, alternating male and female, each one distorted into the shape of a 'T', each one with his or her sex decorated, displayed, and available for whatever whimsical caress or torment a guest might be moved to inflict.

Implements were brought, and hung on the rails. There were dildos, made of rubber, wood, ivory and bronze. Some were slender, some were thick. There were short stubby cones, and impossibly long flexible wands. Some were carved in intricate designs, some had been textured, while others were smooth. Amid the array of false cocks were whips, whisks, canes and paddles.

Dismus tried a silken whisk, beating it lightly on the naked pubes of an upended diminutive albino girl from Mathrassia. The translucent skin of her pure white mound blushed pink under its powder. The boy who hung above her sobbed, 'Do me! Beat my cock!' His cry was echoed along the line. The hanging bodies writhed, thrusting out their pubes as best they could, rattling their chains and creaking their straps with their efforts. Male hips shook, flailing air with stiff erections. Female shoulders jerked, rotating vibrant breasts.

Each captive had been given a measure of mead that had been brewed from the magic honey, but a short while before.

Dismus laid the whisk aside, satisfied. As Krotor had ordered, the walls were now hung with chained lust-incarnate. The youthful victims were no longer merely fine specimens of human beauty. Now they were insanely craving embodiments of erotic desire.

The Chief of Krotor's slaves inspected the pair of wooden frames that had been set in the floor where the Grand Entrance opened up into the Great Hall. A Styxian warrior, captured in battle, dangled in each. They had been selected for the size of their cocks. One's was sheathed in an iron cage that was lined with needles. While he remained limp, his flesh was safe.

Dismus had no doubt that the lady guests would take great delight in kissing and caressing the ebony giant's muscular body. His struggle against the power of their erotic skills would be delightful to behold, but Dismus had no doubt of the eventual outcome.

R'rleeh, one of Vixia's favourites, was a Styxian like the captive. She was especially adept at stiffening reluctant flesh. With her hot breath on the prisoner's cock, with her crafty finger probing his anus, and her poisonous nipples tracing lustful lines on the skin of his thighs, he was sure to rise, will it or not.

The second chained Styxian warrior would likely attract Suisuma, R'rleeh's companion. A circular leather cushion had been fashioned, its hole an exact fit for the black-skinned one's massive member. One side of the cushion had been covered in soft velvet. From the other protruded a hundred small needles. His hips had the freedom to move, if he wished.

Plump little Suisuma would doubtless take great glee in climbing the man's massive frame and introducing his cock's head to her coynte. Then let him thrust, if he dared. One swift jerk would drive the cushion back into his groin, prickling his skin if he was gentle, lacerating it if he was rash.

And if he managed to restrain himself? Suisuma was known as 'The Python'. Her supple thighs could crush a man's skull, and had done so, often. Her internal muscles were preternaturally strong also. Once a man's cock entered her, he was hers until she released him, not that Dismus could recall Suisuma ever being so merciful as to let a man withdraw unmaimed.

Once the Styxian's column of flesh was trapped in the voracious grip of Suisuma's vagina, either her coynte would work, dragging him inexorably closer, or her thighs would wrap his hips and crush him to her. Either way, his time as a full man would be short.

In the Great Hall, the tables were already laid. Some were decorated with life-sized sculptures in spun pink sugar, in the likenesses of couples and trios, frozen in the acts of copulating, fellating, buggering, and performing cunnilingus. Other tables looked the same, but the human tableaux were real, and live, posed unmoving, and then dusted with powdered sugar.

More human playthings were chained to each of the Hall's pillars. Those had been painted with silver, gold, green and blue, transforming them also into living statues.

Elsewhere throughout the Palace, guests, both willing and unwilling, were preparing or being prepared.

The young knew, and the old pretended to believe, that before Queen Vixia had liberated the land, its populace had lived like base animals. It was fitting then, that for the Celebration of Liberation, the guests should dress themselves in the guise of beasts, and thus show their true subservience to the One who had tamed them all.

In the Queen's private chambers, Krotor adjusted the rod of a steel bit between Princess Fotis' jaws. Satisfied that even the gentlest tug on her reins would compel her to turn her head or risk dreadful pain, he turned his attention to her chains. He linked those that hung from her wrists to a ring in the collar around her pretty throat. They were short enough to hold her hands high before her, in a position akin to that a rearing pony might take, pawing air.

Fotis' slender feet had been shod to resemble hooves, in iron-tipped boots that hugged her calves, and kept her on the tips of her toes. Her plump body was criss-crossed with black leather straps. Her fair hair had been pulled high above her head, into a nodding plume. Another plume, made from matching human hair, sprouted from a leather pad at the base of her spine, giving her a frisky tail.

'There's a good pony,' he smirked, stroking the girl's flank.

Fotis whinnied softly, and stroked the floor with one hoof.

Laylanda, still chained, stepped forward, offering herself as next to be prepared. Krotor waved her back to her position against the wall. He chose a Styxian beauty, tall and round-breasted, to pair with Fotis. Where Fotis' harness was black against her white skin, he strapped the midnight-skinned Styxian into white leather, criss-crossing it between her breasts, like Fotis, and added white plumes and a snowy tail. When her bit was firmly in place, both the black girl and the blonde were buckled to the shaft of a tiny golden chariot.

Laylanda stepped forward once more, and was dismissed again. She stood, pouting, scolding herself to be patient. Surely her beloved Queen intended some special costume for her? That was why she was being denied the privilege of drawing Vixia's chariot. Of course it was.

Krotor chose a tall youth from the north. The boy's fair skin was painted a mottled green. His wrists were fastened in the same wise as the ponies'. He was commanded to squat on his heels. Green leather straps were cinched around his ankles and thighs. A short steel rod was fastened between his ankles, holding them awkwardly apart. Steel springs were attached to him, one from the ankle to the thigh of each muscular leg. A mask was fitted over his head, big-eyed and wide-mouthed. Inside the mask, cruel prongs clamped his tongue. When Krotor was done, the handsome youth had been transformed into an ugly frog, able to hop, and croak, but not to stand erect, or speak.

He'd shown signs of pride, Laylanda remembered. Now he was suitably humbled.

Another young man was strapped into a subtly-wrought frame that compelled him to walk on all fours, stiff-armed and stiff-legged. His finely-muscled rump was painted in livid blues, greens, and mauves. Once masked, he was a baboon.

Asha-al-asha, a sloe-eyed sylph whose people's strict religion commanded that they go veiled and robed at all times, was turned into a butterfly. Giant wings, ethereal yet stiff and strong, were strapped to her back. Her wrists and ankles were stretched out and fastened to the tips of the wings. Though she seemed free to flutter, her bonds compelled her to stand with her naked legs astride, her pubes thrust forward, and her bare arms raised, pulled back, and spread.

Her nude body was dusted to perfect whiteness. Krotor

painted her sulky lips, proud nipples and bald vulva carmine. Of all the young nobles who had been sent to Vixia for the celebration, she had been the shyest. Whenever her hands had been free of shackles, they had been cupped over her sex, in a vain attempt at modesty. She had sought corners to stand in, and turned her back whenever she could.

Now, her brilliantly shimmering wings would draw the attention of all who saw her. Once drawn to her, their eyes would naturally focus on those intimate parts that Asha-al-asha habitually sought to modestly conceal.

One by one, the nine noble youngsters were transformed. Two, one of each sex, became a fox and a vixen; there was a lion and a tigress. That left cinnamon-maned Laylanda.

She stepped forward, eyes carefully downcast, and knelt at Krotor's feet.

A nudge from his knee sent her sprawling.

A slave bent over her. Her leather choker and platinum chains were unfastened.

Krotor tossed a ragged black robe at Laylanda. 'Stand, and cover yourself,' he ordered.

Laylanda held the stinking garment at arm's length. 'Is this how I am to be presented at our Queen's Revels?'

Krotor turned his back. He took a clinking sack from a brass-bound chest and dropped it at Laylanda's bare feet. 'The Celebration? I have no way of knowing whether or not you will be allowed to attend. Perhaps not. I only know that Our Insatiable Mistress has commanded me to guard your precious maidenhead, so it seems unlikely you will be exposed to such a debauched company. The others?' He made a dismissive gesture with his hand. 'Their bodies will be used, for the guests' amusement. You, Lady Laylanda, are reserved for the Queen's private pleasures, for some reason. Meanwhile, do as I bid, for it is by Her command.'

Laylanda bit her lower lip. Not to lose her despised virginity? It was too cruel a fate, even for Vixia to ordain.

'Why then, Mighty Lord Krotor, am I to cover myself with this ugly patched rag?'

'Yours is but to do as ordered, never questioning, my Lady, but I am required to instruct you thus. You will cover your body, and hood your head. You will take up this bag of gold, and go forthwith to the market square. There you will meet a man. You will know him by his great size, by the power of his muscular form, and by the new blue linen that wraps his loins. Give him the sack, and tell him ...'

In his Inn, Chan-sahl lay dead, a Vixanian guard's dagger protruding from his belly.

Twelve

Two Slaves knelt to give Brod's cock lingering parting kisses before girding his loins in new blue linen.

'We've had word from the Innkeeper, Chan-sahl,' a feral-faced Mistress told Brod. 'He has found you a fine ship. He begs that you do not go to his Inn, for he is being watched. His daughter will meet you in the market square. You will know her by her black robe, patched with tan, and by your sack of gold, that you entrusted to Chan-sahl.'

Brod left the Temple through its massive front doors. The novitiate, Impah, now disguised as a boy in clothing she had stolen from the laundry and with her hair tucked up under a knitted cap, left by the same rear door that Brod had entered through the night before. She carried all that she owned in a cloth-wrapped bundle.

She was at the market square before him. Feigning interest in a display of copper pots, she saw him meet with a voluminously cloaked figure, and heard their conversation.

'Take your gold,' a young voice said. 'It is untouched. See, those are your knots still sealing it, are they not?'

'I had no doubt of your father,' the man's voice rumbled. 'What of the ship?'

The girl tucked a wisp of cinnamon hair back under her hood. 'My father has spoken with the Captain of the *Indomitable*. She is a fine craft, and loyal to the rebellion. Captain Smy knows your mission. He asks but for his expenses. Half your store of gold should suffice. Give him some token as you board and settle the account when your mission is accomplished. Hurry to the harbour. The *Indomitable* is ready to sail.'

Impah ran. She knew the way well, and Brod was a stranger, so likely did not. She was agile and small. She could dodge through a dense crowd. That some crowd would part before Brod's bulk, but still his stride would be slowed.

She reached the quay and found the *Indomitable*. Captain Smy stood at the head of the gangplank, scanning the dock for sign of his passenger.

Impah trotted up the plank and made a little bow. 'Captain Smy?'

'Yes, lad?'

'I seek the free life of a sailor, Sir. Will you take a 'prentice? A cabin boy?'

Smy grinned. 'You know the duties of a cabin boy, lad?'

'Aye, Sir,' Impah simpered.

Smy stroked Impah's cheek. 'You're soft skinned enough to be a maid, lad. Turn y'self around.'

Impah did as she was bid. She felt Smy's hand squeeze her left buttock through the coarse canvas of her breeks. She flexed back at him.

'A likely pair of cushions,' Smy said. 'Soft, but strong enough to take a lusty pounding. Are y'tight, lad?'

Without waiting for a response, he forced the flat of his hand down the back of her breeks, sought her anus with a finger, and forced an entry.

'Squeeze on that, lad.'

Impah tightened her sphincter, relaxed it, and tightened it again.

'You'll do, boy. Come aboard. See the cook and tell him I said to issue you a bowl of pig-grease and a heel of bread. Be sure y'save some of the grease. Then make yourself scarce while we set sail. Come last watch, bring your tight little arse to my cabin. I'll give you a trial. If you pass, you'll be on the *Indomitable*'s muster. Mark you,' he leered down at her, 'fail me not. I'll have no whimpering on my ship, and I expect a lively ride, y'hear? Them as don't please me walks home.'

Impah found a canvas bale to sit on, above the bustle. From there she watched Brod come aboard, pass over two fistfuls of gold from his sack, and be led to his cabin. It was a sturdy structure, built above deck, near the prow. Landlubbers seldom ventured below, at sea. Most of them found the stench too much for their delicate stomachs.

The ship cast off, was towed by rowing boats to a bowshot from shore, made sail, and wallowed out to the open sea. Spread canvas caught the offshore wind. The *Indomitable*, now in her natural element, lanced through the waves.

Impah laid flat. The bale was big enough that she was out of sight of anyone bar those in the rigging. Her plans would be ruined if some horny tar dragged her off to a corner of the hold to test the bore of her arse. Once her breeks were down her sex would be revealed. Cabin boys were taken on to serve in place of women, but men, being a contrary sex, would never accept a girl as a cabin boy.

Impah resolved, should she be discovered, to persuade the sailor to accept the service of her mouth instead of her arse. She could always plead that the Captain had reserved her bottom for his own use.

It didn't come to that. Half way through the last watch, Impah slipped down, and sought the Captain.

'Impatient for your reaming, are you, lad?' Smy asked, clutching his groin and grinning.

'Captain, Sir, it's the passenger. He came out for a breath, and saw me bending to coil a rope. He told me to come to him, Sir. What shall I do?'

'Curse him, by Sloona's drooling coynte! You'd best go to him, lad. He's paid for the use o' the ship, and I'll allow that means the use of its crew's arses, if that's his taste. Be sure to take the grease. It might ease the way, some. A curse and two poxes on him! If his cock's in size with the rest of him, you'll be no use to any normal man for a tenday at least. I doubt you'll be walking, the morrow. Off with you!'

Blushing at Smy's blasphemy but elated with the success of her ploy, Impah scurried forward to Brod's cabin. Its door was latched, but not locked. Inside, it was furnished with a bolted-down cot, and a chest. The big man lay half-curled on his side, sleeping like a babe. Impah tossed aside her cap, slipped out of her breeks and baggy shirt, and unwrapped the bandage that bound down her bosom. Seated on the chest, she massaged the life back into her breasts. Perhaps it was her own touch, or perhaps it was gazing down at the object of her desire, or mayhap it was memories of what she had watched the night before, but she soon felt her lust rising.

Impah tugged at her own nipples, drawing them out into grotesquely elongated points. Her fingers rolled. Spikes of pleasure stabbed into her distorted flesh. Her head fell back and her back arched. She pulled yet harder, and pinched. Sweet pain jagged down to her nipples' roots. Impah moaned, and then stifled her groans for fear of waking the sleeping giant. Her fingers released her nipples. She clawed down the spread-fan of her ribcage. Her hands gripped the soft flesh of her belly and squeezed, desperate to contain the need that seethed inside her.

It was all so deliciously dangerous! She was naked, alone, helpless. Her safety depended on her being able to seduce a man who did not even know she existed, and in persuading him to become her protector. Should she fail, she would be deemed a stowaway. Custom demanded that a man or a boy who committed that crime would be spread on a grating and whipped, and then required to work his passage until land was sighted. There he would be cast overboard, swimmer or no, to make his way ashore or drown.

They would not be so merciful on a girl. By custom, she too would be whipped before being thrown below to serve as a toy for the crew. No precious provisions would be wasted on her. She would weaken. The crew would soon tire of her. When she was no longer strong enough to respond to their beatings, she would be dropped into the sea as jetsam, with the other waste.

Impah had never been so thrilled in her young life. Fear did to her what it always did. Her vagina spasmed. Her juices seeped.

She left the chest to stand, spread-legged, looming over

Brod's slumbering form. She pressed her palms into her own groin, one each side of her coynte. The pressure parted her. The pouty little nether-mouth yawned. Impah's index fingers moved, creeping slowly, one to sample the wetness between her coynte's lips, the other to find the head of her clit.

Her body bowed back, pushing her pubes forward. Her sex was directly over Brod's head. She knew that, should he waken and look up, he would peer directly into her.

But he didn't stir.

Impah let one finger delve deeper, into hot oiliness. The pad of her other finger rotated on her clit's head, pressing hard. Her knees spread, lowering her core to just a hand's length above Brod's cheek.

A second and a third finger wriggled into her aching slot. The finger on her clit worked faster, and harder. Impah willed her orgasm, demanded it, ordered it. It came. It came with a gut-wrench and a flooding. Her fingers still danced. Impah had to waken Brod before dawn. If so, then this was the way she would do it. She brought to this man-god nothing but her eager body and her boiling passion. She was demonstrating the value of both. What better way to tell a man how great your lust for him was than by spraying his face with liquid proof?

Her nectar splattered Brod's face. He grunted, licked his lips, and snuggled deeper under the covers.

Sloona take him! Well, Sloona would, in Her Aspect of Slave, and in Her incarnation as Impah. If Impah's scent and her dew failed to waken the man, then she'd have to use bolder methods.

Impah pulled the covers from Brod's massive body. She sighed. Her lust, so recently slaked, stirred once more. He was magnificent! Kneeling, she put her face closer to his groin. Moonlight glimmered on the musculature of his heavy thighs. It fell on the length of his gorgeous cock like a caress.

How to proceed? Should she use her mouth, showering that wonderful flesh with lascivious wet kisses? If she did, and if her mouth could stretch wide enough to take some small portion of his huge glans between her lips, what if he woke, and jerked? One thrust of that mighty engine would surely dislocate her jaw, or at least choke her.

Impale herself? Work her coynte onto his staff? That too, would be dangerous. Impah knew that a woman's flesh could expand and stretch to take in the most incredible invader. She had seen that truth demonstrated often, in Sloona's Temple. She was willing, eager, to try the same feat, but not like this. The first time she welcomed Brod's rigid prow into her yielding flesh it would be best to be well prepared. Her way was moist enough, but how to position herself? When the Mistresses had prepared her for her ritural defloration, they had spread her legs wide and eased the rod into her a little at a time. Brod's cock had thrice the girth of that sacred silver Cock, and twice its length. She would need to adjust herself to it gently, at first.

How then?

She recalled the Slave who had been bent before Brod, and the method that the Mistresses had used to feign her buggering. That might serve!

Impah sat herself on the edge of Brod's cot, swung around with her back to him, folded herself to fit inside the curve of his body, and wriggled back. She lifted her upper thigh into the air. Her fingers groped between her thighs and further back, until they found the limp length of burning flesh. Tugging it gently, they drew it forward and laid it on the soft silk cushion of her lower thigh.

Her upper thigh closed, clamping as best it could, though the massive girth felt to her as if she was sitting astride a rail. She arranged the lips of her coynte as best she could, spreading them to fit over a small arc of Brod's vast circumference. Her thumb found her clit and pressed down. Although Brod was not erect his flesh was hard as ivory.

Impah slithered her thighs. She rocked gently, riding Brod's pole like a hobby horse. It pulsed. Brod muttered something. His cock engorged. Impah felt her upper leg beeing lifted on its expansion. Impah clamped harder and thrust back. A brawny arm flopped over her body, crushing the air from her lungs. Squeezing as tightly as she could, she pressed her bum back against Brod's belly and moved her legs together, forward and back, masturbating his titanic member between the loving clamp of her thighs.

'Who?' Brod's sleepy voice asked.

'Your Slave, my Master.' Her hands found the head of Brod's cock and pulled up on it, grinding her pubes down on its neck. 'Take your pleasure, Master,' Impah whimpered. 'I will explain later.'

Brod's fingers fumbled for her clit. His other arm lifted her and wrapped around her. He flickered his fingers over the stiff peak of her breast. He thrust between her thighs, gently at first, and then with growing urgency.

'Spend for me, Master! Give me your seed!'

Her hands wrapped his cock, adding their frantic friction to the writhing of her thighs. He grew yet longer, and harder, and thicker. Impah felt her legs spreading as he enlarged between them. She curled her body. Her face moved lower until she was a ball in his lap with her mouth a finger's length from the eye of Brod's cock. She shook her shoulders, beating on his shaft with the breast that he was not pleasuring. Another tug and she was able to lap at him on his upthrust.

'I thirst,' she moaned. 'Give me to drink, Master!'

Brod grunted a deep, 'Yes', and fountained more of his cream into Impah's avid mouth than she was able to swallow.

Thirteen

Lady Laylanda stood behind Queen Vixia in Her chariot. At first, she had been overjoyed when Krotor had told her that she was to be allowed to attend the revels. That had been before they'd made her ready.

Vixia had supervised Laylanda's preparation herself. Now it seemed impossible that Laylanda would be able to rid herself of her detested maidenhead that night whether Krotor stood guard over her virginity or not.

The Salacious One had decreed that Laylanda should not be transformed into the semblance of an animal like her fellows. Instead, she was given the likeness of one Aspect of Arachne, the Goddess of Spiders, of Weaving, and of Maricides – women who murder their husbands. Laylanda had been metamorphosed into Arachne's deadliest Aspect, that of the dreaded Black Widow.

Vixia had made her bathe in a pool of viscous black liquid. Laylanda had risen from it coated in a glossy ebon skin that dried to so faithful a fit that her natural skin had felt looser. Her hair was plastered slick on her head, almost invisible under its black sheathing. Slave girls had cleansed her face, leaving a perfect oval, then sponged the points and haloes of her nipples. A thin line had been wiped clear, running from the base of her spine, down between her buttocks, beneath her, over her virgin vulva and up to the ridge of her clitoris.

Those exposed parts had been painted dead white. When first Laylanda had been shown herself in a mirror she had quite admired the effect. She had looked, in her own way, almost as inhumanly evil and depraved as her adored Queen.

Her adornment had just begun. They kohled her eyes, drawing them up at the corners. Her eyelids were tinted in shades from black through charcoal, to pale silver. Her lips were made thin, and the red of fresh blood. Fine white lines were drawn all over her slender body in the semblance of a spider's web.

Then they brought out the devices. Invisibly thin wires held a mask secure to her head. It didn't conceal her face. It simply held imitation spider jaws that bracketed her mouth. With those jagged mandibles guarding her lips, no one would dare kiss her.

The next artifact made her shudder even before she understood its purpose. It was a device of straps, a spindle-shaped rubber spike, and two more jaws, these shaped like those of a Venus Fly-trap, with inward curving spines in the place of soft tendrils.

The spindle was oiled. Laylanda was forced to bend over, as if for a caning. The slave girls' fingers were gentle, but Laylanda's anus had never been violated before. She had looked forward to that deep caress, one day, but not before she had shed her other virginity.

She bit her lip and moaned as the rubber forced her sphincter to part, and whimpered softly as its hard bulb widened her rectum. Once it was in place her sphincter contracted around its narrow neck, holding its bulk firmly and uncomfortably lodged.

They took her shoulders and straightened her. That too, was pleasure-pain. The spindle was a solid distending lump. Bent over, it had been a discomfort that she had been adjusting to. When she was erect it seemed to grow larger and force her rectum to distort into an unnatural configuration.

They pulled the rest of the thing up between her thighs and buckled it in place over the bulge of her mound. Like the cupped hands of a preying mantis, it guarded her. A child's finger could have passed between those needle teeth. Nothing thicker could.

Vixia, grinning, demonstrated that even a finger could not penetrate that threatening cage unscathed. A thin wooden rod, poked between, barely touched Laylanda's vulva before the jaws snapped shut, gouging it viciously, cutting so deeply that a tap snapped it.

Laylanda swallowed. Any man who was so foolhardy as to let himself be tempted by her coynte would straight away be shorn of his manhood, in an incredibly agonising manner. Vixia had changed Laylanda from a delectable virgin into the embodiment of alluring depravity. At the same time, she had set a mechanical guardian over Laylanda's virginity that would be impossible to pass.

Finally, a thin glossy black collar had been fastened around Laylanda's throat, with a leash that Vixia clipped to her tightly cinched gold-mesh belt.

Laylanda was not the only spider. Her Majesty wore three more. Rings had been inserted through Her Vileness's pierced nipples. The jewelled clip that gripped her clitoral shaft, squeezing its head from its sheath, also bore a ring. Thin strands of black silk tethered live tarantulas to each golden loop.

The arachnids had been trained, or ensorcelled. One squatted over each nipple. The third crouched, gripping the skin of the Queen's pubic mound in its tiny claws. The spiders jiggled and swayed as Vixia moved, frotting the stiff black bristles that grew on their bulbous bellies against Vixia's most sensitive points, her nipples and her clit's head.

Apart from the three beasts and her glittering belt Vixia's body was naked. Her arms and legs were, however, covered. She had dipped all four limbs into the same pool of liquid midnight as had bathed Laylanda. As she had withdrawn, slave girls had dusted her hands, arms, feet and legs with powdered rubies. The same glittering dust had been pasted onto her eyelids.

Laylanda knew that Vixia would doubtless demand caresses during the revels. She prayed that it was not her tongue's service that Vixia would require. Much as she craved the taste of Vixia's honeyed coynte, the thought of out-staring a spider as she lapped Her Majesty's clit terrified her.

Krotor swept into the antechamber and bowed low before his Queen. Laylanda suppressed her giggles at the sight of his stiffly brocaded robe, swinging like a bell, exposing hairy white shins. It wouldn't be wise to show amusement at a man who would be striping her bare bottom with his rod the next morning.

'O Queen of Whores,' he started, using the latest title that Vixia had conferred on herself despite the protests of Sloona's Priestesses, 'the Revels await.'

Vixia cracked a short whip. Fotis and her dusky companion neighed, trod air with their forelimbs and strained forward. Their straps cut deeply into the soft flesh around their breasts and grooved their shoulders. The chariot creaked and rolled.

'We have various entertainments for your amusement, Your Vileness,' Krotor continued, walking backwards. 'In this cage we have my illustrious predecessor, Pasnar-of-the-iron-member. As Your Majesty decreed, he has been subjected to a variety of interesting torments over the past year. In honour of this special Celebration he has been spared the tongs and needles for a day, healed, given of the magic honey, and brought here for all to see. His prong is, as all will observe, as hard as the day Your Evilness ensorcelled it.'

Krotor poked his rod through the bars of Pasnar's cage and smote his metal cock. It rang like a gong, doubling Pasnar over in agony.

At a crook of Krotor's finger, a naked sylph pressed her bare belly against Pasnar's cage. Bellowing lust, the prisoner charged. His iron spike thrust between the bars a moment after she skipped giggling aside.

'The poor fellow!' Krotor shook his head. 'He is as lusty as ever, my Queen, but even should he be so fortunate as to find a willing coynte, he is still as incapable of reaching his climax as ever.

'And here, Salacious One, we have a collection of freaks gathered from throughout Your lands. This Elygian, purchased at great price, is blessed with a cock that dangles, as you see, to far below his knees. Unfortunately for him, he has never been capable of achieving a full erection. With your gracious leave, Greatest of All Whores, the Rune Gravers shall use their arts to rectify this. Once they are finished, instead of never being erect, his cock will be constantly so. It should make an amusing sight, Your Majesty. I estimate that once engorged, his weapon will stand as high as his head.

'We have a particularly tiny Tiblan maid, eagerly awaiting his transformation. Later this evening, if it is Your will, we will be able to watch a most fascinating coupling. May we proceed?'

Vixia waved her assent. Karina and Betohl, the brother and sister Rune Gravers, came forward with their pots of ink and magic needles.

Krotor announced, 'Next we have another interesting situation.' He turned to a plumpish female slave. 'Show your Queen your treasure.'

The woman knelt, bent backwards, and pulled the lips of her sex open wide. She had three clits, in a vertical line, each fully developed.

'She is to be mated,' Krotor said, 'with this man, who, as you see, has two fully-functional cocks. He will be able to bugger her at the same time as he fucks her, Your Majesty. Not only will this provide amusement, but both subjects are fertile. It will be most interesting to see what their offspring will be like. One sage predicts twins, a boy with three cocks and a girl with six clits, or perhaps with two coyntes, with three clits each. In due course they too will be mated, and so on, until we produce a race of people who are nothing but sexual organs.

'And next, two true hermaphrodites. Each of these pretty young things has both male and female organs. One can but envy them, Your Majesty. To fuck, and be fucked, at the same time. Ah me, that must be quite exhilarating.'

'If it is your wish to try that experience for yourself, it could be arranged,' Vixia offered, her fingers already curling as if ready to cast a spell.

'Thank you, O Debased one,' Krotor stammered. 'You need not trouble your Royal self on my account.'

After that there was a woman with breasts so large that she couldn't reach her own nipples with her fingers. A harness had been constructed for her. Its straps supported her massive mammaries straight out in front. Their weight forced her to lean backwards and walk in an obscene splay-legged waddle.

Having been shown these new exhibits, Vixia cracked her whip three times, signalling Her permission for the general revelry to commence. Musicians played. Acrobats who walked arched over backwards on their hands and feet, face up, carried trays of wine balanced upon their bare bellies.

Naked boys and girls scurried about, using tapers to ignite bronze bowls of herbs and incense. Coils of smoke wreathed up to cloud the air. The yellow smoke came from the aphrodisiac pollen, but there was also green, that bemused the senses of those who inhaled it, confusing fantasy and reality. The purple fumes were a stimulant. With it in their lungs, the celebrants could frolic until their bodies dropped from fatigue poisons. White smoke contained an essence that sharpened the senses. Sniff it, and all colours brightened, all touch excited, all appetites became voracious.

Vixia unclipped Laylanda's leash from her belt and tossed it to her. 'Amuse yourself, child. There is much to see if you are curious, and I am sure you are.'

And there was, all of it inflaming. Two courtiers who were costumed as stags unhitched Fotis and her black companion but left them in their pony harnesses. The two men rammed their rigid members into their ponies' arses, pulled their heads high by their reins and trotted them off, racing around the Great Hall.

Asha-al-asha, the modest bufferfly, was clipped to an overhead pulley and lifted up to flutter helplessly above a group who flirted and caressed among themselves with occasional gropes overhead to maul her delicate breasts or insert spirit-soaked grapes into her timid sex, command her to squeeze out the juice, and catch the drippings in their upturned laughing mouths.

There was a display by a quintette of acrobatic contortionists who taunted their audience, daring them to try the sexual positions that they demonstrated. Two more contortionists, a man and a woman, curled into separate balls and performed auto-fellatio and auto-cunnilingus. If the noises of their lip-smacking and gobbling were any measure, each was well content with self-love.

Laylanda pushed her way through a crowd of laughing women, each one costumed fantastically, to find out what amused them. Two creatures were tethered to posts. One, a goat-legged satyr, they were teasing into a frenzy by offering it their coyntes, breasts and arses, and then skipping out of reach before it could catch them. Inevitably, perhaps on purpose, one was too slow.

The cloven hoofed man-beast caught a slender matron who was masquerading as a python. He had her down on her back and straddled in less than a blink. A hairy knee parted her painted thighs. An inflamed yard skewered into her. His hips thrust. Goat-legs clamped her thighs together. A short-tailed arse lifted, and lunged. The beast's hips juddered and then blurred. The woman writhed up at him, squealing her erotic joy.

Perhaps it was the smoke, because it seemed to Laylanda that the woman changed before her eyes, her arms melting into her body, her legs uniting and becoming flexible, so that she truly became a serpent, with breasts, that coiled around the untamed son of Pan, undulating her passion as he pistoned into her.

The other beast was a centaur. Three leopard women, perhaps sisters, crouched, shared in fellating the mighty pizzle of the chained man-horse. A fourth woman, older and enough alike to be the trio's mother, pulled them aside. She knelt down under the beast and raised up her rear high enough for him to lance into her sex. The man-half neighed triumph. He beat his fists on his naked chest as he bucked, tucking his tail down and whipping at the woman's thighs with it. She soon slumped, defeated, to be replaced by one of her salacious daughters.

Laylanda ached. Her fingers pressed down on her black-coated belly, squeezing her own flesh, but she dared not touch herself where she so desperately needed touching for fear of losing her fingers.

A man in a gorilla mask turned her from behind. One hairy hand closed on her rubber-sheathed breast but when he saw the vicious cage that enclosed her aching coynte he turned aside to reach for a prancing gazelle-woman.

The noble lad from the north, the one who had been made into the likeness of a frog, squatted on a stone mushroom. One of Vixia's ladies-of-the-bedchamber was taking advantage of his splayed thighs and dangling genitals. Costumed as a racoon, she had laid herself backwards across the stone hump. She had taken the head of the lad's green-tinted cock between her lips. Her hand squeezed his testicles. He straightened his legs as best he could, fighting their springs, and then recoiled downwards, spearing his shaft into her mouth. She squeezed again and again, rhythmically, keeping him bouncing too slowly for him ever to climax but fast enough to maintain his erection.

Laylanda wandered into the Grand Entrance. She didn't know whether she sought to feast her eyes on yet more depravity or to escape such sights. Her need was a surging tide, lifting her to greater and greater levels of desire. She was drunk on lust, but there was no way for her to find relief. Surely even the Insatiable One Herself was not so tantalised. If She was, then no excess could not be forgiven Her.

Laylanda was discovering Vixia's special truth, that lust unslaked curdles to cruelty. At that moment, Laylanda would have sacrificed a thousand innocents if doing so would have granted her one tiny orgasm.

The two long walls of the Great Entrance were vertical orgies. Lords and Ladies clambered high, using the splayed young bodies that hung there. Despite the drugs that saturated the air, there were those who were not crazed. Some toyed. Two bird-women, a flamingo and a macaw, were masturbating a pair of the suspended young men. They were playing a game, bending the boys' cocks down, aiming them at the yawning coynte's of two upended girls.

Two Lords, dressed as a peacock and a lizard, were gaming on which of the Ladies would prove to be the better aim. The stakes were a pair of Tiblan slaves.

Another woman left off her languid licking at the underside of a chained lad's cock and left him humping air. Laylanda was tempted to climb him and thrust his waving member between her thighs. She did not, not because she cared a fig-seed that her action would have maimed him, but because it would have been to no avail. His cock would have been severed before it did her any good.

She took a goblet from a passing slave, drained half, and poured the rest over her own jet-sheathed belly, letting the cold liquid trickle over her clit and between her thighs. The spiced wine, rather than cooling her coynte's fire, stoked it. She shuddered with lust and staggered back into the Grand Hall.

A dog-woman with four pairs of damson-hued nipples was riding what seemed to be an automaton – a bronze man who had likely been created by one of Vixia's less-malign spells.

Hope rose in Laylanda's breast, but was dashed when she saw that although the magical toy had a tireless metal body, the eyes that burned in his bronze sockets were human. The cock that protruded from a circular flange at his loins was mere flesh. If only his staff had been as impervious as his body she might have found a lover capable of enduring the bite of her metal-toothed protector.

Lady Laylanda was inspired. She pushed through the mob, heedlessly stepping on writhing bodies, ignoring the sights, the sounds, and the smells of sex. There, at the far side, Pasnar was still rattling at the bars of his cage while Ladies of the Court teased him mercilessly. Laylanda elbowed a masturbating vixen aside, grasped the bars in both fists, thrust her caged pubes into the narrow gap, and called, 'Here, Pasnar! Take me!'

The ex-Seneschal didn't even see Laylanda's viciously fanged defender. He rushed at her, steel cock in hand, and rammed it. There was a terrible screeching as metal teeth bit metal cock, but the cock was harder. It stabbed between

Laylanda's gaping lips, found her oozy channel and pierced, ploughing through her virginal constriction as if it were but a cobweb. Laylanda screamed her joy as the wonderful hot hardness drove yet higher through her hungry flesh, impaling her to her womb. She clutched the bars for fear that the delicious weakness that flooded her would make her faint and fall. Her hips juddered, beating soft thighs against hard metal, but she ignored the bruising. Now, at last, she was finally free of that cursed obstruction to her happiness, her maidenhead. Ecstasy boiled in her veins. She was so close to her climax that just a few more moments and ...

Hands dragged her back. She spat and screamed, legs flailing, hands clawing.

'Laylanda!' Vixia's voice was soft, but it froze. 'Laylanda', Vixia repeated, 'you have chosen to lose your virginity. You have gone against my wishes. Very well, if mindless fucking is what you want, then that is what you shall have. If lust drives you, then you will be driven harder than you have dreamed. You want to be like your Queen, do you? You want to share my torment? So be it.' She turned her head. 'Bring the Rune Gravers, Betohl and Karina. I have a task for them.'

Fourteen

The widow Rafflesia pointed her finger at Darmo and Flist. 'I accuse,' she said.

Hibiscus shivered in her sister Jasmine's arms. It made no sense, but she felt guilty. If she and her sister had not contrived to be chosen by Lake that night, he might still have been alive. That final tribute to his superiority might well have poured one last bitter ladle of jealousy into the two cousins' cup, overflowing it. Now all she and the others who had loved Lake could do for him was wear the black lotus of mourning, and ensure that Darmo and Flist paid for their terrible crime.

'I accuse,' Anemone, Lake's adopted mother, said.

Jasmine followed suit, as did Hibiscus. Durcas was next. That was five. Six were needed if the vile sea-slugs were to be found guilty.

The Widow Drusinia looked about her, as if hoping another would point. As her hesitant arm lifted a horn sounded. Everyone fell silent, heads cocked. It sounded again, a long wail. The High Point lookout had spotted a slavers' ship on the horizon.

The trial was forgotten. Mothers scooped up their babes and ran for the deep forest. Children fled. Fathers and the young unwed of both sexes raced for their huts.

The Islanders would snatch what valuables they could easily carry and vanish into the trees. The slavers would burn and loot, but, Father Sun willing, leave without the human cargo they hunted.

Hibiscus and Jasmine sped home, smashed pots rather than leave them for the slavers, grabbed the family bolt of silk and the trade-goods cooking pots, and set off after their father, who had already carried away both of the iron tools.

A short dash from the edge of the forest, they stopped. Darmo and Flist barred their path. Darmo carried a canvas sack that the girls recognised as the one the Elders stored the pearl harvest in. Flist's cudgel was bloody. Human hairs clung to it, signs that the old men had not surrendered the Islanders' treasure willingly.

The girls might have dodged around and outrun the men, but they could not have evaded their killing-sticks. They allowed themselves to be herded towards the beach. There was no point in their arguing, pleading, or offering their bodies. Darmo and Flist were now murderers at least twice over. Whatever their crazy plan, it was driven by desperation. There was no reasoning with blind-and-deaf gibbering panic.

The four got to the beach just as a longboat ground its iron-wood keel into the sand. Two score cutlass-waving sea-rogues boiled over the boat's sides. The ruffians stopped and stared, dumbfounded at being greeted.

Darmo pushed Jasmine forward. 'We have slaves for you,' he shouted. 'Two fine young healthy beauties, not virgin, but prime meat, skilled in swiving. The rest have fled. We snatched the best for you.'

A sway-eyed man in grimy emerald silk pantaloons and a plumed tricorn bowed low, grinning. 'How kind, young Sirs. Is there perhaps some small service a humble sailor might render, in return?'

Darmo puffed out his flabby chest. 'These two will fetch a fine price, will they not? They are yours, my friends, in exchange for passage on your ship.'

'Passage? And where are you gentlemen bound?'

'Away from the Island. Anywhere civilised will suit us. Your next port of call?'

'It's a long haul. These two would be worth but half the journey. Would that suit you?'

Darmo took two steps back at the implied threat, dropping behind Flist. He let his club fall and put the edge of his killing-stick against the back of Flist's neck. 'Half way for two? That'd be a full voyage for one then, would it not?'

Flist froze.

The gaudy sailor said, 'You'd betray your mate? I admire that, but methinks not. I see your friend carries a sack. Have you ought else to trade?'

Flist laid the sack on the sand, opened its neck, and pulled out two palms-full of pearls. 'Would this pay my passage?'

The sailor rubbed a bristly chin. 'The sackful might, if they're first water. Bring them closer, so that I might judge their value.'

Flist and Darmo pushed the girls ahead. The ruffians gathered round, to pinch and poke at Jasmine and Hibiscus as well as to peer into Flist's canvas bag.

The slavers' leader admired a few choice pearls before dropping them back into the sack. 'Very well, young gentlemen, there's no doubt there's value enough here to pay your passage to where you're going.' He turned to his men. 'Right lads?'

There was a chorus of 'Right ye are, Cap'n Purd.'

'Then let's be off. I've no mind to dredge the churn for whey when the cream's been skimmed off and served up to us. Stow the wenches, lads, and send these two pretty gentlemen on their way.'

Hibiscus and Jasmine were swung onto burly shoulders and heaved over scuppers, into the bottom of the longboat. The gurgles and screams that they heard from the beach told them where the slavers had sent Darmo and Flist.

The row out to the slavers' ship was a nightmare. The two girls lay face-down, spluttering in noisome slop. They could neither sit up nor raise their heads, let alone essay a leap over the side. Horny heels ground down on their buttocks and backs. Grimy toes tested the smoothness of their tender skin.

The longboat lurched over the swell, lifting and slapping down. Ragged rowing rolled its passage. Mother Ocean's waves slopped over the sides, saturating the girls' silks.

'The little one has a nice arse,' a coarse voice grunted. 'I'd give a silver bit or two for the use of it, for a day.'

'You've nary a chance, Frag,' another growled. 'Them as your ugly dong buggers gets damaged. If it was me, now, I'd show the bigger one a time she'd never forget, and teach her a thing or two about the fine art of cock-sucking. Did you note the ripe lips on her? Real fine, they'd look, wrapped round my fat stump.'

'You'd reckon on teaching her owt? Don't you know these Island girls? All they do, day and night, is suck their menfolk dry. When all the balls is empty, they turns on each other for pussy-gobbling. There's none on 'em, past twelve summers, as couldn't pull you inside out with the strength of their sucking.'

'Keep dreaming,' a third voice interrupted. 'Y'ken the Cap'n's rules. These girlies be prime cargo. Content y'selves wi' the hags on deck, and wi' the poxy cabin boy. These go to market unmarked, lice and scab-free. Think of it – there'll be gold enough when we sign off *The Claw* to buy us the use of a dozen harlots apiece for a ten-day. Save y'scummy selves for fat Hildi-Gobble-Cock at the Bag o' Oats and her three randy sisters.'

A toe dug between Hibiscus' buttocks. 'Aye – you're right, but when I bend young Heth over a barrel tonight, it'll be this fine plump arse I'll be dreaming on, not his scrawny flanks.'

'And I'll think on the other while I take his mouth, by Sloona's sacred portal. He gums real good since Big-foot Ky knocked his front teeth out.'

The slavers tied alongside *The Claw* and swarmed up its boarding net. Four grabbed the girls' ankles, two apiece, and dragged them up dangling face-down, arms wrapping their heads to protect their faces. On board, Purd turned them over, one at a time, with his bare foot.

'They ain't exotics,' he said, 'but they'll do. I reckon on 'em fetchin' two gold crowns apiece, maybe three if they're kept healthy-like. The bolt o' silk goes in the aft lock-up, wi' the rest o' the loot. The pearls'll be safer in my chest. We did well enough off the last haul we give to the Queen, eh boys? Wait till Her Majesty sees these. I could be a duke 'ere I'm done.

'Sluice the wenches off, lads, and escort 'em below gentle-like. Any man as so much as bruises a tit'll feel the tickle o' me rope, y'hear? Or mayhap I'll feed him to my pet ogres.' He made a gesture towards the two squat monsters that sat swathed in bronze chains on the poop deck. 'You fancy some hot fresh man-meat?' he called to them. Both deformed beasts looked up, licking the lips of fanged mouths that were wide enough to take a haunch of venison, sideways.

Two men dropped leather buckets over the side, drew them up, and doused the trembling girls. Dripping wet, their hair hanging lank and their brief skirts clinging to their thighs, they were led down a creaking companionway and along a dim narrow passage to a stout wooden door. A muscular Styxian unbarred it and shoved them sprawling into total darkness.

Hibiscus lay on the straw-strewn wooden floor, sobbing.

'We're still alive,' Jasmine comforted her.

Something made a soft mewing sound.

Hibiscus sat up. 'What's that?'

There was a scraping, and a spark. Someone blew softly. A tiny flame flickered and then grew strong. A glossy-skinned Styxian girl with breasts like mobile black orbs held up a stub of candle. 'You speak the true tongue?'

'Of course,' Jasmine said.

'Thank H'Rath! Some of the others talk, but in tongues I do not know. My ears are as hungry for the sound of true speech as my eyes are thirsty for daylight. Even this candle is the last of our poor stock. We guard it well.'

'Others?' Hibiscus asked. 'Others talk?'

The Styxian stretched her light out sideways. It was taken by the whitest hand the Islanders had ever seen. The girl who now held the candle squinted and raised it high, as if the pale flame was harsh to her eyes. She was child-sized, but her breasts and hips were those of a fully-developed woman. Her skin was white as wave-froth, and translucent as the shells the Island people used to protect flames in the wind without dimming their brightness.

Hibiscus thought that if this tiny girl was to stand before Father Sun his rays would shine right through her. Her hair was whiter than an Elder's, though long and luxuriant.

Her eyes, when she blinked them open, had enormous inky pupils, rimmed by thin yellow irises. She trilled something and nodded.

Jasmine crawled closer, into the weak circle of light, touched her own breast, and said, 'Jasmine'. Turning to draw her sister closer, she said, 'Hibiscus'.

The Styxian said. 'H'neeth', or something like it, though the final 'th' blended into a click.

When the albino gave her name it was a whistle that Hibiscus could not imitate, for its pitch was so high it slid beyond the range of her hearing.

The tiny white one passed the candle on, to another of her own kind, whose eyes had pale green where she had yellow. Another whistle, and the candle moved again.

The next girl hesitated. She took the tallow gingerly between two fingers, as if unused to being so close to fire. Her fingernails were long, strong, and curved. Her eyes were slanted, with slit pupils. Her hair was striped in two colours, yellow and brown, and cropped close to her narrow head. When she smiled, her canines were half as long again as her other teeth, and sharply pointed. She purred something, showing a delicate sharp-tipped tongue.

Hibiscus guessed that it had been this captive whose mewing she had heard. When the cat-girl handed the light on, rolling onto one shapely hip, Hibiscus saw that she had a tail, just a slender one, about as long as her hand. It was furred and banded in the same colours as the smooth fleece on her head. A thin line that looked to be soft as velvet ran up the length of her spine to blend in with the pelt on her skull.

There were two more cat-girls, and then a trio of blonde giantesses, each as tall as a big man, but formed with exaggerated feminine contours, with fat-nippled breasts that could make pillows, waists no thicker than tree-trunks, hips wide enough to birth orcas, and dimpled buttocks broad enough that both of the midget albinos could have curled on them to sleep.

Their voices were feminine but deep and vibrant. When they spoke it was as if silver gongs conversed.

The last to display herself under the light was a black-haired golden-skinned girl from the silk lands, but darker than most, almost copper, and taller. Her body was slender and supple as an eel, virtually breastless, but with black nipples as long and thin as the thorns on a cut-bush. Both tender spikes had been drawn through golden rings that gripped their bases, close against the girl's haloes.

When she saw that Hibiscus was looking at them, she smiled and drew soft fingers along one's springy length, as if very proud of its abnormal growth.

Whether she could or not, she made no attempt at speech.

The candle returned to the Styxian, H'neeth, who snuffed it. 'There is a pile of straw-stuffed palliasses against the far wall,' she said. 'Help yourselves. You'll soon get used to groping around in the dark. The white-skinned ones can see, even in this darkness, so if you can make signs to them they might understand.

'They feed us twice a day – salt pork and boiled greens – with fruits, sometimes. There is fresh water for drinking in the corner. Take care, the barrel next to it is sea water for our ablutions. We are well taken care of, being valuable live-stock.'

'Where are they taking us?' Jasmine asked.

'To market. I'd guess the slave-pens on the Great Island of Lothia. We'll fetch the best prices there.'

'As slaves?'

'It might not be so bad. I've heard the Grand Chan of Xta buys there. It's said he keeps a dozen wives and a hundred concubines, apart from his many body-slaves. The Chan is an old man. His harem is renowned for its comforts. I could stand one night a year in his bed, if left to lead a life of pampered ease the rest of the time.'

'Even pampered, you'd still not be free,' Jasmine said. 'And what of your womanly needs?'

'I'd manage. I like men well enough, but being confined in the company of so many lush female beauties would have its compensations.'

'You mean the finger-and-tongue game,' Hibiscus guessed.

'Is that what you Island girls call it? It's as good a name as any. My people call it "eating persimmons", or "fighting with pomegranate pips".'

'I understand "eating persimmons",' Jasmine said, 'but "fighting with pomegranate pips"?'

Hibiscus felt a hand on her knee, and then higher, smoothing up her thigh. Much closer, the Styxian beauty husked, 'Perhaps I could teach you? Do you girls play – what was it? The "finger-and-tongue" game?' Deft fingers loosened the knot of Hibiscus' skirt.

'Er, sometimes,' Hibiscus allowed. She could feel H'neeth's body-heat radiating onto the skin of her breasts and her humid breath in the crook of her neck.

'Would you like to play, with me?' The ebony-skinned one was much closer now. Hibiscus felt that if she so much as twitched, their bodies would touch.

'We are not alone,' she hedged, suddenly nervous. She had played the game, of course, and enjoyed it, but only with her sister so far. Grief at losing Lake had driven such thoughts from her mind, or else she and her sister would likely have slept with the Widow Rafflesia, as had been their plan for the night after they had lain with Lake. She had anticipated that with a mixture of lust and fear. This offer was even more frightening than Rafflesia's. She had known the Widow all her life. The black girl was a total stranger. That made it more scary, and yet more exciting. Hibiscus wondered what a black girl's coynte would taste like. Would the flavour be spicier, saltier, or even bitter, perhaps?

'No – you are right. We are not alone,' the Styxian said. 'I doubt we will be, ever again. Do you fear giving offence to the others? No need, little one. There is nothing for us to do down here, in close captivity, in the utter dark. I have even been denied the solace of conversation. How do you think we slaves-to-be have amused ourselves, through the long days and nights?'

Hibiscus sucked in her tummy. H'neeth's hands were

busy there, solving the riddle of the knot that tied Hibiscus' last garment. It seemed only mannerly to give those fingers room to work. 'You mean ...?' she asked, knowing the answer.

'Of course. We are all of us comely, are we not, each in her own way? We comfort each other as best we may. The cat-girls were reluctant at first, but soon learned to join in our sport. I promise you, Hibiscus, that every female here, of whatever breed, is eager to sport with you and your sister. A new playmate livens any game. We but await some sign that you are willing. Are you?'

Hibiscus' triangle of silk fell loose from her loins. She lifted her bum from the deck to allow the black girl to tug it away.

Behind Hibiscus, Jasmine said, 'I'm willing, for one. More than willing. Once we get to our destination we may well be starved for a loving touch. Let us take what joy we may, while we may, in each other. What say you, sister?'

Hibiscus parted her lips to speak. Before she made a sound, a thick hot tongue filled her mouth. She found herself being laid back flat on the deck, her head cushioned by her sister's silky thigh. Her cheek felt no damp silk. Jasmine must have disrobed in the dark, which was sensible. It wouldn't do to catch a chill.

'Mmmmm,' the Styxian moaned between Hibiscus's lips. 'Your mouth is sweet, Island girl. Is is true that your people dine on flowers?'

'Only on the orchids between each others' thighs,' Jasmine interrupted. 'Try my sister's nectar for flavour, if you will. I warrant it's as sweet as any honey you have tasted. But H'neeth, before your mouth is too busy, explain to us please, the "battle of pomegranates".'

'"Fighting pomegranate pips",' the black corrected. Come join our embrace, Jasmine, and I will show you.'

Jasmine slithered over. Hibiscus felt her sister's cool skin slide over her body. When the three women were cuddled together, H'neeth greeted Jasmine with a long deep kiss and then eased down between the two sisters, licking at one then the other as she descended, until her face was pressed between two soft bellies.

'Let me just . . .' she said, 'ah yes! Feel where I touch, Jasmine? Is not that little bud that I feel creeping from under its hood much like the pip of a pomegranate? Is it not soft outside and yet hard within? Is it not sweet and juicy? Does it not slip in my fingers' grip? Now I must find your sister's sweet pip, like so. Move closer, my loves. Belly to belly, if you please. Mound to mound. Raise your thighs, if you will. My fingers need room to play. Good. Now, if I take two slippery pips, thus, and bring them together, like so . . . Now I have them both between my thumb and finger. I pinch, gently. I slide one on the other. I – you gasp? Is it so good, then? And if I am careful, I can get the tip of my tongue to them both, like so. Mmmmm.'

Her tongue flickered as she hummed.

Hibiscus crushed her sister in her arms, raining frantic kisses over her face and neck. 'More,' she squealed. 'Ah – divine! I love your pomegranate game, ebony beauty. And – oh yes! I feel your fingers, my dusky love, parting me. Yes, stab me, for Mother Ocean's sake. Do it . . . Oh? How many hands have you?'

Delicate fingers turned her face sideways. A long pointed tongue stabbed her mouth. She returned the kiss, her tongue exploring a musky-flavoured cavern of flesh with incredibly sharp teeth.

Hibiscus' hand found a pendant breast. She let her fingers wander to its nipple, and flicker there. Her play was rewarded by a deep purr. How sweet that melodious vibration would be, were it focused on the stamen of her sex! Her clitoris would be the tremulous reed in a flute of love. she resolved to try that particular pleasure just as soon as she might.

Teeth found the lobe of Hibiscus' ear, and nibbled. Her free hand was taken in someone else's and drawn across a flat chest, to a springy spike. There was hot breath on her bum. Two tongues, at least, slithered across her back. Sharp nails raked gently across the arch of her ribs.

A wet mouth sucked and nibbled at the sensitive skin behind her left knee. Palms parted her buttocks. Something hot and squirmy probed her sphincter.

Hibiscus felt herself and Jasmine being drawn apart by the press of bodies, except for at their cores, where H'neeth's busy fingers still worked their pomegranate-pip magic.

Hibiscus was rolled onto her back, with Jasmine following to sprawl at an acute angle across her thighs. Large soft palms stroked her cheek. A billowy mass of satin flesh smoothed across her face. The nipple that nudged her lips was half the size of her own fist. Feeling as if she had been transported back to her own suckling childhood, Hibiscus opened wide and drew the resilient knot into her mouth.

Jasmine was jerking at her now, squirming her clit in the Styxian's grasp. Hibiscus heard her sister give a deep grunt. Scalding wetness sprayed over Hibiscus' nether lips. The knowledge that her sister had reached her joy, coupled with the delightful sensation of H'neeth's avid tongue lapping every last drop of Jasmine's spending from the lips of her coynte tipped Hibiscus over the edge. Her belly convulsed. Her vagina knotted. She gave a choking little cry as her own juices gushed.

The Styxian gobbled the blended nectars.

Hibiscus let herself sigh and relax, still nibbling on a giantess' teat, when two fresh tongues slithered the creases of her groin. The giantess pulled away. Her nipple was replaced by two more tongues, one squirming into each corner of Hibiscus' mouth and probing as if they planned to meet each other.

Oh well, if she was to be allowed no rest! Hibiscus rolled over and knelt up. The tight curls that her groping fingers found felt as if they were the Styxian's. Hibiscus crawled over, pushed the black girl onto her back, and slavered down an ebony belly with the flat of her tongue. She'd wondered about the flavour of a Styxian coynte. Now seemed the ideal time to satisfy her curiosity.

Even as her probing tongue found the answer to her question, she was already pondering how different a catwoman might taste, or a diminutive albino?

Two fathoms above her head, a sailor called out that he had spotted a drifting dinghy.

'Let it drift,' Captain Purd ordered. 'It ain't worth the towing.'

'Nay Cap'n,' a bearded man said, 'I recognise the warts on that ugly old face. It's an old shipmate o' mine, off the *Blue Swan*. Best haul him aboard, Cap'n. It'd be as well to know what sunk that craft. If some sea-rover's turned his coat and is attacking slavers, we might be next. Anyhow, Half-hand Droodge ain't a bad carpenter. We's got us a cracked spar or two could do wi' splicin'.'

Fifteen

They bore Laylanda to another chamber, where four wooden pillars, each half the height of a man, formed the corners of a square. She was laid on the floor in the middle, on her black-coated back.

Her arms and legs were drawn out. Slave girls wrapped her wrists and ankles with suede and then with plaited leather thongs. The ends of the ropes were lifted to diagonal grooves in the tops of the pillars. Oversized wooden tubs were tied to the dangling ends.

Laylanda watched in horror as four brawny male slaves each lifted a rock and then placed their burdens in the tubs. Leather lines slithered through grooves, lifting her feet and hands off the stone floor.

The second quartet of rocks pulled her limbs taut. The third load partly raised her, so that only her bottom was still resting on the flagstones.

This device was not the rack, but resembled it closer than Laylanda liked. Surely her beloved Queen did not intend to rend her limbs from her body?

Perhaps, and Laylanda shuddered at the thought of even the lesser punishment, perhaps her disciplining would cease once her joints were dislocated?

Leather creaked and stretched as the fourth and fifth set of boulders was added. Laylanda was lifted. Plaits ran through grooves. Now Laylanda was stretched wide at the greatest height she could achieve. Her joints ached. Her tendons were tight as harp strings. Her ribcage was a spread fan. It became hard for her to take a breath.

Laylanda was sure that one more loading would yank her limbs clean from their sockets.

Queen Vixia mused. Her gem-crusted Royal finger made a sign. Each slave sorted through his store of rocks and selected one that was half the size of those that had gone before.

Laylanda whimpered as this final half-load strained her, drawing her out until it felt as if the skin behind her knees, in her groin, inside her elbows and under her armpits was about to tear. Her cleft had been tugged open to its widest stretch, and tugged again. The tiniest more strain and she would surely cleave along its line, bisected to her breastbone.

Was that to be the nature of Vixia's justice? Laylanda had contrived to open her legs when Vixia had ordained that they stay tight clamped. She had plotted to sunder her hymen when Vixia had decreed that it remain intact.

Was Vixia's revenge to be Laylanda's opening, further and wider and deeper than any maid could dream on? Was her tight little slit to be rent into a mighty fissure?

Laylanda had no doubt that Queen Vixia was cruel enough to inflict that bifurcation upon her, and skilled enough in her magical arts to heal her in that divided state. To go through life as such a living antithesis of virginity would be ironic indeed, and no doubt appealing to the Queen's warped sense of humour.

She had sought a man to ease the hunger in her narrow crease. Once Vixia was done, no man, no beast, would be mightily enough endowed to fill the vast gape of her titanic void.

Queen Vixia said, 'Enough.'

Relief juddered through Laylanda's tortured body.

The Queen's fingers unfastened the mandibles from Laylanda's jaws. The Queen's hands loosed the buckles that clamped the toothed device to Laylanda's groin. It was Her Depravity Herself who plucked out the rubber spindle from Laylanda's rectum.

There was no discomfort in that unplugging. Like the lips of her coynte, the cheeks of her bottom had been spread wide – so wide that the invader almost fell into Vixia's palm.

Eunuchs brought pitchers of sharp-smelling unguents. Naked girls bathed Laylanda's body. The glossy black coat dissolved and was rinsed away.

'Her body hair,' Vixia said.

They brought braziers, and cauldrons, and wax. Hard yellow lumps were melted into amber liquid. Ladles poured. Heat, an iota cooler than scalding, a degree short of unbearable, was poured onto Laylanda's skin. Her legs, her thighs, her pubes, her torso and her arms all acquired a hard translucent coat.

Had she been able, Laylanda would have writhed.

Vixia's ruby talons picked at Laylanda's belly as one might worry at a scab. An edge came free. Vixia took a firmer grip.

She ripped!

The pain was a sheet of fire on Laylanda's skin, and then gone almost before she felt it.

Once Laylanda's pubes had been plucked bald, the Queen gave over the task to lesser beings. That first tearing had been the most agonising and so Vixia had reserved the pleasure of inflicting it for Herself.

With five pairs of hands peeling hard wax from her tender skin Laylanda's depilation was soon done.

'You are almost ready for the Rune Gravers,' Queen Vixia told her. 'But before that, I have two gifts for you.'

Two slaves held salvers. The Queen of Depravity took a flask from one. She filled her mouth with yellow liquid, stooped over Laylanda's head, and kissed her.

Distilled desire poured into Laylanda's mouth. She drank of it, eagerly. The Empress of Harlots scooped yellow salve from a dish on the other tray and smoothed it over, and into, Laylanda's coynte. Just as the girl's throat had worked to take the aphrodisiac into her body, so too did her vulva writhe into life to mumble the magic ointment to her vagina and that too seemed to swallow and gulp.

Laylanda became an inferno.

So intoxicated was she by the unbearable concupiscence that racked her that she barely heard Betohl, the Rune

Graver, whisper in her ear, 'We must enchant you, by Her command, but be consoled, fair one. What my sister and I scribe upon your poor body shall be one level less severe than She demands. You shall retain your sanity at least.'

A needle buzzed on the naked head of her clitoris. Its incitement was more than she'd dreamed possible, but even so it was less than she now desired. Maddened or no, Laylanda came to the realisation that no erotic stimulus, no matter how intense, would ever again be enough.

And that was Vixia's punishment.

Sixteen

A knock sound at Brod's cabin door. The young giant's abdominal muscles twitched but he did not rise. He frowned and deliberately willed his muscles to sit him up. The action required but the slightest exertion, and yet it was more effort than he was used to putting forth. Brod was still stronger than any man who had ever lived, but for some reason he felt a shade less powerful than on the yester-eve.

The knock came again. 'Are ye awake in there, Sir? I have the ship's chirurgeon-barber wi' me, to tend to the cabin boy, an' it please ye, Sir.'

'To tend?'

'Wi' salve an' cotton waddin' for his arse, Sir.'

Brod leaned over the side of his cot and grinned down at Impah, where she lay curled on the deck. 'Does your arse need salve, "boy"?'

Impah smiled, and shook her fair head. She mouthed, silently, 'Not yet'.

'The "boy" is fine,' Brod called out.

'Then, if you've done wi' the lad, the Cap'n has chores for him.'

'Done with him? Give your Captain my regrets, sailor, but this youth has barely started on the tasks I've set. Have your cook prepare something to break our fasts, and have him leave the vittles outside the door. I don't want to be disturbed unless there's good cause.'

Brod swung off the cot and stood. The deck moved gently beneath his feet. Below that – he sensed the yawn of a deep abyss.

143

Brod suddenly understood the cause of his weakness. He was Heir to the Throne of Earth. He was wed to Mother Earth. She gave him his strength. Now he was far from Her, on an alien element, water. It was no wonder that his vigour was sapped.

He turned to look down at Impah's slight and naked form. Thank Order his power had two sources. The strength that he didn't draw from Earth through the soles of his feet, he sucked in through his cock from the magic power of the orgasms he gave to women. It was fortunate indeed that this cabin "boy" was a girl in disguise, and a randy one. With the help of her coynte, he could lessen, in some measure, the draining of his vitality.

'Mother Earth sent you to me,' he told her.

She stretched, and yawned. The lifting of her breasts twitched Brod's cock.

'Perhaps,' she said. 'Perhaps it was my Goddess, Sloona.'

'And mayhap the philosophers have it right, and all the Goddesses who side with Order are but aspects of one Goddess. It matters not. Whichever Goddess sent you, She was kind, and wise, and I give her my thanks. I need you, little one.' He stroked his own lengthening flesh. 'My cock needs you.'

'And my coynte craves your cock, O my magnificent one, but she begs he be gentle.' Her fingers curled over her mound protectively. 'My portal will always be open to you, but I pray you not batter down its tender doors with your mighty ram.'

Brod looked down at his throbbing cudgel, and then at Impah's tender little slit. 'How shall we manage this?' he asked. 'The clasp of your thighs was a delight, and the ministrations of your tongue and your fingers gave me great joy, but I need to sheath this sword. I fear your delicate scabbard was formed for more slender blades, and shorter.'

Grinning impishly, Impah spread her legs until her toes pointed at opposite walls. Her fingers plucked the lips of her sex apart, stretching them obscenely. 'Fear not, magnificent one. This channel is elastic. One day, perhaps, it will open wide enough to eject a babe. If it can achieve that gaping, I am sure it can be persuaded to encompass the thickest and longest plaything that Sloona ever attached to a man for his woman's pleasure.'

Brod knelt between her thighs and bent his head closer to her mound. 'And what form of persuasion would it prefer?'

Impah kneaded at her own sex. 'Like wax, my love, it softens in the hand. Mould it with your fingers. Warm it with your breath, for heat also serves to melt.'

Brod hunched down. He bracketed Impah's sex, four fingers on her mound and two thumbs beneath her slit. As he squeezed gently, she opened. He put his mouth to the wet gap, and breathed in, sucking her humid aroma into his mouth, and then exhaled, blowing his hot breath into her depths.

Impah humped up at his face. 'Oh yes, my Lord! I soften! I melt! More heat, I pray you, and I will turn to liquid.'

His tongue lapped. 'You are become part liquid already, little one. Sweet and salt and spiced. And yet – and yet I see one small pink pill that hardens, stubbornly. I shall have to work it the more, and defeat its obstinacy.'

His lips clamped on the head of her clitoris. His breath inflamed it. His tongue trilled on it.

'Ah – ah – ah! Oh, oh yes! Teach it. Make it surrender! Whip it with the scourge of your tongue. Beat it harder, and faster, and harder, and . . .' Her sweet young voice became deep and guttural. '. . . and force it to submit, my Lord, my Master, my, my, my . . .' A groan shuddered through her belly.

'Yes, my man. The wax is soft. The passage is oiled, and as loose as it can be. My limbs are limp and supple. Mould me to your pleasure, I pray you. Shape me to the form of your desire.'

Brod lay down beside her on his back. He turned, grasped her hips in his broad hands, and lifted her effortlessly. With her slight form held above him, he bent up his legs. He sat her on his knees and spread her legs wide, one to each side of his body.

With his thighs slightly parted, he bent his weapon almost parallel to them. 'Slide down,' he said. 'Be easy. There need be no hurry. A rope is not threaded through a needle in a moment.'

Impah spread her legs still wider. She let her bum slide down Brod's thighs. The head of his cock met the steamy softness of her sex's lips. Impah reached between her legs and adjusted the lips of her coynte, draping and spreading them across his glistening dome.

'Take my hands,' she said. 'Grip hard, and when I command it, pull down with all of your might.'

Her hips rotated. She found a position in which the eye of Brod's cock peered straight up into her vagina. 'Three, two, one. Now!'

Brod tugged down and jerked his hips up at the same time. There was a brief moment of incredibly tight constriction and then a soft soundless plop, as his swollen bulb passed through the narrowest cincture of her passage.

Impah squealed, sighed, and looked down. 'I have the half of it,' she said with a satisfied grin. 'Hold still, my love and let me complete this happy task.'

Her hips wriggled. She gripped Brod's hands and pulled herself, slowly, grindingly, inexorably down.

For Brod, the slithering feeling as his cock was forced deeper and deeper into the slick rubbery yielding was an ecstasy that was almost too much to bear. He fought the urge to thrust, holding himself rigid.

The lips of Impah's sex inverted as they were dragged by their friction on his shaft. She twitched, settling herself into less discomfort. There was more cock to take in, though she had two thirds of its length inside her. She already felt bloated by it. Her vagina was a glove, pulled by error onto a too-large hand. Well, the glove would just have to stretch.

'Take my shoulders,' she gasped.

Brod obeyed.

'Now – force me down.'

'Are you sure?'

She nodded. Her breath was too precious to waste on words.

Brod pulled. Another finger's width of his gigantic shaft disappeared. And another. And another.

Impah threw her head back and bit her lip. It wasn't pain, but the strain was so intense that she felt she had become nothing but a skin, filled with male flesh, stretched taut to bursting, and then – ah – the bliss! Her distorted, tucked-under clit felt the rough springiness of Brod's pubic curls.

She had taken him all.

She sagged back against his raised knees. 'Give me but a moment, my love, to gather my strength. Let my body adjust. Let me breathe. Yes, that's better. I draw my strength from you, my Master. And now, if I just pull up my legs and get my feet flat on the floor – yes.'

She braced. The long muscles in her slender thighs bunched. Impah rocked forward, to get her weight directly over her massive impaler, and she lifted herself, very slowly, just a fraction, before she squelched back down.

'I will get the way of it, I promise, if you will just be patient.'

Brod stretched back and locked his fingers behind his own neck. 'Take your time, little one. We have a long voyage before us.'

The sun was low in the afternoon sky and Impah was curled asleep, recovering from her last few orgasms, when someone pounded at the cabin door.

'Sir! We are pursued. A pirate closes with us. Will you take up arms and aid in our defence?'

Brod shook Impah awake. 'Here is a knife,' he said. 'Hide yourself under the cot. Don't be afraid. I've fought more men than a ship carries on my own, and I'm sure that our crew is well-used to fending off pirates. They don't really need me, but I'll join them for the sport of it.'

'Take care!'

'Rest, little one. Battle makes me horny. Think on the Congress of the Ram with the Lioness and be prepared to execute its first three positions on my return.'

As Brod left the cabin an iron-headed harpoon thudded into the deck between his feet. A whoosh and a crack above his head told him that some massive missile had smashed through the smaller of the ship's two masts. Rigging groaned and squealed as a shattered spar dragged through a tangled web of rope. A line snapped and cracked like a whip. A freed sail billowed and sighed as it drifted and slowly descended. A cloud of patched canvas draped itself gracefully over the *Indomitable*'s prow.

Sling-shot pellets rattled against wood. A crossbow's quarrel skittered along the deck, lost momentum, and rolled to a gentle halt against a dead sailor's crusty knee.

Brod stooped, wrenched the harpoon out of the planks, stood, and hurled it back whence it came. The attacker, the *Sea Serpent* by her figurehead, was half a bowshot across the waves and closing. Her rigging was thick with men. Some held short recurved bows. Others gripped cutlasses or boarding-pikes and were ready to swing across on ropes.

On the enemy's deck, a crew was winding back a catapult that was laden with pebbles and small rocks. These lighter missiles would not have the reach of the boulder that had crippled the *Indomitable*, but once within range they could clear the ship's deck.

The tactic was obvious. A boulder to destroy their rigging and leave them wallowing – a rain of missiles to prevent retaliation – a catapult of stones to stun or kill – followed by a mass boarding. If the assault was not broken within the next few moments the battle would be over.

Brod tore into the tangle of rigging that blocked the deck. It had taken an eight-man catapult to hurl that great boulder, but Brod found it, and heaved it high. Hurling boulders had been his main sport when he'd been but a lad. His feet thudded the deck. He ran to the scuppers and threw.

Brod had aimed for the *Serpent*'s catapult, but his missile fell short. He truly was weaker now, despite his night of swiving. The great stone arced. Brod thought it was going to miss entirely but it crushed into the other ship's hull, exactly on the water-line.

Teeth of broken timber held it for a moment before letting it tumble into the sea. Waves gurgled gleefully into the gaping hole.

Both ships wallowed. No longer under human control, they perversely drew closer, as if eager to start the hand-to-hand slaughter. The catapult's crew moved with frantic precision, levering the great machine around and lifting its iron tail to depress the path its missiles would take.

The *Sea Serpent* lurched as ocean dragged her port rake. Four of the men at the catapult reversed their attentions. The sudden cant now aimed their engine at the *Indomitable*'s side, where such puny missiles would do little harm. The other half of the crew shouldered the catapult's bulk to hold it from sliding down a slanting deck.

One man screamed as an iron runner crunched three toes off his bare foot.

Brod found a neatly coiled hawser. He freed a broken spar from a mound of tangled rigging and tied the rope's end to its middle, where it was banded by bronze. Standing tall, heedless of the deadly rain, Brod swung the tethered baulk around his head on the hawser's end. Once, twice, thrice, and release. His missile soared, dragging a line that was as thick as Brod's wrist. The spar speared into rigging, sagged, and caught.

Brod leapt up onto the ship's side, tugged twice, and launched himself. Even as he swung across the gap, he was swarming up his line. When he pendulumed over the *Sea Serpent*'s side he was three times his own height above its deck.

He dropped.

His clubbed fists felled two men half an instant before his feet slapped deck. Weaker, he was. So far from his Mother Earth, Brod was reduced to the strength of five or six men instead of that of a dozen.

A hairy man swung a length of chain. Brod let it smack into his open palm. His fist closed. He heaved. As his assailant's wrist was manacled to his chain, it did not come free. The man became a part of the weapon, to be whirled around Brod's head and smashed into his mates – a human flail.

Four times Brod was charged. Four times his assailants were bowled back with broken limbs. The chain-wielder had been a big man, but no human arm is built for such strain. His tore free from his shoulder.

Brod spun his chain until the air thrummed.

Within a few breaths the deck around Brod was cleared except for one lanky pirate with a long slender blade. The man was bald as a pebble, but the black ringlets of his beard hung halfway down his chest. He was better dressed and cleaner than the rest of the pirates, so Brod took him to be their Captain.

The man lunged under Brod's whistling metal arc. Brod jerked a chain that weighed half as much as a man into a new path. It clipped the Captain's sword, flicking it away as easily as if it had been a reed.

Brod took the man by thigh and shoulder, lifting him high.

'Are you their Captain?' Brod bellowed.

'Aye, I am.'

'Then call on your men to lay down their arms. Let us end this useless slaughter. Your craft is sinking. Surrender is your only chance. We will be merciful, I swear.'

'Break my back, if you will,' the Captain panted. 'My mates will fight to the death, with me or without. You think they'll trust to the Witch's mercy? Sooner die clean and fast than die lingering, providing sport for the Vile One.'

'I am not in Vixia's service,' Brod protested. 'I seek to destroy Her. It is you, pirate, who serves the foul Witch.'

Despite his position, the Captain managed a sour laugh. 'Indeed? Then perhaps our flags fly from the wrong ships.'

'Flags?' Brod looked back towards the *Indomitable*. There, high on the remaining mast, flew the Whip and Manacles, d'argent and d'or on a sable field. He looked high above his head, peering through the *Sea Serpent*'s rigging. The Captain's ship was sailing under a white and green flag, a white tower on a field of grass – the emblem of the White Lodge. No base pirate could fly that righteous symbol. The Gods of Order would not allow it.

'Then . . .' It came to Brod that he had been instructed not to return to the Inn, and perhaps why.

He set the Captain gently on his feet. 'I have been deceived,' he said. 'I owe you an apology, and an explanation, but meanwhile . . .'

The two ships ground their hulls together. Brod took up his chain and charged back to the *Indomitable*. 'Follow me, *Sea Serpent* rebels,' he screamed. 'Death to Vixia, and all who serve Her!'

Seventeen

'Do you lust for either of them?' Vixia asked.

Laylanda inspected the pair, Fotis, Princess of Iliam, and Rolel, Marquis of the Marshes. She knew that they had asked for their fetters. Both thirsted for the fluids of Queen Vixia's body, and perhaps they now yearned for hers also, since she had been saturated by the yellow essence.

Being naked and constrained in Her Vileness' presence gave them some small chance of being granted a sip of Her mouth's liquor, or a few droplets of Her coynte's ambrosia.

There was a better chance that they would hang in their manacles all day, ignored. It might be that Vixia would tantalise them, offering Her intoxicating kiss and then snatching it away.

However slight their chances, they took them eagerly. Their addiction gave them little choice.

They had been fastened with thongs, spread-eagle, to the rims of wheels that were mounted on one wall. If Vixia chose to use their bodies, they were available at whatever angle She selected.

'Well Laylanda?' Vixia prompted.

'Of course, Your Vileness. I lust for them both.'

'And they both desire you, Laylanda. That has been my gift to you all, but especially to you.

'Which do you think is the greater need, Laylanda? Do you want them more than they want you?'

'Since you gave me over to the Rune Gravers, Your Supreme Malevolence, only You, in all the world, knows more intense lust than I.'

'Does that not anger you? To yearn for their bodies more than they ache for yours?'

Laylanda made tight fists. 'Of course, Your Majesty.'

'Then you must revenge yourself on them, must you not?'

'With whips? Or thin rods?'

'No child. That satisfaction is hollow and fleeting. Their lust insults your lust, by being lesser. Avenge yourself through lust, Laylanda. Increase theirs, but deny it surcease. Slake your own, for that brief moment that it can be slaked. Shall I instruct you? Shall we do it together? Which one will you use, little Slut-Princess?'

Laylanda's emotions reeled. 'Little Slut-Princess'? It was, without doubt, a term of endearment, and likely the first one to pass Vixia's cruel lips in a century or more.

Laylanda put her turmoil aside to be contemplated upon later. She had a decision to make. 'I choose Princess Fotis,' she said. 'Before You changed me, Your Depravity, I felt a certain closeness to the girl.'

'A wise decision.' Her eyes narrowed. 'It is always more satisfying to hurt someone you have felt affection for. Then follow my lead.'

The Queen stood with her sinuous naked body less than a hand's thickness from the young Marquis' nude torso. 'Look into my eyes,' she said.

Laylanda took the same position, before Fotis.

Vixia pinched the youth's nipples. Laylanda followed suit with Fotis. The girl's peaks were pale pink, scarcely darker than the skin of her blushing breasts. Laylanda's had been a similar tint before they had been tattooed. Now they were deep coral and had grown into cones the size of doves' eggs. Since Betohl had dyed them with his magic inks they never softened. They knew varying degrees of hardness, but never relaxed.

'Use your nails,' Vixia advised.

Laylanda did as she was bid, digging her thumbnails deep enough into Fotis' tender spikes to leave white crescents when she released them.

The tormentors kissed the tormented, long and deep,

still toying with their flesh. Laylanda felt Fotis slump in her bonds as if her body was melting. From the corner of her eye Laylanda watched Vixia's play. The boy whose mouth she was ravishing with Her Royal tongue did not soften. He stiffened in his leather bonds. His youthful cock rose up. Vixia parted her legs for it and trapped it between her thighs. She slithered her limbs against each other and on his shaft.

The Queen reached down between her body and her prisoner's. Two fingers hooked beneath his pallid stalk to snuggle it up against and between the lips of her coynte. Her thumb pressed down, trapping the head of her clit under its ball, squeezing it onto his hardness. Her hips began a slow insistent rhythm.

Laylanda understood. The friction on the Queen's bud was intense. The silken caress that the boy's dome felt was likely pleasant enough, but too subtle to ever bring him to completion. Vixia was fucking the lad, while denying him the full pleasure. It was not love-making. It was the rape of a male by a female.

But Laylanda's victim, Fotis, was a girl. How was Laylanda to achieve the same effect? How could a girl rape a girl, taking pleasure without returning it?

She gripped her own clit's shaft and pulled back on it, forcing its head from its sheath. That sensitive organ had been but half the length of one joint of her smallest finger. Since her Graving, it had grown to thrice its former span. It shead had been the tiniest sweetest pea. Now it had become a swollen pink bean.

With its new size, Laylanda had found she could easily frig it, like a boy masturbating. That was what she did. Her fingers manipulated her stem, inserting it between the wet folds of Fotis' inner coynte-lips. She rubbed it hard and fast, gliding its head on slick softness, taking care that it flicked Fotis' minute love-bud only one stroke in a dozen.

'I'm going to come,' Vixia told the Marquis. 'I'm going to get my pleasure. I'm using your cock for my delight. Soon, very soon, I am going to spill my scalding juices all over your nice hard cock.'

Laylanda's teeth worried at Fotis' plump lower lip. Without releasing it, she growled, 'Your coynte is hot and slippery on my clit's head. I'm fucking you with my clit. I'm going to take my pleasure soon. I've going to flood you with my spending.' She twisted the girl's nipple with her free hand. 'When I come, I am going to mash our coyntes together, lip to lip. I come very wet now. You will feel me gush into you, my sweet little bitch. You want me to come inside you, don't you?'

Fotis gasped, 'Oh yes!' She humped and twisted, desperate to bring her clit's head to Laylanda's, but was denied.

'I'm very close,' Laylanda hissed. 'I can feel it building.' Her fingers blurred. Pre-orgasmic juices, hers and Fotis's, were whipped into a froth that coated both sets of coynte lips with white foam.

'I'm going to come – now!' Laylanda juddered. Her thighs spread. She humped up, parting Fotis' lips, spreading them wide over her own mound so that her coynte was inside her victim's, and let herself gush.

'Now turn them!' Vixia commanded. 'Don't let it stop. You can keep coming.'

Both Vixia and Laylanda spun their prisoners on their wheels, upending them.

'Like this!' Vixia ordered.

Her fingers locked together beneath the Marquis' neck, dragging his face up into her crotch. Her gaping slot slid across his face, to his mouth. She held him there as she squirmed her hips, working her elongated clit between his lips, fucking his mouth.

His cock wagged before her feral face. She shook her head, batting its head with her cheeks. Her lips caught its tip, and sucked hard, twice, before releasing it. The lad had time to feel his jism boil and then subside as she teased and then denied his cock.

Laylanda, Vixia's willing pupil, treated Fotis in a similar fashion, swivelling her hips on the girl's face, lapping twice at her straining clit, and then withdrawing her tongue's favours.

Both tormentors juddered the last spasms of their orgasms.

'I'll leave them both to you for a while, Laylanda,' Vixia said. 'In the chest you will find a pale blue ointment in an onyx jar. The flesh it coats will engorge as if it were drawn by a poultice, but will lose some of its sense of feeling. A cock or a clit, so treated, will ache for pleasure but be numb to any but the most intense stimulation. Before long both of these living toys will be begging you to scourge their most tender flesh. But half a watch later, when the power of the salve wears off, their flesh will regain its sensitivity, but enhanced. It will feel the slightest breath as an intense caress, but will be unable to engorge. The Marquis, in particular, will suffer then. Men find it most frustrating when they are overcome by avid desire and yet their precious cocks remain meek and limp.

'Amuse yourself, my dear, until I return. I have a small duty to take care of.'

Queen Vixia strode from the chamber and ascended to the scrying room in her tower. There she sat on a bench and pulled down an iron ring that was studded with stones of jet. With her head within its compass she could see whatever was within range of the stones around the iron band that Brod wore upon his forearm.

She saw Brod cave in Captain Smy's chest with one back-handed slap. She watched as the young titan threw a belaying pin with such force that it pierced a sailor clean through. Vixia saw Brod take up a bale of camel hides and use it to propel four men over the ship's side. She observed the deaths of a dozen more of the *Indomitable*'s crew at Brod's hand and at the hands of the *Sea Serpent*'s crew.

Brod leaped back to the sinking hulk he had holed. He wrapped its mizzenmast in his brawny arms and heaved it up out of its seating in the deck. He had to let it tumble and drag it, just to free it of the rigging, but once it was loose he swung it over to the *Indomitable* in one great heave.

With that to replace the mast the catapult had smashed, Captain Daud ap-Dan tugged thoughtfully on his beard and assured Brod that the *Indomitable* would be sailable again within a day, and the pursuit of Raven could continue.

Queen Vixia raised up her scrying ring. Captain Smy and the *Indomitable* had been good tools, in their time. She shrugged. Tools break. The vital thing was that Brod's quest continue – that Brod should save Raven, Heir to the Throne of Air, and return with her to Vixania, where She, Queen Vixia, had a volcanically warm welcome waiting for them both.

Eighteen

'Father Sun scorch this accursed darkness,' Jasmine swore. 'My ears tell me that I am surrounded by acts of love and yet I can see none of them. Love loves the light, does it not?'

'When there is beauty it does,' Hibiscus agreed from the other side of the hold. 'You are right, sister. Our eyes are amid a feast of love and yet are denied the pleasures of watching. Tell me what you are doing, Jasmine, and who to, and what sweet things your present partner is doing to you, if you will. I'll try and see your sport in my mind. Then I'll describe for you what games I am playing.' She chuckled. 'I'll wager you any stake you choose that my pleasure is stranger than yours.'

'A wager? Very well – the stake shall be the loser's face between the winner's thighs, for as long as the winner can stand it.'

'I like your stakes,' H'neeth interrupted. 'If you will allow, I'll join your wager, and start, if you like. I warn you two, I shall win. I've been lusty since the day I became a woman. I've had two score or more lovers, both men and women and one who was neither, but no one has ever before done to me what is being done to me now.'

Hibiscus and Jasmine eagerly agreed to include H'neeth in their wager.

'I am sitting lap-to-lap with the silent one,' H'neeth began. 'The tall slim girl from the East. The one with no breasts and skin like soft copper. We have been kissing and fondling each other. Her mouth is sweet and spicy and very wet. Though she speaks not, her tongue is very able I promise you. You recall her nipples?'

'Long and spiky,' Jasmine said.

'Cruelly banded with gold,' Hibiscus added.

'And very sensitive,' H'neeth told them. 'When I but brush their tips with my flattend palms it sets her a-quiver from nape to arse. I suckled one a short time past and she reached her peak of pleasure from that alone. It is as if she has no nipples, but has been blessed with three love-buds, one crowning her tight little cleft and two more mounted on her chest.'

'That is interesting,' Jasmine said, 'and I will surely put what you say to the test, but I have heard stranger tales. All of us get pleasure from our nipples being played with. She just gets more than most.'

'Ah – but I have just begun,' H'neeth said. 'Huh! Oh yes! I – I simply told you what this girl and I have done, not what we are now doing.'

'Go on,' Hibiscus urged.

'She has plucked out two of the long silky hairs of her head,' H'neeth continued. 'As I have been talking, she has tied them around her nipples. My hands have been on her chest, feeling what she is doing. Now – now as I speak – she is doing the same to me. She has tethered her left nipple to my right one, and is now pulling – oh – so tightly – yes – my right nipple is now firmly tied, and anchored to her left one.'

'Doesn't that hurt?' Hibiscus asked.

'Oh yes! It hurts good. My poor nipples are strangled at their bases. The blood pounds in them. They throb. There is an ache in them like none I ever felt before. When I touch them – it is like they are hard beads. When I pinch – aaahhh. Father-Mother-Sister-Brother that felt so good-bad I was close to coming from the lovely pain.

'And now her palms are flat upon my chest, pushing me back away from her. The hairs that join us are taut. My nipples, and her nipples, are all being tugged so haaaard! Ouch! Oh damn-the-Gods it's good!

'And now – oh yes. Yes – she's shaking her shoulders. My breasts are wobbling and being pulled out and, and, and. Oh! I came. It felt as if those threads were not tied around my nipples, but pierced clean through them, and then ran down through my body, to my clit. Each tug on my nipples drew on my clit. Each pull was like a plucking, and my bud the string on a lute.

'She isn't stopping, the little slut, though I can feel that she too had a climax. What? Oh yes! The sweet harlot has plucked out yet another hair. She had made loops at each end and put it to my fingers to feel. I understand! She is asking my permission to continue. Yes! Yes! Do it, damn you. I can stand it.

'Now – now she has pulled my clit's head out yet further from its sheath. Her fingers – she is – oh – such delicate slender fingers. She has the loop over my clit's head, and draws the noose tight around its neck. Her hands are in her own lap now. I know what she is doing. I must be patient and still. Yes. Her hand is taking my fingers to her core so that I may feel that she is bound in the same way as I. And now she is moving. Her body sways and undulates. I feel a sweet drawing upon my left nipple, and now my right, and now on my clit. Oh yes! I see it now. That first pleasure was but to prepare us. Having climaxed once, we are more patient. This exquisite agony is going to go on, and on.

'She is still. Her hand presses my shoulder. Ah – I see! Now it is my turn to move. Like this! Ah – I am on the brink! And so I still myself.

'Jasmine, tell us what pleasure you take while my lithe love and I tease ourselves into delirium.'

'Like you, H'neeth, I will first tell you and my sister what has passed. I was with one of the giantesses, laying on her, suckling one breast while fondling the nipple of the other. Someone joined us. I did not know who until I felt a small face nuzzle at the great rubbery polyp I was squeezing in my fist. It had to be one of the tiny pale girls by the size of her features.

'Not being greedy, I surrendered my toy, but as my hand withdrew tiny fingers enwrapped my thumb and drew it back. The little one folded my fingers except for the middle one and made my hand into a fist. She guided me, wobbling the pad of my finger on the tip of giantess's fat cone.

Her hair brushed my arm. Her mouth stretched to its widest, and engulfed my fingertip and the nipple together.

'She is small, but her suck is strong. She drew hard. Her tongue flickered from my finger to the giantess's nipple. After a while, she alternated – a suck at my finger – a draw on the giantess's nipple. Both became slippery with her saliva.

'Perhaps her oral play put the thought into the large one's mind, for she drew up my other hand and put it to her mouth. Being so big, her mouth engulfed me to my wrist. The flat of her tongue was as wide as my palm. I stroked. She lapped.

'Holding my forearm, she slowly pumped my hand into her mouth. I caressed her tongue. It was hot, and wet, and slippery. She sucked on my hand as if it was a sweetmeat, or perhaps the cock of her lover.

'The attentions that my second lover was paying to my finger were also as lascivious as if her mouth had been working on a man's rigid stem. I worked it back and forth, slowly, between her sucking lips, encouraging the illusion. They soon realised my import. As you were speaking, H'neeth, the giantess lifted me up off her body and arranged me flat on my back. I spread my arms, bent at the elbows, so that my forearms were rigid and erect.

'The small one was first to take advantage. I sensed her standing over me and then squatting, though she did not have to bend very far. Her two hands guided my finger to the heat between her slender little thighs. She lowered herself slowly. Her slit is so tiny, Hibiscus, that I had to work my finger up into its tenderness very carefully so as not to hurt her. Still, I managed to part that soft tight slot and impale her. She finally settled herself and seated her delicate little coynte in the palm of my hand. She is so light that I can take her entire weight without strain. Even now, as I speak, she is squirming her tiny delicious body on the spike of my middle finger while the ball of my thumb rubs over her mound and the tip of my little finger tickles between the cheeks of her bum.

'The giantess, being so long of leg, had to squat so low that now she is almost sitting on her heels. For her, I made a tight fist. She rubbed my knuckles over the soft lips of her coynte, soaking them with her oils, and then lifted my hand to her clit. I grasped its stem and frigged on it as if it was Lake's cock, Hibiscus.

'My palm became slippery. I pressed its heel on the head of her clit and revolved it. That seemed to please her, for very soon I felt a splatter of hot juices rain on my arm and shoulder. She was not done with my arm and hand though. She tucked my fist up into her great gaping coynte and rammed down.

'There was some tightness, but not a lot. Father Sun knows how the men of her race are equipped!

'Can you imagine what it feels like to have your arm, to the elbow, far up inside a gigantic vagina? When she squeezes it's like a hot wet rubber clamp. She is not smooth, in deep. There are convolutions, and nobbles, and such. When she clamps on me, my hand is so compressed I feel its muscles must cramp, but I will endure, for her sake.

'And now she is convulsing on me. She's working up and down like some enormous engine of flesh, and all the while the tiny little pale one is treating my finger in the same frantic fashion. I have become two cocks, Hibiscus, one puny and one mighty. I am soaked to my waist in female spending. Sweet fluids trickle my arms. My face and my breasts are slick with woman-juice. I am drunk on the heady aroma of my lovers' spending.

'Tell me, Hibiscus, is not my loving even stranger than that of H'neeth and her coppery paramour?'

When Hibiscus replied her voice was husky. 'Strange indeed, but stranger? I find it hard to judge, sister, but it matters not, for what I am doing surpasses you both. I will win the contest, as you two will surely agree.

'When first you spoke, Jasmine, all I was doing was stroking a cat-woman's back. I love to hear, and feel, her purr. She has very fine fur all the way up the ridge of her spine. When I rub down, it's like silk. Stroking up, the top layer is still silky, but it's stiffer underneath, like coarse velvet.

'She likes my caresses both ways. I had her arching and trembling and then I thought to discover what that fur would feel like on the insides of my coynte's petals.

'I bestrode her waist, parted my sex, and lowered myself. Still caressing her nape, I pressed down and slid gently backwards and forwards. Moving back, the soft hairs tickled me. When I pushed forwards, tiny bristles prickled my wet softness.

'As I listened to your stories, Jasmine and H'neeth, I was gliding, and then grinding, getting wetter and wetter. I arched over this lovely pet and gripped her furry nape between my teeth. My nipping seemed to excite her. Perhaps that is the way her mate takes her. She writhed beneath me. I thrust down hard enough that my coynte could feel the bones in her spine.

'I reached back, seeking her sex, so that I could return some measure of the pleasure that she was giving me. My hand found something stiff, upright and hairy. It was her stubby little tail.'

'She likely lifts it for her lover, to expose herself,' H'neeth guessed. 'I have observed cats and monkeys do the same.'

'Perhaps. Still, I had no cock to give her, but it seemed she had something very like one to offer me. I planted my feet flat on the deck, lifted my rump, steered her tail, and impaled myself on it. Oh Jasmine, you must try it! It slides out so easily now that it is coated with my spending, but as it goes in – oh Jasmine! My inner lips, my tight passage, all are scoured so gently but so very deliciously. When I grind down hard the fur at the base of her tail prickles the head of my clit. Oh Jasmine, I swear I have come six times already from riding it! And still I – oh!'

There was a pause during which all the sounds that Hibiscus could make were as animal as those of the catwoman.

'She too has had pleasure,' Hibiscus eventually continued. 'She seems to love the clawing of my nails upon her back and buttocks. She's lifted herself up so that she can reach under herself to her own coynte and clit. I can tell by the rumble in her chest when she nears her pleasure. It gets stronger and stronger, pauses, and then bursts forth in a thrumming groan.

'Ah! There she goes again. And I – I too spend!

'Oh, my sweet sister, oh my ebony love, who now wins the contest?'

H'neeth chuckled. 'May we call it a draw? Finish what you are at, both of you, and then let us find each other. All three of us must pay the price, each with our face between another's thighs, must we not?'

Hibiscus assented. There was no word from Jasmine.

'What say you, Jasmine?' H'neeth asked again.

'I – I may be a while.'

'You are still acting as two cocks – pleasuring your giantess and your pale little friend?'

'No more. I was inspired. With the one being so large and the other being so small, it seemed to me that it might please them both if I persuaded the bigger to bugger the smaller with her enormous clit. The proportions are right. To this wee pucker, the giantess' love-bud is as big as Lake's cock is to my own rear entrance.'

'And?'

'Just a moment. I must lave the two – the target and the arrow – with my tongue. Yes – it is in. The giantess is being gentle. Now it is my turn. If I position myself with care, I can get both of their faces where I need them. Yes! Oh, Jasmine! The giantess' tongue fills my coynte like a squirmy wet cock. I am filled with writhing tongue. Oh – it feels so good!'

'And the little one?' Hibiscus asked.

'Her mouth is small, sister, but quite large enough that its lips fit tight around my clit. Ah! Oh yes! Yes, I will be with you both in a few moments, I am sure. Keep talking so that I can find you. I – I'm coming.'

Nineteen

Laylanda used two fingers of each hand to stretch Queen Vixia's anus wide open.

'Enough! Now do it!' the Insatiable One ordered.

Laylanda pursed her lips, took careful aim into the distended pink funnel, and jetted a thin stream of golden mead out of her mouth and deep into Vixia's rectum.

'Ah yes,' the Queen sighed. 'That was quite pleasant. So, little whore, what would you have me do to you in return?'

Laylanda lapped up a glistening drop that had spilled. 'If your Lewdness pleases,' she said, 'show me some magic.'

'Erotic magic?'

'Of course.'

'Very well. Fetch me the golden phallus that you will find in the chest at the foot of my bed.'

Laylanda brought it to Vixia's bed, quivering. Since the Queen had transformed her she had taken many cocks, both real and artificial, but this one was surely impossible. It was as long and as thick as her thigh, with a smooth dome that was larger than her knee. It had been formed in intricate detail, with bas-relief veins and a dimple in its bulb that would have taken her little finger to its first knuckle.

'I don't think –' she began.

'Fear not. It is but a container. Hold it steady.'

Laylanda held it in both hands. It was heavy, but not so weighty as if it had been solid gold. Vixia poured oil into her palms and caressed it. Laylanda watched closely as Vixia's fingers stroked slowly at first and then more quickly, more urgently. To her amazement, she saw the eye dilate. Hard metal was reacting to the Queen's touch as if it had been living flesh. The thing throbbed. The eye gaped even wider. Queen Vixia frotted hard and fast.

The golden phallus twitched – and ejaculated! It spewed forth a stream of pink pearls onto her black satin sheet.

'It is empty,' Vixia said. 'Put it aside.'

The Queen's taloned finger stirred the glistening pink pool. 'Pick one up,' she said.

Laylanda obeyed, selecting the largest. To her surprise the rest followed. They dangled from the one she held in a dew-drop of shiny pink balls.

'Touch them,' Vixia urged. 'Try them in your fingers.'

Laylanda rotated one. It moved freely, turning this way and that, but whichever way she twisted it, the pearl still clung to its mates.

'Shape them,' Vixia said.

'Shape them?'

'Into any form your wicked little heart desires.'

Laylanda moulded the glob in her hands. She formed it into the semblance of a snake, or perhaps it wasn't a snake exactly. Vixia touched the pearly cylinder where it lay on her bed. 'Now pick it up again.'

Laylanda did as she was bid. Now it held its shape, though every single pearl was still able to move freely. When she caressed its length the revolutions felt oddly erotic under her palm.

Vixia took it from her. 'The silver fyrinx,' she said.

Laylanda knew the instrument and its power. When Vixia coaxed tiny trills from it, any cock that was close by rose and swayed to its song, as a cobra dances for an Indirian snake-charmer.

'Lay on your back with your legs parted wide,' Vixia purred. 'Be perfectly still.'

She laid the pearly snake between Laylanda's delicate breasts. Her lips pursed. She blew softly into the fyrinx's mouthpiece.

The long mass of pearls quivered. A few began to revolve of their own volition. The friction made a soft dry rustling that became louder as more and more of the pearls became enchanted. Rolling on three score tiny balls, the thing crept, undulating down Laylanda's naked body.

Laylanda lifted her head to watch its progress, though her skin knew exactly where the magical worm was. Each pore that it passed over felt its dry caress. It crossed her midriff. It slithered over the gentle rise of her belly. It climbed the naked hairless mound of her sex. As it passed over the ridge of her clit she felt it open along its belly, so that her clit was stroked on both sides and above.

The unnatural thing reached the lips of her sex. It reared up for about the width of two fingers pressed together and dipped. Its blind head nuzzled, parting her.

Vixia's tune commanded. The pearly serpent nudged and flowed into Laylanda's body.

She watched with wide eyes as the last small pearl, the tip of its tail, disappeared. Laylanda sank back on the pillows and surrendered herself to the incredible sensations. It wriggled deep into her. No part of its skin was still. Each and every pearl revolved, this way and that, some spinning rapidly, some rotating with tantalising slowness.

It squirmed. It writhed. It filled her.

Laylanda was caressed in places that had never felt a touch before. The thing expanded and contracted. It put out probing tentacles that explored recesses of Laylanda's body that she didn't know she had.

And it kept moving.

Vixia's tune grew louder. Its beat came faster. The thing in Laylanda gyrated in time to the music. It undulated. It convulsed.

And so did Laylanda. Her vagina squeezed. As her climax convulsed her, her joy undid the enchantment. The snake of pearls collapsed, unjointed, was no longer one but simply a thousand totally separate, inanimate, pearls.

A handful spilled from her coynte. Her spasmodic contractions, the gut-deep echoes of her orgasm, spat more out. Her sex trickled hundreds of oily pink pearls onto the black sheet. A final squeeze plopped out the last three. One of those, the largest, clung between her inflamed lips, adhering to her flesh by the stickiness of her discharge.

Vixia laid aside her fyrinx. She plucked out the final glistening pearl and sucked on it. 'Well?'

Laylanda groaned, 'That was wonderful, Your Majesty. I have a gift for you, in return for my pleasure.'

'A gift?'

'The Rune Gravers, Your Vileness. Betohl and his sister Karina. They have deceived you. When you bade them engrave my skin with erotomania to the fifth degree they showed me mercy. They only marked me to the fourth level.'

'And this is how you repay their kindness? With betrayal?'

'Yes, Your Majesty.'

Vixia pinched the flesh of Laylanda's inner thigh. 'Excellent. I knew when I chose you that deep down inside you were utterly vile. I am never wrong about such things.' She took up the fyrinx once more. At Her first note, the pearls twitched back to life. They began to roll together.

Twenty

Droodge, the half-deaf carpenter, pounded an iron-wood spike into the splice he'd made near the top of *The Claw*'s mizzen mast. As he twisted to tuck his maul into his belt he saw a black speck on the horizon. He cupped his hands and bellowed, 'Sail ho!'

Sailors gathered at the ship's side. Droodge scrambled down to join them. 'Nah, it ain't a sail,' he said, 'I mistook myself, but it is a ship – a ship wi' no sails raised. That's the *Blue Swan*, or I'm a poxy whore.'

Captain Purd said, 'You're that, right enough. Tell me that strange tale again – o' the witch as maddened ye. I thought ye sun-tetched from driftin' so long with no provisions, but I'll allow there's sorcery here now. That craft is making better way than we are, an' she's got nary a stitch o' sail on her.'

'Haul away from her, Cap'n,' Droodge said. 'The *Blue Swan* is cursed, I tell ye.'

'Cursed or no, she'd make a fine prize, eh lads?'

'There's a siren aboard, I tell ye,' Droodge protested. 'D'ye want *The Claw* to go the same way as the *Swan*?'

'A siren? All the better. D'ye know what Queen Vixia'd pay for a real living siren? A siren's song is lust-magic. That's just what our lovely Queen collects. Just one o' 'em sea-witches'd fetch us more gold than all them exotic beauties we got stowed below.'

'You'll change your tune the moment ye hears her voice,' Droodge said. 'She crazed and drowned the *Swan*'s entire crew, remember.'

'But you escaped, on account of being so hard of hearing, didn't you?'

'Aye.'

'So a deaf man'd be proof against her? Aside from her song, she's no more than a girl?'

'Aye, Captain. D'ye plan on stopping up a boarding party's ears? I doubt that wadding nor wax'd do it. She's got a song as'll cut through 'em. Only a man with no hearing at all would be safe, Captain.'

Captain Purd squinted at Droodge. Drawing his stiletto, he said, 'And you're half-way deaf already, ain't you?'

Blood was still trickling from Droodge's ear as he made his way across the *Blue Swan*'s heaving deck. He paused to clutch at a mast and vomit. Did the splash of his spewing make enough noise to alert anyone below? He had no way to tell. His ears heard no better than his elbows.

Clutching his carpenter's maul, he staggered down the gangway. There were no lights below deck but he knew his way to the Captain's cabin by feel.

When he got to the door there was a glimmer showing beneath it, and a pale beam of light shining through a knot-hole. Droodge put his eye to it. If the Gods were with him, the witch'd be sleeping, mayhap.

She wasn't. The cabin was lit by a score of candles, a scandalous waste, and a hazard. In the flickering light he saw the witch, and someone else, a man. It was no one Droodge recognised. None of the Swan's crew had so finely formed and muscular a back, nor was so trim o' waist 'n' hip. Could be it was the witch's mate, a male siren, if such a creature lived.

Mate or not, they was mating, for a surety. The man was standing, holding the witch's wrists, and her jutting out in front of him like a ship's figurehead. Her legs were straight back and spread either side of the man's thrusting hips. Nigh on all her weight had to be bearing on the man's cock, so he wasn't human, whatever he was.

Droodge thought of going back to *The Claw*, but what to tell Captain Purd? The agony in Droodge's left ear reminded him that the Captain could be a cruel man when the mood took him, or even when it didn't.

He took a firmer grip on his maul and eased the door

open. Mayhap it screeched its hinge. He had no way to tell. The man turned his head. Quicker than he could think, Droodge swung. The maul struck the man's temple. He crumpled, sending the witch sprawling on her face. Droodge stepped over him. His maul descended once more, thudding her skull above her hairline, where she'd not be marked so as to show. Droodge unslung his bundle and stuffed the rags from it into Raven's mouth. Five turns of thin line around her head bound it in place. Six more lengths secured her wrists and ankles.

Droodge turned to the man. There was no point in tying him. The blow had caved in his skull.

Twenty-One

Captain Daud ap-Dan poured spirit-of-wine into a matching pair of aurochs horns that were mounted on bronze claw bases and into a crystal goblet that had just the tiniest chip at its lip.

'The last repair is done,' he told Brod and Impah. 'We are under full sail at last. The *Sea Serpent*'s figurehead is set in place. The *Indomitable*'s old one is kindling for the galley. Here's to the new *Sea Serpent*, may she one day sail an ocean that's free of Vixia and her scum.'

All three drank. Impah, kneeling beside Brod, spluttered into her goblet. The spirits that the Temple served were always diluted.

Brod kneaded her naked back and said, 'My heart still bleeds, Captain Daud. I'd give my right arm to bring back those brave men of yours that I slew.'

Daud dabbed at his lips with a fistful of curly beard. 'Save your arm for smiting our foes, Brod. It was none of your doing. She's the Queen of Lies, that one. There's many as does her will without knowing it. You had no way to tell that the *Indomitable* was in her foul service.'

'If I'd spent more time on deck instead of in my cabin, I might have guessed. They were an evil looking crew, the lot of 'em.'

'No more ugly than my own men,' Daud assured him. 'Evil can wear a wondrous beautiful face – as Vixia herself proves – and Good can be masked by dirt and scars.' He poured again. 'It was an honest mistake you made, Brod. My men are all sworn to die in the fight against Vixia, if need be. Those as you slew just went the sooner. At least they died clean. Let's drink to 'em, poor sods.'

He and Brod drained their horns and refilled them. Impah sipped at her goblet.

'Captain Daud,' Brod asked, 'How many days to the Great Island of Lothia?'

'If the wind is with us? Barring storm or an attack by one of Vixia's pirates, six to eight, by my reckoning. With any luck we should catch up with the *Blue Swan* a full day before Lothia – in five or six.' He squeezed the juice of a lime into his drink and stirred it with his grubby finger. 'Brod, are you sure this Raven is the true Heir?'

'As sure as I may be, without proof. Her song struck me down, and I doubt any but an Heir could do that, Rune Graven or no. We must find her. The White Lodge is sure that with all four Heirs gathered, the Rebellion has a fighting chance to destroy Vixia. If any of us are missing, Vixia is undefeatable. It's part of the prophesy. Hypocrate is certain that the four of us make the sides of the omen's "square", that must become a ring, to slay Vixia, though how that is to be accomplished, he knows not. He tells me it is a puzzle the geometers cannot unravel, no matter how they toil with their edges and compasses.'

Daud leaned forward. 'So – once we have the two of you – Earth and Air, together – then we needs must find the other two.'

'There are tens of hundreds of loyal rebels scouring land and sea. Sooner or later all four of us Heirs are sure to be found.'

'I pray it be so. I know of the search. This good ship is part of it. We were headed south on that very errand when we met up with the *Indomitable*. Seeing her foul flag, we delayed our quest for the chance to spit on it. It is by order of the White Lodge that we harry Vixia in every way that we can.'

'You had a clue? To the whereabouts of one of the other Heirs?'

Daud shrugged. 'We've chased a score of rumours this past year. I put little store by yet another.'

'What nature of rumour?'

'A thin one. It's a tale from out of the Southlands. The desert nomads tell of a strange woman, that is all.'

'How strange? In what manner?'

'It is said she walks the burning sands, alone, barefoot, naked, unprovisioned. Half a day in that heat would kill a strong man were he not covered from the sun. The tale is that she heads north, towards the Bedoo. Where she came from, none knows, but the oasis gossip is that she had been walking for eight moons without food or water. If she is not just a mirage, she is surely more than natural.'

'Does the rumour have a name?'

'None that any knows, but she has been described.'

'And?'

'Tall, beautiful – as all legends are – skin the colour of burnished copper, with a great mass of hair like gold thread fresh-drawn from the fiery furnace.'

Brod's fist slammed the table. 'She must be the Heir to the Throne of Fire.'

Daud dabbled a hunk of hard black bread into a bowl of oil and then dipped it in the salt dish. 'Brod, be not so sure. Just three moons past I sat on the slope of a volcano and watched three girls, none yet a woman, paddle ankle-deep through molten lava. I know not how the feat was done, but none proved to be the Heir of Fire.' He paused to gnaw and chew before continuing.

'In T'rona, last winter, I hung for half a watch in a woven withe basket from the limb of a tall tree. A girl had fashioned for herself silken wings and a cap of eagle feathers, to prove her mastery over Air. She fell to her death.' Daud rinsed down his bread with a mouthful of sour Jiddian ale and followed that with another swig of spirits-of-wine.

'Hope is good, Brod. It keeps us fighting and searching, but my hopes have been shattered so often that now I press on simply because I know not what else to do. A man cannot lay down and die just because his quest sees no end.'

Brod slapped Daud's shoulder, gently. 'But I was found, was I not? And before the new moon rises we will have saved my Raven, Heir of Air. Mayhap your "walking woman" will prove to be Fire. That will leave us but one last Heir to discover, and then we can attack the Evil One.

I feel it in my bones, Daud. We are not met by chance. There is a Power that guides us. If you have no hope left, try faith.'

Impah snuggled her cheek against Brod's thigh. 'My Goddess, Sloona, is for you and the White Lodge,' she said. 'I know it seems likely that some of Her Priestesses sided with Vixia, and betrayed you, Brod, but perhaps Sloona allowed that. Their treachery brought me to you, Brod. Without me you would now be less mighty.'

'How so?' Daud asked.

Brod ruffled Impah's hair. 'In this way, Daud. My strength comes from Earth, and from women, Her daughters. The ocean weakens me. That sapping of my strength is allayed, in part, by Impah here. It is as if all females are conduits to the Ultimate Mother, my Holy bride, Earth.'

Daud's eyebrow raised. 'Is this some magic rite that you perform, you and women?'

Brod laughed. 'Aye – magic enough. It's an old magic, that you no doubt practise yourself whenever you get the chance. It is a simple spell, friend Daud. When I lay with a woman I rise refreshed and renewed. Is it not the same with you?'

'Of a surety!' Daud pushed back his stool and rose. 'Well, you must be at your mightiest when we catch up with the sea-dastard who has your Raven captive, must you not? I leave you in Impah's pretty hands, Brod.' He bent and whispered in Impah's ear. 'Make him very strong, Impah, for all of our sakes.'

As soon as the cabin door closed Impah scrambled up into Brod's lap. She twisted to face the table, sprawled across it with her rump lifted high, and drew the bowl of oil closer. 'Dip your fingers, if you please, Brod,' she asked. 'Oil them well, to make their entry into my arse the easier.'

'Impah, my cock was a sore tight fit in your sweet little coynte the first time I laid with you. That narrower entrance tempts me, but would be impossible.'

Reaching behind her, Impah loosened Brod's loincloth. Her other hand steered his fingers into the bowl. 'I know that, dear Brod, and I thank you for your kindness, but all things have beginnings. Even the tightest knot may be loosened if it be teased at for long enough. Your finger is as thick around as most men's cocks are. This morn it will be but one finger that stretches my rosebud. If we persevere, by nightfall two, or perhaps three may gain entry. Captain Daud's reckoning is that we won't catch those that have your Raven imprisoned for perhaps six days. Who knows what wonders we may achieve in that time, if we are diligent?'

Brod gave no reply. He was already bent forward, one broad hand spreading her buttocks. The tip of his tongue tantalised Impah's sphincter, persuading it to relax. It softened. Brod stiffened his tongue, and prodded.

'Ah yes!' Impah sighed. 'Now your thickest finger, Brod, deep as you will. I swear by the spread of Sloona's sacred thighs, I am ready for it.'

Twenty-Two

Karina and Betohl, brother and sister Rune Gravers, stood stark naked at the foot of the steps before Queen Vixia and Her favourite companion, the Lady Laylanda. Nor were the Queen and her pet overly clad. They wore nothing but the paint upon their faces and matching green satin sashes, draped around their hips, loosely square-knotted over their mounds, and trailing before them to dust the marble floor.

When the Rune Gravers had tattooed Rena, a year earlier, they had taken great pains not to mar her beauty. Their enchanted needles had deposited potent inks beneath her skin, but in such a way as to enhance her comeliness, not spoil it. Once the scrolls and spirals had been etched into the tenderness of her lips, her nipples, her haloes and the rim of her anus, the designs had been hidden with permanent dyes of the same deep red. When they had worked on her pubes, they used an indelible blush pink to cover over the fine lines of their patterns. They had tinted the head of her clitoris with vermilion.

The other designs, the ones that had both strengthened and inflamed her internally – within her mouth, her rectum and her coynte – had been left undisguised – visible to any who cared to open her flesh and peer into her intimate orifices.

When they had done with her she had been transformed into a nymphomaniac, but with hidden strengths that had enabled her to survive, and endure, the insatiable desire that was liquid fire in her blood.

Certain portions of the cryptic symbols had been soluble. In the course of the frantic coupling that Vixia had condemned Rena to, tiny parts of the patterns had been dissolved in body fluids. She never totally regained her sanity, but she had at least recovered some degree of self-control.

When Vixia had commanded that they take Lady Laylanda to the fifth degree of erotomania, they had likewise cheated. They had elevated her to only the fourth degree. Laylanda's tattoos were also disguised. She, like Rena, now had lips of the deepest red, crimson nipples, and an always-blushing pubis.

Karina and Betohl's engraving of their own bodies was not, however, in the least manner concealed. Their ceremonial skirts had been stripped from them. They stood naked. Thus revealed, it was plain to see that not a single patch of their skins had been left unadorned by their art. From head to toe, they were living tapestries, decorated in ten thousand intricate interlocking designs of blue, green, purple, lavender and scarlet.

Despite their mottling, they made a handsome pair. Both were sturdy, in peasant fashion. Betohl's muscles were mobile slabs upon his stocky body. Karina was broad-shouldered and heavy-breasted. Her waist was not narrow, but seemed so by contrast to the opulence of her bosom and hips. Her thighs were not slender, but their tapering musculature was not without its own special charm.

'What shall we do with them, Laylanda?' Queen Vixia mused.

'Mate them with wild animals?' Laylanda suggested. 'A lusty stallion for her, and a sabre-tooth that's in heat for him?'

Vixia patted Laylanda's hand. 'A lovely thought, my dear, but no. They have enhanced themselves, you see. The patterns on their skins protect them from pain and give them unnatural strengths. Karina's embrace would likely break the stallion's back. Betohl could easily fuck a sabre-tooth into submission.'

'If their power is in the designs on their skin, why not flay them first?'

Vixia ran a fingernail down Laylanda's spine to the pad

of muscle at its base. 'Oh, my dear child! What an apt pupil you are, to be sure. But unfortunately I have need of their services. Whatever we do to them, they must survive.'

'Then?'

'It is the good in them that has led them into disobedience, you see. I had thought them totally depraved, but some hidden trace of charity remained. That is why they took pity on you, my dear, and I suspect on at least one other before you. So, you see, it is their virtue that we must destroy.'

'Their virtue? How will we do that?'

'With shame, of course. Guilt drives out virtue. We must force them into some act that they consider unforgivably heinous. Overwhelmed, their consciences will die. Once their consciences are dead, what will remain will be just their natural pure evil, distilled to a strong essence. Those who know that they are beyond redemption have no choice but to turn to Chaos, and Havoc, and to *me*!'

'But I still don't understand, Insatiable One. I have seen them at Your orgies. I have seen them each take on a dozen partners with no regard for age, sex or species. What debauchery is there that they have not already eagerly embraced?'

'How observant you are, little whore. You have seen them lay with men and women, with young and old, with comely and ugly, but have you ever seen them lay with each other?'

Both Betohl and Karina flinched.

'Is that all?' Laylanda asked. 'Is incest so terrible a sin, to them?'

'Have you tried its delights, tiny harlot?'

Laylanda looked at her feet. 'I have not had the opportunity since you changed me, Your Majesty.' She lifted her head and looked the Queen straight in her glittering eyes. 'If that be your will, bring my family to your Court, O Queen. I will lay with every one of them, each while the rest are condemned to watch.'

'I don't doubt it,' Queen Vixia said. 'I know the depth of your depravity, child. That is not the issue. It is their last trace of morality that we must crush. Yours is already dust.'

'I can see that your powers could force Betohl to mount his sister, My Queen, but would that suffice? Could they not afterwards excuse themselves the act, if it was done by compulsion?'

'Well reasoned, except for two things.'

'And those are?'

'Like most siblings, they harbour secret lusts for each other already. They deny those perverse passions but will be forced to confess to them before I am done. You see, Laylanda, I will merely start them on the road they have long craved to travel. They will complete their journey on their own.'

The Vicious One raised a taloned finger. Three naked slaves approached, a boy with the penis of a grown man and two Tiblan matrons whose faces were sealed into grotesque silver masks. The youngster kneeled before Vixia, presenting a jade bowl. The Queen took a yellow flask from one matron and a blue one from the other. She poured both into the bowl, where they blended into a deep green mixture.

'The yellow aphrodisiac is one that you know well,' Her Supreme Depravity told Laylanda.

Laylanda nodded and licked her lips.

'The blue liquid limits the power of the yellow. It does not lessen its power, at first. The dilute green potion inflames lust just as strongly as the pure yellow, but its effect wears off quite rapidly.'

'How soon?' Laylanda asked.

'It is better that these two do not know that,' the Queen said. Her evil eyes narrowed. She bent her mouth to Laylanda's ear and whispered, 'One thousand heartbeats, but hearts beat faster, when swiving, do they not?' Her tongue licked the edge of Laylanda's ear. Her teeth nipped at the girl's lobe. 'And Betohl's heart might beat faster, or slower, than his sister's.'

Laylanda shivered. 'So,' she guessed, 'that is your second secret. You will treat these two with the green potion. They will couple under its erotic influence. When it wears off they will be in mid-embrace. Will they then disengage, driven apart by their consciences? Will the temptation overwhelm them? Who would know that one more thrust was under their own volition? And if one, why not two, or three?

'Your Majesty, you are brilliant. Each of them will know that he or she betrayed the other, and will suspect having been betrayed in turn. It will be a dark secret, festering between them.'

Vixia drew the point of her fingernail down the crease between Laylanda's buttocks. 'Well reasoned, slutling. You have the half of it. Karina will be dosed, but not Betohl. His passion for his sister will be entirely natural, and obvious. A woman may conceal her lust, and perhaps her climax. A man may do neither. Betohl's shame will be clear to see. Left with his sanity, if he truly has no desire for his sister he won't attain an erection. If making love to her really disgusts him, he won't climax. We shall see, shall we not?'

Vixia's finger lifted. Four burly guards brought what looked to be a suit of bronze armour. As they fitted the metal pieces to Betohl, Laylanda saw that it had no fastenings. Each portion clung where it was placed and melted into the next. When they stepped back, Betohl was sheathed in a bronze skin, except for his eyes, the inside of his gaping mouth, and his dangling cock. Even his lips gleamed metallically.

Laylanda recognised the magical suit as what she had taken for an automaton at the revels. It had concealed a living man inside it!

Queen Vixia made a sign. Betohl – or his false skin – flexed muscles, turned, postured, and bowed to Her Depravity.

'My will now controls his every movement,' Vixia told Laylanda. 'Only his tongue and his cock are still his to command. It will be interesting to see what he does with them.'

She turned to the guards. 'Spread the woman.'

They lifted Karina into the air, holding her horizontally, arms and legs splayed wide.

Vixia handed the jade bowl to Laylanda. 'The honour is yours.'

Laylanda bobbed a curtsey and descended the steps. 'Lift her legs,' she said.

The guards tilted their victim, presenting her shapely rump.

'Spread her arse.'

Strong fingers pried Karina's buttocks apart. Laylanda tilted the bowl to her mouth, filling it with green liquid. She pursed her lips and ejected a thin stream. Her aim was true. The jet splashed into Karina's rectum.

'Lower,' Laylanda said.

The next stream splattered the insides of Karina's coynte and then wandered higher, to bathe her clitoris. Karina writhed in the guards' grip, not to escape, but from the lust that was already building within her body.

Laylanda circled the Rune Graver. 'Open your mouth,' she commanded.

The order was unnecessary. Karina's jaw was already wide agape. Her tongue lolled, eager for the aphrodisiac essence. Laylanda filled her mouth once more, and once more squirted. The green stream jetted between Karina's lips. Fast as it flowed, Karina gulped.

The next mouthful splashed Karina's left nipple, and then her right. Laylanda's final draught was not spat, but allowed to trickle slowly from her lips, smearing an olive trail upwards from Karina's deep navel, between her breasts, over her throat, and finally to her mouth once more. Laylanda let Karina suck the last few green drops from the tip of her extended tongue.

Laylanda licked her own lips. Her voice trembled with barely controlled passion as she said, 'She is prepared, Your Majesty.'

The Queen smiled sweetly. 'Let us be sure it has taken effect. Put her face between your lovely thighs, my dear. She must despise you for your betrayal. If her lust is stronger than her hate, she is ready.'

The guards tipped Karina down. Laylanda lifted her sash and bestrode Karina's head. The Rune Graver slobbered like an animal at Laylanda's coynte.

'Good,' Vixia said. 'And you, Laylanda, are you also inflamed?'

'My – my mouth,' Laylanda croaked.

'Then we mustn't waste your need, must we. Pillows!'

Slaves scurried, fetching satin cushions and silk pillows in various shapes and sizes. They made a couch of them beside where Vixia stood. She sank onto the heap and beckoned to Laylanda.

Spreading her thighs wide, she pointed to Her own dimpled mound. 'Let this be your cushion, sweet little harlot. Pleasure me with your tongue as we watch.'

Laylanda obeyed, snuggling into a position from which she could lap her Queen's golden clit while still being able to look over her Majesty's shapely hip at the obscene exhibition that was about to start below.

At a sign from Vixia's magic fingers, Betohl stood straight, his hands behind his back. The guards set Karina down on her trembling feet.

'Your brother is yours,' Vixia purred. 'He will not resist. Do with him as you have ached to do all these years, Karina. Satisfy your secret needs. Is his cock not handsome, and all the more desirable for being forbidden to you? It is yours now, to suck on or to ride, whichever takes your perverse fancy.'

Shaking her head in denial, Karina half-crouched, looking about wildly. Her left foot moved. She took a single step towards her brother. Strain twisted her face. She bit her own lip until it bled. 'No!'

Her face turned towards Vixia, pleading, but her right leg took a step. She glanced at Betohl. Her expression begged his forgiveness, but she took a third step. Her eyes changed. They focused on the length of tattooed flesh that dangled between his metal legs. Lust blazed in them. The back of her hand smeared the blood on her chin as she staggered another pace nearer, and another.

'Fight it, dear sister!' Betohl groaned.

'I am fighting it.' She leaped at him. Her arms wrapped his neck. She pulled his face down to hers.

Betohl's lips clamped tight. Vixia made a sign, and they parted. Karina mashed her patterned lips to his metallic ones. Her tongue plunged into his mouth, and out, and in, and out, making ferocious mock-love to it. Her nails screeched on his bronze back, clawing him closer.

'I don't want to do this, I swear, brother,' she gabbled into his mouth. 'I don't want to, but I must!'

'I forgive you,' he mumbled around her writhing tongue. 'It is not you who commits this terrible sin, but her. Take from me what you must to assuage your need. I love you my sister. I love you now, and still will after this is all done. Vixia cannot defeat pure love, no matter what she does.'

Karina pulled her head back, leaving smears of her bitten lip's blood on her brother's metal mouth. Her eyes blazed at him. 'Confess,' she screamed. 'Confess your lust. You have wanted me just as I have wanted you, since we were children. The sin is not mine alone. Share the shame with me, Betohl, my brother, my love.'

Betohl strained to avert his head but the bronze skin would not let him. 'I have known that unnatural lust, Karina, I confess it, but I have always fought against it. I have never touched you, except as befits a loving brother.'

Karina's hand wrapped his limp cock. 'I have lain awake at nights, brother, yearning to do this.' Her fist pumped his foreskin. 'And this.' She dropped to her knees before him. Her mouth found the tip of his cock and kissed it, almost chastely. Her lips parted and mumbled, drawing him into her mouth slowly, a fraction at a time.

'Will shame keep him limp, do you think?' Vixia asked Laylanda, 'Or will years of pent-up lust work their magic?'

'Shame has power only after lust is sated, Your Majesty.'

'Well said. And we two are proof against shame then, are we not? Our lust is never sated. Look! You are being proved right, my little harlot. He stiffens!'

Karina was drawing her sucking lips back along her brother's shaft. It was emerging with twice the girth it had as it entered.

'See how she squirms her coynte on the arch of his foot,' Laylanda observed.

'Hush child. Put your mouth to its duties. Purse your sweet lips and take just the tip of my clit between your lips. Suck shallow but fast – quick little tugs. Yes. If you are diligent, my sweet, you will be rewarded. I will cover your lovely face with the gift of my spending.'

Betohl was still resisting. Though his sister's mouth had drawn his cock to its greatest length and full thickness, still he held himself immobile. Vixia made a subtle sign. Betohl's hands clamped behind his sister's nape and pulled her face into his groin.

'Yes!' Vixia gloated. 'Fuck your sister's mouth, Betohl. Let your lust run rampant. She is Graved, is she not? She will not gag, no matter how deep your cock probes. Harder, Betohl. Work your way into her throat.'

Karina made animal noises – a plaintive mewing as her brother's cock withdrew and a deep satisfied grunt each time it thrust against the back of her mouth. Vixia made Betohl withdraw entirely, take his flesh in a metal hand, and pump it. Karina lifted herself to get at least the bulbous head between her lips.

'Shall I have him come in her mouth,' Vixia mused, 'or splatter his hot seed all over her face? Perhaps . . .' Her fingers moved. 'On your knees, Karina!' she ordered. 'He'll mount you, I promise.'

Karina swung around, knelt on all fours, and tilted her rump up. Under Vixia's inexorable influence, Betohl dropped to his knees and took aim.

'Her arse!' Vixia ordered.

Betohl did not even try to resist. He parted his sister's cheeks and stabbed. She writhed against him. Her back undulated. Her belly heaved. She juddered.

Vixia stroked Laylanda's hair. 'Did you know,' she purred, 'I released my control over Betohl some moments ago? Does he show any sign of his virtuous disgust? Of course he doesn't. And, Laylanda, the potion lost its power over Karina even sooner. For the last little while the only compulsion that either have felt is that of their own lust. I'm sure that they both realise that. I would say our little experiment has proved a complete success, wouldn't you?'

Her hips gave a little twitch.

'Yes, my dear. You may lick my juices off your chin now. When you are done, my dear, watching all this delicious incestuous buggery has given me a deep rectal craving. Let us see if your tongue can be stretched long enough to reach it, shall we?'

Twenty-Three

Rough wood chafed the soft skin of Raven's upper arms. She ignored the discomfort and worked her way lower down the post. Raven knew something of bondage. Any who dwelt at Vixia's court learned the basic skills, either as a binder or one who was bound. She had often relished both pleasures, when she had still enjoyed Vixia's favour. Whoever had tied her had done well.

They'd wrapped her arms around the wooden pillar behind her and then lashed her, forearm parallel to forearm, from elbows to fingertips. Her nails were not going to pluck any knots loose. She wasn't going to be able to abrade through her bindings, not in less than a moon. Had they used rope, that would have been possible. They'd used thin cords, and not just one long length, turned around and around. They'd used perhaps fifty or so short pieces, each individually knotted. Given an entire day, undisturbed, she might have rubbed one of them through. She was never left alone for the length of a full watch.

Her voice wasn't going to win her free, either. She was gagged with a mouthful of horrid rags. They hadn't tried to feed her. She'd hoped that when they gave her water she'd be able to somehow gather one mighty note that would strike them dead on the spot. They were too crafty. Every so often two men came to where she stood in the dark. The one with no front teeth held the lantern. The fat man who smelled of old scorched grease brought a pail and a ladle.

He poured water over her face until her gag was soaked through, and then some more. Raven was always thirsty, but each time they came she managed to suck just enough precious liquid through the rags that a drop or two trickled down her throat.

They knew something of her nature and took every precaution against her power.

One last wriggle and her rump dropped the final span to plop jarringly on the wooden deck. She stretched out her long naked legs and fumbled through the darkness with her toes. Lake had been laying to her right when last it had been light. If he hadn't rolled – there! Her ankle felt flesh. An arm? Her toes explored. No, it was a shoulder. Its skin felt clammy, but with not the dire chill of a corpse. Lake lived.

Raven squirmed around on her bottom, ignoring the slivers that pierced her back. With both legs extended she could – yes. She got the soles of her feet to either side of Lake's neck and gripped gently. At least now his head would not flop with each roll of the ship. And that was all she could do for him.

After a while her thighs cramped. She flexed them as best she could until the pain passed. Then it was her left calf. Eventually both legs went numb and she could not know whether she still protected Lake or not.

The two men came again. Raven blinked in the glare of a single horn-shielded candle. Poor Lake's hair and half his face were covered with clotted blood. His skin looked greasy. At least they'd bound him. They wouldn't have bothered if they hadn't thought he'd recover.

Would they?

Then she couldn't look at him any more. If she didn't turn her face upwards towards the ladles of water they simply splashed it onto her face. The one time they'd done that she'd almost drowned. At least she'd held back from vomiting. With her mouth blocked, spewing could have proved fatal.

When they'd done they emptied the scummy dregs from the pail over Lake's face. He didn't stir.

The one with no front teeth said, 'What think ye?'

The fat one prodded Lake's side with his toe. 'Dead by noon, like as not. Men don't bring the price a' girls nor pretty boys, neither. If he did live he'd be tetched, for a surety, wi' that great dint in his skull. 'E ain't worth the bothering o'er, brother Gap. Take hold, will'ee?'

'Ye plan to feed 'im to the Capt'n's pets?'

'You can, if ye like. The last man, aside from the Captain, as tried to toss them monsters a tid-bit lost a hand and half a forearm. I've got no mind to spend the rest o' me days wi' a stump and a hook.'

'Me neither.'

'Then it's over the side wi' 'im. They say if ye feeds the fishes enough, it proves y'gainst drowning.'

They each took one of Lake's ankles and dragged him away. Raven would have wept, but her body lacked the moisture to make tears.

Lake's head was roaring white agony. That pain was the entire universe to him, for an age. Eventually the torment abated some, enough for him to think and realise that he was lying on the seabed, half sunk into ooze.

He remembered being in the *Blue Swan*'s cabin, making love to Raven, and there'd been a screeching noise. Then? Then a face and something coming at him. Then nothing – until now.

Perhaps the *Swan*'s crew had returned? They'd surprised him and Raven and struck him down? He'd likely been thrown overboard, though why they'd bind a man they took for dead was beyond him. What would they have done with Raven?

Raped her? The thought caused a pang, but not a great one. Raven was no shrinking virgin. They'd bound and raped her already, hadn't they? And she'd shaken it off like milk that'd spilled on her fingers. His Raven was not averse to a little violence in her loving. Twice in their love-making she'd demanded, 'make me', and three times, 'Use me. Do with me as you will.' No, the Heir to the Throne of Air would likely thrive on their raping, and ask for more.

Perhaps they'd killed her. Perhaps they'd tortured and killed her? Perhaps they'd taken her prisoner again, likely well gagged this time. They wouldn't have cut her tongue out. That would have lowered her value.

He had no way to guess Raven's fate, but his path was clear. If she lived, he would have to rescue her. If they'd slain her, he had to avenge her. Lake made a decision. If Raven had died clean, he'd break the arms and legs of every man aboard the *Blue Swan* and then maroon them on some remote sea-washed rock to die slowly of exposure. If she'd died in pain, then he'd make sure that the scum's deaths were thrice times as painful.

But first he had to free himself from the cords that bound his arms, and then he'd have to find that accursed *Blue Swan*.

Lake wriggled free of the mud and writhed through the water. Even bound, he swam faster than a hunting shark. Mother Ocean washed and tended his wound. His skull knitted. Flesh and skin grew back. Before long his headache was just an awful memory.

The waters inked into night and then brightened into day. Lake surfaced. Father Sun marked the east. The *Swan* had been headed west-by-north-west. Lake got his bearings and dived once more.

He broke the surface again at noon. There was a speck on the horizon. Land or a ship? Whichever, there would likely be people. People could free his arms. Lake swam.

He was perhaps ten bowshots from the rocks when he heard the voice. At first he thought it had to be Raven, for the song was one of lust and longing, drawing him with supernatural strength.

The voice was deeper than Raven's. A siren? Lake veered away, and then paused. Was he not Lake, son of Mother Ocean? Was not a siren Mother Ocean's daughter? Was he not male, and a siren a mere female? He was surely more powerful than she. He would use her song to guide himself, but be proof against its magic allure. How surprised the siren would be, to draw a male who was immune to her spell. Perhaps, out of kindness alone, he would make love to her. It would not be because he had become enchanted. It would be from simple charity. It would, wouldn't it?

He swam faster. Lake's erection grew. His mouth became thirsty, but not for water. What would a siren's kisses taste like? What would be the salty savour of a siren's fishy coynte?

Lake threw himself from the water to flop belly-down on a rock. The song ended on one long exultant note. Lake rolled onto his back. There she was, sitting above him, combing out her long green hair. Her shoulders were almost white. Her full breasts were tipped with emerald. Her belly was rounded, with a navel deep enough for a rockpool. Below that – her scales shimmered in the afternoon sunlight. Her tail was broad and flat, with flukes that tapered so finely that Father Sun's light showed through them.

A melodious contralto asked, 'Who has delivered me so fine a package? Is it my natal day, that I am sent my greatest desire bound up with cords?'

Lake said, 'Untie me, sweet siren. I know not in what wise we may couple, but I promise you, if you will instruct me, that it will be such a loving as you have never enjoyed before.'

'You show no fear? What manner of man are you? Do you not know that it is a siren's nature to take her pleasure on any man she catches, until he dies from it? You will sate my lust, man, and then fill my stomach.' She rubbed her belly suggestively.

'If such is to be my fate,' Lake said, 'then let us at it. You are comely indeed, and I am strong. If I am to die in your arms, I will die happy. Perhaps though, it will be me who survives, and you who perish from ecstasy.'

She laughed with a watery gurgle. 'Indeed? Man, even among human kind, no mere man can out-swive a randy woman. No matter how big his balls are they empty eventually. I'll flatten yours, I swear, before night falls.'

'With the suction of your mouth? The thought pleases me, but how am I to pleasure you in return, sea-witch? Is there a coynte hidden beneath those scales? And if there is, how is my cock to find and pierce it?'

She smiled. 'Watch!' Her hands lifted her breasts and pinched their green crests into urgency. She stroked down her human hips and onto her fishy flanks. As she caressed herself the glittering scales lost their gleam and softened. Soon, patches of the palest green skin showed through. Eventually she had shapely legs and pretty feet, though her limbs were still joined from thigh to ankle.

She gave herself a little flip and dropped from her rock, landing lithely, but with her lower limbs still united.

'I see,' Lake said. 'If you now kneel, I may find entry from behind. Is that the way of it?'

'By no means. It is lust that transforms me. I am part-way changed by my own touch. To complete my mutation, I need the touch of a human male – you.'

She gave a little hop and then toppled forwards onto her hands. Like a beached sea-lion, she crept towards Lake, humping her body and dragging herself with her arms. Her hands reached his feet. She lifted her upper torso and pulled herself atop him, writhing her way up his body.

Her skin was soft, smooth and quite cold. The change had not heated her blood. Outwardly, she was a beautiful woman. Inside, she was still cold-blooded as any fish.

Lake smiled to himself at the thought. He'd heard tell of human women who had been accused of the same, but never before lain with one.

Her face reached his groin. Lake braced himself, unsure how so chilly a mouth would feel on his cock, but she passed it by, nuzzling her way up his belly, dragging her lush breasts over his thighs, planting tiny kisses on his chest, his throat, and then reaching his mouth.

'Will you kiss me willingly?' she asked. 'Or must I sing you into mad lust?'

'Give me your lips,' Lake said. 'The sight and the feel of your lovely body has inflamed me enough. I thirst for your kisses and long to see your lovely legs part for me.'

The siren smiled almost wistfully. She licked her jade lips and covered Lake's mouth with her own.

Her tongue was an inquisitive eel. The nectar of her mouth was salty-sweet. At first Lake thought the coolness unnatural, but as his passion grew he found that the contrast between his heat and her chill strangely refreshing and oddly exciting. He was reminded of an unusually severe winter, when he had greeted the Widow Forsythia as she had risen from the ocean one dawn. Her skin had been goose-bumped from the chill waters. When he had cupped her ample breasts in his warm hands they had felt more solid than before and her nipples had been chips of ice. He'd massaged slowly, letting his heat thaw them. That passage of warmth from one body to another had been almost like the flow of bodily fluids. He had gifted her with his heat.

So it was now. Lake imagined that to the siren his mouth must have felt scalding hot, like the intoxicating tea that the elders brewed from fermented chi leaves. Indeed, the siren drank from his mouth as if she had been long athirst.

She drew up from him. Her hips wriggled. 'Almost,' she said. 'Suck.'

Her hands guided her breast to his lips. Lake took her nipple into the wet furnace of his mouth, pursed his lips on her cold hard flesh, and drew as hard as he could.

'Yes!' she sighed.

Lake felt her thighs part, spread, and bracket his.

'I am open and ready,' she said. Her hand fumbled down between their bodies, clasping his hot cock in her cold hand.

'You mean to mount me so soon?' Lake asked.

'What else? I am ready. You are hard. Why should we not begin?'

'Do you know nothing of the more subtle ways of a man with a woman? Untie my hands and I will show you how a man can give you pleasure.'

'Untie you? I think not. If you are loose you will likely struggle. I would then have to sing you into submission or damage you. I want you to last, man. It is easier to leave you bound.' Her hand took his cock once more.

Lake twisted under her. 'Very well, if you will not untie me, then let me get my head between your thighs. If you think you are ready for my cock now, wait till I have used my tongue for a while. Then you will be truly ready.'

'Your tongue? But your cock is much larger. What can your soft tongue do for me that your hard cock cannot?'

'Put my head between your thighs and I will show you.'

Her sea-green eyes narrowed. 'This is no ruse? You do not seek to bite me where I am tenderest, and attempt to force me to release you? I warn you man, draw one drop of my cold blood and I will bite. You'll swive just as well minus a toe or two I'll warrant, and when you are used up, instead of slaying you cleanly before dining on your warm flesh, I'll nibble on you piecemeal, starting here!' She squeezed the bulb of Lake's cock hard enough to make him wince.

'Indeed I do plot to escape you, siren, but not in that way.'

'What!' she screeched.

'You have consumed many men, have you not? The Ocean hereabouts is thick with craft. There must have been many natural wrecks, survivors of sea-battles, and yet others who you have lured to their dooms with your songs?'

'Indeed there have been,' she grinned. 'Many.'

'And every man you have taken from the waters you have swived into exhaustion before devouring?'

'I have.'

'Well, I am kinder. Release me, and I will make love to you until you swoon from the joy of it. Then I will escape.'

She laughed. 'You have spirit, man. I like you. Very well, I will reward your vanity. Swive me until I faint, if you can, and then, when I wake, I will loose your knots. Then we will have at it once more. If you can pleasure me until I collapse a second time, you shall have your freedom as my gift.'

'Done and done,' Lake said. 'Will you swear by Mother Ocean?'

'That is a terrible oath, but I so swear. So, man, show me your magic. Be swift, for I grow impatient. Never before have I wasted so much time in debate with one of my victims. I warn you to prove yourself quickly, or it shall be done my way and our pact is broken. It was your head between my thighs that you wanted, was it not? How should this be arranged?'

'The first time? The first of many? As I am on my back, bestride my face if you will. It would be easier if I had my hands free to direct you, but I will tell you what to do while I am still able. After that, I am sure you will get the way of it.'

She knelt with her soft cool thighs bracketing Lake's head and half her weight on his face. He found his nose pressed into the soft folds of her coynte. He sucked air, filling his mouth with her salty aroma and considered how he was to achieve his object.

Through muffled ears he heard her say, 'When is this magic to start, man?'

He decided it was best to begin immediately, using what was available. Lake's tongue stretched out. It probed between the cool globes of her buttocks and found its target. He swirled its tip around the rim of her sphincter. His power drew on the blood in her veins, compelling it to follow his tongue's caress. Under the twin influences her knot relaxed. Lake strained, able to probe but shallowly, for she did not yet know to tug her own buttocks apart and press down to give him deeper access.

'Yes, that is nice,' she said, 'but I doubt I will find my climax from it. Nevertheless, I will grant you more time to prove yourself, man.'

Lake twisted his head to one side to find air and then tilted his head back as best he could, to get his lips to her coynte. He nibbled, very gently, for it would not do to startle her into thinking he was about to bite. His lips mumbled a pendulous lip into his mouth, where he nibbled on it as he hummed into her depths.

The siren fidgeted on his face – with pleasure, he hoped.

'That tickles,' she complained, 'but is not unpleasant. Your reprieve is extended.'

Lake braced his feet flat on the rock and pushed himself along. His tongue dragged across the slickness that led to the juncture of her coynte's lips. He sucked a deep breath and tilted his head up. Thank Mother Ocean the siren had a clit like a human woman, though perhaps longer than most, and with a pea-green head that barely poked from under its sheath. His lips found it, and sucked it in.

'Oh!'

If his hands had been free Lake would have been toying with her nipples with one hand and tickling her rectum with the fingers of the other, speeding her towards her first climax.

His hands weren't free, so he relied on his power. His tongue flickered on her clit's head. His command of her bodily fluids pumped it harder, and harder. Splitting his attention, he drew briny blood to her nipples also. They had to be so tight they'd feel like bursting. How much of this erotic torment could she stand? He wasn't teasing, but deliberately urging her to her climax as quickly as he could. Any human woman would have sobbed out three orgasms already from what he was doing to the siren. Was she, being also a child of Mother Ocean, somewhat immune to his power?

She jerked her hips, pistoning her clit between his lips. That was better. Lake summoned up all his strength and mentally sucked the fluids from the walls of her spasming vagina. Once the flow started it continued on its own, flooding Lake's face in a salty gush.

The siren screamed and collapsed to one side. Lake rolled towards her, burrowing his face back between her thighs.

'No more! I must rest for a moment,' she begged.

Lake was merciless. He found her clit and worried at it like a dog at a bone, shaking his head from side to side, elongating it to the point it must have been ecstatic agony for her. Yes! Like a human woman, the siren had withdrawn but a little way from her plateau of pleasure. His persistence lifted her back again. She screamed her joy twice more before he released her.

The siren lay panting in the sunshine. 'You have proven your word,' she said as she passed out.

Lake found a rough spine of rock and set to work abrading his bonds. He had the siren's word on his eventual freedom, but what worth is the oath of a being with no soul? Four strands had parted when he heard the siren speak.

'That is not necessary. You have my word, on Mother Ocean. You have passed the first part of your testing. I will release you now. Repeat that miracle just once, and you will be free to depart.' Her sharp little teeth gnawed through the rest of the cords. 'Will you lay now, that I may mount you?' she asked.

'Is that the only way of loving that you know?'

'I know that a man may mount a woman, just as I mount my victims. All before you have been unwilling so I have pinned them and ridden them. If you would rather be on top, I am ready to try that novelty.'

'Perhaps later. You have much to learn, siren. Shall we continue your schooling?'

Lake knew that when a man has demonstrated his ability to give a woman her climax once, she is in expectation of similar joy when next he makes love to her. The second time is always easier, and the third easier yet. He experimented.

The siren's next orgasm came from his sucking at her teat, with a little help from his magic's fondling of her clit. After that he had her on all fours. When she sprawled from under him, sobbing her pleasure, she turned to him. 'What you did to me with your mouth, man – is there some way I might return that pleasure to you?'

He taught her the art of fellatio, and found her mouth most satisfying, despite its coolness. As a reward, he introduced her to the pleasures of buggery, milking at her breasts with his hands and at her clit with his mind as he plunged into her arse until he flooded it.

'I am undone,' she admitted. 'Go, man, but return to me some day, if it please you. You have my word that you may come and go from my rocky home as and when you wish.'

'You have not yet fainted for the second time,' he reminded her. 'I owe you that.'

'I forgive you the debt. I confess, my body can take no more pleasure this day.'

'Then I will give you one last gift. Is it true that you cannot complete your transformation into woman-shape except you be lusty?'

'It is.'

'And when you caress yourself, you may achieve but part of the change? You need a man's touch to finish it?'

'True.'

'Then I will teach you how you may raise your own lust higher than before. It may be that you learn the power to divide your limbs and walk on two legs whenever you will.'

'How can that be?'

'Clamp tight your thighs, my siren. Press them together as if they were wedded.' She did as he asked. Lake leaned over her and took her hand in his. 'You see, this little bud is still exposed. Take your finger like so – and press – and wobble – and . . .'

'Oh yes!' she gasped. 'I see how it could be. O man, you have paid for your life tenfold. I release you now with my good wishes.'

'My thanks, but first . . .' He wrapped her tight-clamped thighs between his. His hand pressed his cock down between them. It found her slit, and nudged in, not deeply, but far enough to give them both pleasure. As he pumped the upper edge of his staff rubbed on her clit. Lake bent his head to her breast and sucked. His hand squirmed beneath her bottom, found her anus, and probed. Stimulated three ways at once, the siren soon climaxed yet again. This time she did swoon.

Lake jolted her between his thighs until he jetted his seed into her unconscious body, kissed her forehead, and dived off the rock.

Perhaps it was making love to a sea-creature that had enhanced his powers, for when he swam now, he left a roiling wake that was half a bow-shot long.

Twenty-Four

Tomo, Century-leader of Queen Vixia's Fifth Royal Devastators, cursed his commander under his breath. He'd never do it aloud. If he did, there was bound to be some handy ear that was attached to a mouth – a mouth that would whisper tales as a sure route to promotion.

Tomo cursed Commander Deet that the boys he was likely buggering in the comfort of his villa would give him the clap, or worse.

It was all very well that the mission was an easy one. If there was combat, it would only be against the untrained hill-men who styled themselves 'Bee People'. That wasn't the problem. The problem with leading a Century that was nine-tenths raw recruits wasn't that they couldn't fight. It was their marching that was the problem.

With a Century of seasoned men under him, he'd have been up the Havoc-cursed hills, done the job, and be halfway home again by now. It would be easy enough. Cut down a few hill-men if they were foolish enough to show themselves. Find a cluster of the bees nests. Make smoke to drowse them. Empty out the honey. Spend a quiet afternoon napping while his men gathered pollen from the yellow flowers, and back in time to try the new concubine his wife had promised him for his birthday.

A fine way to spend his birthday – dragging a hundred shirkers upslope!

'Is that them?' Rhee, his second-in-command called out.

Tomo stomped along the line of scruffy recruits to the front of the column. Aye, it was them all right. The air was buzzing. There was as big a cluster of nests as he'd seen in five years of honey-gathering. With a crop like this no one would miss a pot or two. He could sell one pot for a month's pay, and use the other himself. It had been a long time since he'd smeared his cock with honey and let some pretty little chit go crazy with passion from gobbling it off.

Mayhap he'd give his wife, Onda, a taste, her having been so good to him this year. There's nothing like two thirsty mouths sucking at his cock at once to set the juice aboil in a man's balls.

Tomo didn't like the location, seeing as it was between the walls of a ravine. Old soldiers like the high ground, but it couldn't be helped. This was where the nests were, so this was where they'd be harvested.

'Set a watch,' he told Rhee. 'Get them smoke-pots fuming. Get a detail scouting for the flowers and watch 'em close, mark you. I want no man licking his thumbs while he's gathering pollen. This bunch is bad enough, without they're randy all the way back, though it might put some spring in their slovenly steps.'

Tomo found some nice springy bracken and stretched out. He'd barely fallen asleep when he was wakened by Rhee.

'Leader – there's no honey!'

'What?'

'No honey. We smoked the bees, like usual, and I broke the first nest open. It was empty. No honey, no combs. I split four more – all the same. All dried up inside, they was, like they'd been abandoned a season since.'

'They can't be old nests. There was bees around when we got here.'

'Yes Leader, but none now. We ain't seen no bees since we started the smoke. There's usually some as drops. Y'can often see 'em crawlin' on the ground, all woozy-like.'

Tomo scratched his head. 'No honey? No bees? Nonsense! Look, there's a swarm now.'

And there was – not one swarm but a dozen clouds of swirling specks, buzzing upslope towards them, coming from downwind where the smoke wouldn't have carried.

That was when the first javelin took a recruit through his throat.

Tomo looked up. Both ravine rims were lined with men, and there was one woman. A tiny thing she was, and all glittering at the waist, like she was wrapped in gold. She weren't no girl, no matter how small she seemed to be. She had hips and a bosom that'd stiffen a man's yard right fast, even seen from afar.

The Century-leader was an old campaigner. He knew how to calculate odds. He had a hundred men, most of them untried. There had to be twice that number on the cliffs above them, and downslope there were the bees, hovering now, as if waiting in ambush. It was a queer thing, for a certainty. It was almost as if the bees and the hill-men were working together, under one command.

The golden-girdled woman raised her arm and brought it down sharply. Javelins rained. A good part of Tomo's force took heel, straight at the bees. Another third died where they stood, pierced through twice and thrice each.

Tomo and Rhee ducked into the bracken. They knew the chances. They lay and watched as their men died amid the broken nests. Those were the lucky ones. The ones who fled into the bees died much worse. Some, after their first sting or two, turned on their mates, ripping off their leathers and mounting those who didn't resist. With the bee venom in their veins, even those who had never looked at another man became so desperate to plunge their cocks into flesh that they cared not a fig seed what sex that flesh was.

Others took a dozen stings, fast. That much lust cannot be assuaged, or even contained. Their bodies contorted. Muscle fought muscle. Bones broke – arms, legs, but mainly backs.

Tomo crawled through the bracken, followed by Rhee. 'What we going to tell the commander?' Rhee asked.

'Tell that limp-cocked old sodomite? Tell him that a hundred of his men were routed and killed by a band of primitives and a few bees, all led by some sort of crazy girl in a gold girdle? You tell him, Rhee. He'll skin your balls and pickle 'em while you're still wearing 'em, and that's before he hands you over to the Queen's torturers, or worse,

Her Vicious Majesty Herself. I'm off – off to where they've never heard of bloody Vixia and Her bleedin' spells. I don't know where such a place might be, but if there is one, I'm going to find it.'

Twenty-Five

'Sail ho!' the lookout cried. 'Belay that. Two ships, one towing the other.'

Brod, in his cabin, set Impah back on her feet and snatched up his loincloth. Still knotting it, he strode across the heaving deck. 'Can you see a figurehead?' he bellowed.

'They're sailing away from us, Sir. We'll be right on 'em before we'll know who they are.'

Captain Daud ap-Dan touched Brod's massive arm. 'My guess is it's the *Blue Swan* and some poxy ally o' hers what's been dismasted. If it ain't, it's still likely a pair o' slavers what's mates, in these waters. I doubt me the second craft is a prize. When there's a sea-fight there's usually only one craft left afloat when it's done, as well you know. As there's two of them, that means two crews. That doubles the odds against us. What say you, Brod? Do we attack?'

Brod shook his head. 'I've brought enough harm to you and your men, Captain Daud. I have no choice but to attempt a rescue, but there's no need for any more of your men to die. Spare me a rowing boat. Trail them till nightfall and I'll board them alone.'

'Are you mad? My men and I are sworn to Vixia's downfall and the restoring of the Four Heirs to their thrones. D'you think we'd put one Heir in peril, on a mission to save another, and just sail away? I look to your judgement, not your leave to turn tail like some mangy mongrel.'

'I doubt you not, but it seemed to me that one man, boarding in secret, would stand a better chance than an open attack.'

Daud shook his head. 'Secret? You think to sneak up on two ships, in dead of night, board them both, search out your Raven and spirit her away before the alarm is given?'

'That was my plan, though I figured on having to fight free.'

'This ain't the forest, where you can take cover all the way to an enemy camp. We're at sea, Brod. We've seen them and they've seen us. There'll be double watches on both them craft till we drop over the horizon and for a day after – triple at night. With a hundred eyes scouring the waves for you, you think to sneak up on 'em?'

'Then what?'

'One craft's a cripple. We've the legs on both, as they've one set of sails pressed into double duty. We attack now, fast as we can catch 'em. Every moment we delay gives the poxy swine more time to prepare for us. We use our speed to swing west and then east. We'll come at 'em from their port. We sail between 'em. There's a hawser as joins 'em. Either it'll snap and leave the stern ship becalmed, out of the fight till we're ready for it, or else it won't.'

'And if it doesn't break?'

'Ask me again when we can see better. If the line's long enough, and we hit it dead centre with enough force, both of 'em'll swing, crash together, and likely sink.'

'Sink? But what of Raven?'

'I've never seen two ships collide side-by-side, but my reckoning is that they'll lock and wallow, going down slow. That'll keep 'em busy, by the Glorious Great Fire of Lyx! You and me and my roughest men'll make a boarding party, find your Raven, and back to the *Sea Serpent*, quick as may be.'

'Won't the *Serpent* be tangled in that towing hawser?'

Daud scratched his chin through his beard. 'A good point, Brod. I'll have a man hanging from our prow, ready with an axe to free us.'

Brod slapped Daud's back. 'An excellent plan, Captain. I can see we'll have to make you an admiral in the new Arcadian Navy when the revolution is victorious.'

'Plan? Aye, that's what it is, just a plan, useful as tits on a fish. There's ten score things as could go wrong, and a dozen of them as will. We have a plan just so's we have a direction to start by. Once we're in action, its just do your damnedest and kill as many of Vixia's foul scabs as you can afore you die. I'm off below to put a fresh edge to my sword. What arms do you favour, Brod?'

'A sturdy staff if you can find me one, iron-bound if possible. Shouldn't you be on deck, Captain Daud, directing your men?'

'My chief officer will sail the *Serpent* for now, Brod. There's plenty of time, you see. This isn't like a land battle, where it's see the enemy and fall on 'em. It'll take half a day to catch 'em. I pray it works to jitter them. My men already count themselves as dead and so fear nothing. Slave-trading scum are brave enough when it comes to raiding a few villagers. Wait till you see how feeble they are, faced with true fighting men. They're twice our count of bodies, likely, but we still outnumber that rabble when it comes to cut and thrust.'

The *Serpent*'s carpenter soon had a spare spar trimmed to suit Brod. He had no iron to band it, but hammered a sheath of lead onto each end and then bound over the soft metal with copper wire. No man but Brod could have lifted it when it was done. He gave it a few trial twirls and decided it would serve to cave skulls well enough.

The deck was abustle with men bringing missiles up from below or sharpening dirks, boarding pikes, cutlasses and assorted edged weapons. Brod wound the catapult for its crew and loaded it with a net full of jagged flints. The engine's commander told him that it was intended for the enemy's rigging, as they had no great stone to hurl.

'Like as not it'll do the task better,' he said. 'It'll make a nice enough mess of their mainmast if my aim be true, and then shower down on their scurvy heads.'

'I wish you luck with it,' Brod said. 'Your aim could carry the battle for us.'

The commander grinned lopsidedly. 'That's the sure truth. That's why the catapult and its crew's the prime target for the enemy's bows and slings. Just pray for us that our catapult's reach is longer than their bows'.'

The deck lurched as the *Sea Serpent* tacked east. That would be the longer leg, as they'd be sailing across the wind. Brod went to his cabin to say his farewell to Impah.

Somehow or other the girl had acquired an evil-looking rusty blade that was as long as her forearm. 'You won't be leaving me here, Brod,' she protested. 'I'll be boarding with you. You'll need someone to watch your back.'

'If you're behind me I'll be looking over my shoulder,' he said. 'Who'll guard my front?'

'Forget me. I'll be there, but forget me.'

'Impah – you stay here. That's an order.'

She gave him her most submissive smile. 'Brod, my God, my Lord, my Love, I'd cut my own throat if you told me to. Better, I'd perform acts of love for you that would break my back, split me in twain, or choke me, if that would give you a pinch of pleasure. I was born to be your slave, to obey your least command, but not that one. Order me all you like, beat me if you wish, but when you board that slaver I'll be two paces behind you, and stay there until I die.'

Brod turned on his heel and slammed out. He returned a few moments later carrying a coil of cord. Impah looked at it, smiling softly. 'You wish to bind me, my Brod? I am skilled in such things. If your slave may make a suggestion?'

'You may. How would you be most secure, but still comfortable?'

'Comfortable?' She stamped her foot. 'Master, I had thought you meant to bind me for our mutual pleasure, in perhaps the Thonged Web, or the Crouch of the Cricket. I see now that you mean to abandon me and leave me behind like a cur on a leash.'

'There would be no use your resisting,' Brod warned her.

'I see that. Bind me to that sea-chest then, if you must. Tie me tight, and face up, and then grant me one last wish, if you will.'

'A wish? Apart from letting you follow me, anything.'

She lay herself on the chest, arms and legs dangling. 'Bind me first, please Brod.'

Brod took a dozen turns around and under the chest, pinning her four limbs securely, though not as tightly as she begged. He finished off with a line across her thighs and another beneath her pert young breasts.

'Well?' he demanded. 'What is it that you want?'

'I am sworn to Sloona in Her aspect as The Slave,' Impah reminded him. 'As such, I am devoted to giving my man pleasure. Any I receive in return is of little consequence. I am merely an instrument. I am the humble receptacle that receives your seed when, where and how you wish it. I am sworn to give you pleasure, as the Book says, "Any where, any time, any how".'

'You've received a plentiful measure of my spending these last few days, sweet Impah. I'm sure that Sloona is well pleased with you.'

'Perhaps. Mayhap She would consider that my own pleasure, the joy you have given me, has been too great.'

Brod scratched his head. 'Are you telling me that I have failed you, by giving you pleasure?'

'By no means, Brod. You have done so because you wanted to. I know that. What I ask of you now Brod, just this once, is that you take your pleasure while giving me none.'

'How?'

'Shed your loincloth, please Brod. Stand astride my face. Let those wonderful balls of yours rest upon my unworthy chin.'

Brod shrugged, but did as he was bid. Few men would have refused so reasonable a request.

When Impah spoke again her breath was hot behind Brod's scrotum. 'Now take yourself in hand, my Master. Stroke your own flesh. Look down on my helpless body as you play, if you will, my Master. Consider it nothing but the eager receptacle that awaits your liquid gift. Cover my flesh with your spending, Lord, and I will be content to wait beneath that wet blanket until you return victorious.'

'Would you not wish me to take a different position, Impah? Do you not wish to watch?'

Brod was well used to the visual game. When he had

taken shelter at The Widow's Welcome Inn, with plump and randy Mahia and her slender depraved daughter Leiala, that had been one of their favourite sports. Brod had spent many a happy evening pumping himself while watching as the two debauched women frotted their own coyntes and clits until the air had been thick with the sweet musky smells of sex.

Impah nibbled the loose skin of Brod's scrotum. 'I have other duties,' she explained. 'I have set myself the task of making your self-pleasuring more enjoyable than you could achieve alone.'

She planted a long sucking kiss on the sensitive skin between Brod's balls and his anus, where he bore the mark of Earth.

Brod took his shaft in his right hand and stroked gently up towards his bulbous glans. Impah made her mouth very wet. A saliva-laden tongue slavered the base of Brod's balls, slid back, and flattened as it twisted sideways to slide between his muscular buttocks.

Brod looked down past his wagging cock, at Impah's sweet girlish breasts, partly lifted by the cord that passed beneath them. He squeezed himself and pumped faster.

Impah pushed her hips up, straining against the cord that bound her thighs. She knew she could not break it. She just wanted to groove it more deeply into her soft skin. All men, even those as kind as Brod, have some cruelty deep within them. Her self-torture was designed to rouse that vicious streak, for it is a sure goad in the service of Sloona the Slave.

Brod stroked with a will. His eyes burned at Impah's naked mound. Her clit had emerged, a sure sign that even untouched she was still being excited. As Sloona knows, the most potent organ in love-making is the mind, and Impah's was revelling in her service to the man she worshipped.

Brod squatted a fraction, opening his sphincter to Impah's probing. Her tongue took full advantage, rimming and stabbing, stabbing and rimming. The squirmy invasion incited Brod even more than his self-love did. That, and the three engorged points on Impah's body, her clit and her two nipples, urged his lust. When Brod made love to a woman he always held back for as long as he could, prolonging her pleasure. The special joy of this love-making – for it was love-making, she was getting her pleasure from his – was that he need not consider such restraint. He flailed at his own cock, willing the milk in his balls to boil over.

And it did. A great gout of foaming hot cream jetted and flopped, splashing Impah's body from her mound to her breasts.

'Thank you, my love,' she breathed into his slowly closing rectum. 'I am content. Go slay the slavers. Rescue your Raven. Think only, when you return, to release me, if you will.'

'What? What mean you? You think I mean to abandon you?'

'You will have Raven, will you not? When you have an Heir in your bed, what need will you have of a humble Slave of Sloona?'

Brod grinned. 'Impah, you are a foolish girl. Yes, I love Raven. There is a bond between Heirs. That does not mean that an Heir forsakes all other loves. There are two amazons and a girl who was a victim of Vixia's cruelty waiting for me in the rebel quarters. I love each of them, all in different ways. I think they care for me, but while I've been gone they've each given their bodies to a dozen lovers, I'll warrant.

'Yes, I'll swive Raven the moment I have the chance. My balls are large, Impah. There'll be enough left over to keep you happy, I promise, and when I am not with you, you are free to love any man or woman as takes your fancy. Love is freedom, not fetters. I thought you understood that.'

Impah gave a contented sigh. 'Then I am doubly happy, Brod. You must understand though, for a Slave of Sloona "fetters" are a vital part of love. Promise you will let me teach you how to bind me with fitting severity, when the battle is done and won.'

Brod hefted his still-stiff shaft. 'Give me a day and a night for this to settle its overdue score with Raven, and I'll bring you enough cordage to tether a herd of mastodons.'

Twenty-Six

Captain Daud said, 'I've bad news, Brod.'

'It's not the *Blue Swan* out there?'

'No, it's the *Swan* all right. She's the craft in tow. It's the other ship as bothers me. She's *The Claw*.'

'You know of her?'

'Her Captain's a slimy villain by the name of Purd. He's a special favourite of Vixia's.'

'All the more pleasure in killing him then.'

'But the harder. The story is that he stole himself a treasure in pearls a while back. Being crafty, Purd didn't try to sell 'em. He made a gift of 'em instead – to Her Supreme Vileness. She paid him back with better than gold. She gave him two monstrous great ogres from the Northland Forest to be his pets. The beasts live on human flesh and that alone. Purd feeds 'em a captive once in a while, but not too often. He keeps 'em hungry.' Daud stroked his beard.

'When it comes to a battle,' he continued, 'Purd rubs some evil-odoured grease that Vixia gave him into his men's hair. The ogres don't like the smell of it none, so when he unchains them they goes for the likes of us, what's trying to board *The Claw*. Are you up for it Brod? I'll volunteer to take ten men and harry one beast. It'll be up to you to slay the other and then come to our aid. An Heir might stand a chance against an ogre, but no mortal does.'

Brod whistled his copper-bound spar through the air. 'I'll cope, but have your bowmen do their best to give the monsters a prick or two to slow them down will you? Make it easy for me.'

Daud slapped Brod's shoulder. 'That's the spirit. I'll give the order, but they'll have small enough targets. An arrow won't pierce an ogre's skin. My boys will have to aim for their eyes.'

Brod fixed a grin to his face. On land, far away from this damned unsteady Ocean, he'd have felt confident enough. Floating, with half his strength sapped, he wasn't so sure. Still, it would never do to let the *Serpent*'s crew know that. A battle begun in confidence is half won, as Theocritus had taught him.

The catapult was aimed with a slew to port. When it was released it would rock the *Serpent*, perhaps slowing her, but that was a chance that Captain Daud had decided to take.

The *Serpent* lanced through the waves as if she was aware that speed was life and death. A volunteer clung to a boarding net that hung from her figurehead. It was his task to decide if, and when, to climb down with his axe and cut the hawser that towed the *Blue Swan*. He'd given his few paltry possessions to his mates before taking his position. All agreed that he was a dead man.

A few spring-thrown darts from *The Claw* splashed into the waves. An arrow clattered harmlessly on the *Serpent*'s deck.

'Hold your fire, men,' Daud ap-Dan shouted. 'Ready on the catapult. Marksmen, as soon as the catapult strikes, your first target is the ogres, but if you've no clean shot kill whoever you can. Helm, two points starboard if you please. Steady now.'

The *Serpent* surged over *The Claw*'s sluggish wash, aimed into the gap between the two slavers.

'There's no one aboard the *Blue Swan*,' a lookout called.

'Starboard crew, move to port, quick as you like,' Daud bellowed. 'Steady all. We'll hit that hawser on my count. When I get to five, release the catapult. Eight, seven, six, five . . .'

A man knocked the chock free. The catapult swished. Few eyes followed its missile's flight. Those men who weren't pulling bows or hurling javelins were watching the towing hawser where it sagged under water for about the length of a tall man.

A man cried, 'Curse it! A clear miss!'

The hawser hit the *Serpent*'s bow an arm's reach below the waves. There was a grinding, and a long moaning scrape. The *Serpent* shuddered to a halt and wallowed with her prow uptilted.

'Did we break it?' Daud demanded.

A javelin from *The Claw* nicked a line as it flew and was deflected away from Daud's unprotected back.

'No Captain. We've damned well ridden up on it. It's fast beneath our keel. We're spewing-well beached on a sodding bugger-it-to-Hel rope.'

Sling-shot pellets rattled. One man cursed his broken finger and passed his double-bitted axe to his left hand.

Daud spat orders left and right. 'Find a way to cut it. Right that catapult and rewind. Boarding party to me. Grapnels stand ready.'

A wave lifted the *Serpent*. The ocean's troughs dropped both *The Claw* and the *Swan* lower. Daud's men in the rigging took advantage of their momentary elevation to let loose a volley at *The Claw*'s deck. Mother Ocean changed her allegiance, dropping the *Serpent*. *The Claw*'s hull loomed above the *Serpent*'s crew's heads. Rocks and darts rained down.

A dozen of Daud's crew threw grapnels on looping lines. Half of them bit wood. A weighted and hooked boarding net missed its mark and hung useless from the *Serpent*'s side.

Boarders scaled lines up *The Claw*'s side or swung down onto her decks from the *Serpent*'s rigging. Brod crossed the heaving gap in one mighty leap. Daud was three breaths behind him.

'The ogres,' Daud panted. 'Aft!'

Brod's spar crushed one man's shoulder and tore the head from another on the back-swing. Daud lunged low and ripped through a man's femoral artery with the point of his blade. Behind Daud, the man with the crushed finger and the double-bitted axe gurgled his last around an arrow that had split his larynx.

Brod bellowed, swung his spar in great circles, and charged.

Six valiant men from the *Serpent* had reached the ogres already. Two were now headless corpses. Another pair screamed like gutted horses as monstrous double-thumbed hands plucked them to gobbets of flesh. Brod levelled his spar like a lance. He galloped along the deck, taking no note of *The Claw*'s crewmen that he brushed aside like gnats. Lead that was wrapped in copper wire hit an ogre in its breastbone. The monster juddered back a single step.

Brod let his spar's end droop to the deck and then swung it up as hard as he could between the ogre's warty thighs. There was a horrid popping sound as both of the beast's scaly testicles burst. Brod ducked low and swung once more, this time at an angle against the inside of the ogre's knee. The creature staggered howling towards the side. Brod followed, raining a flurry of blows, heedless of where they landed just so they drove the monster to the scuppers. Its taloned foot hit the rail. Brod poked its belly. It toppled between *The Claw* and the *Serpent* into the waves and disappeared.

Brod whirled. Daud was harrying the second monster, dancing beyond the reach of its long arms, slashing when it was careless. The single thick finger that lay twitching on the deck was proof of his blade's keenness.

The monster seemed not to feel the pain. Even as it snarled and groped for Daud, it still chewed at the bare foot that protruded from between its grinding jaws. It sucked hard, dragging the severed member into its mouth. As the last toe disappeared from sight, the monster let out a mighty roar and charged at Daud. There was no time for Brod to reach his friend. He drew back his arm and hurled his spar as if it were a javelin. The lead-weighted missile took the beast full in its ugly mouth, snapping off a curved fang and lodging in the ogre's throat.

Brod put his shoulder down and charged. He hit the beast at its pot gut. Brod's feet slithered in blood as he scrabbled forward, urging the ogre half a pace at a time towards *The Claw*'s side. The rail caught the backs of its knees. The creature gave one horrified shriek and followed its mate into Mother Ocean's wet embrace.

The Heir to the Throne of Earth picked up a boarding pike to replace his lost spar.

Daud said, 'Brod.'

Brod turned. The battle was still going on in *The Claw*'s prow, but barely two dozen of the *Serpent*'s crew were left standing, fighting three times that number of slavers.

Between Daud and Brod and the losing struggle stood Captain Purd. He was flanked by ten of his men, six with recurved short bows and four with crossbows. All ten missiles were aimed unerringly at Brod and Daud. At fifteen paces, likely none would miss their marks. The Captain and the young titan let their weapons clatter to the deck.

Twenty-Seven

Captain Purd said, 'Let's end the slaughter. If you'd be so kind as to have your men lay down their arms, I swear I will be merciful.'

Brod touched Daud's arm and tried not to let his astonishment show on his face. Behind Purd and his bowmen a naked man was climbing up over the side. He was tall and fair and wet. A finger at his lips warned Brod and Daud to make no sign.

Captain Daud ap-Dan stroked the sweaty tangles from his beard. 'What terms do you offer then?' he asked Purd.

The slaver Captain lifted a brow. 'Terms? Oh, I will be most generous. I'll have your ship and all that's on her as my prize, of course.' Purd paused to swallow, as if something was stuck in his gullet. 'I'd expect your men to kindly repair the damage they've done to my poor ship, as well.'

Brod waited for the naked stranger to make some move, but all he did was crouch, staring intently at Purd's back.

Purd coughed. 'I'd – I'd – ahem. I'd want the young giant as my prisoner.' He rubbed his throat. When he spoke again his voice was thick and his words slurred. 'You and you' men, Captain – I'd – I'd set you adg-adrift. Longboat. Two oars. A dozen loaves and – and water. Two full bawews. Barrey-y, barrel of . . .'

He clutched at his mouth with both hands and fell to his knees. Blood spurted from between his fingers. His bowmen turned to him in amazed horror. The naked stranger rushed them from behind as Daud and Brod snatched up their weapons and charged from in front.

A hasty arrow whistled between Brod's thighs. A more

steady aim creased his shoulder. Brod swung his pike as if it was a scythe. Three bowmen fell with broken legs. A mighty fist battered another's armoured chest flat enough to burst his heart. Brod ran yet another through, stamped the man's body off the hooked blade, and turned.

The rest of the bowmen were dead at the hands of Daud and the stranger.

'How?' Brod asked.

'Later,' the naked man told him.

The stranger and Daud snatched up bows and let arrows fly into the backs of *Claw* crewmen as fast as they could draw and release. Brod tried to follow suit, but the bows weren't built for such as he. The first one snapped in his hands, and so did the second.

Brod tossed the pieces aside and grabbed up a bloody axe from the deck. He was no marksman, and lacked the skill to make his missile strike blade first. It didn't matter. He couldn't miss the press of backs that hemmed in his allies. No matter what he threw, if it was heavy enough it killed, no matter whether it struck blade first, shaft first, or sideways-on.

The Claw's crew soon recognised their defeat. Expecting as much mercy from the victors as they would have given, they rushed the side and threw themselves over. The *Sea Serpent*'s men dispatched the enemy wounded, tended their own, and set to the urgent repairs. Storms came quickly in those seas. Three crippled ships, interlocked, wouldn't have survived the first tall wave.

Brod grabbed the stranger's arm. 'Now tell me,' he said. 'What did you do to Purd?'

The man grinned. 'I have a certain skill,' he explained, 'with making people's blood flow where I want it to. I'd never tried using my power as a weapon before, but it seemed worth trying. I simply engorged the man's tongue in his mouth until it choked him.'

Brod swallowed hard. 'I think it burst first,' he said, 'but the end was the same. My thanks to you, but who are you?'

The man held out his hand. 'I'm Lake – and you?'

Brod took the proffered hand. 'Brod. Very well, "Lake" is your name, but what are you?'

' "Brod"? I know that name. Can we talk later? I came to rescue a friend. She must be somewhere below deck.'

'I too came to make a rescue,' Brod said. 'Let us search together.'

They found horn lanterns in the galley, and smouldering punk-sticks to light them. Once below, Brod bellowed, 'Raven!'

A muffled voice cried, 'Help!'

'That's not Raven,' Lake said. 'She'll likely be gagged, if we are lucky.'

'Lucky?'

'If she lives. You know something of Raven's powers, Brod. If she is alive, and can sing, she is free. None could resist her voice.'

Brod whirled on Lake and took him by his shoulders. 'You seem to know who I am, and who Raven is. Best tell me who you are, now.'

Lake tried to shrug, but Brod's iron fingers held his shoulders. 'Is it not obvious? You are Earth. Raven is Air.'

'And you?'

'Why – I am Water, of course.'

Brod drew Lake into a brief embrace and slapped his back. 'Three! Three of us!'

'Two,' Lake reminded, 'until we find Raven.'

The first door was stopped by a simple oaken bar that any able-bodied man could lift, but Brod was impatient. He flat-handed it open, letting slivers fly. All that was within was a dozen sacks of oka beans.

When he burst the second door he found coils of cordage. Brod grinned, remembering his promise to Impah.

'There are living bodies behind this door,' Lake called. 'It's chained.'

Brod snapped the iron links between his fingers. When the two men peered within they saw that the hold was filled with women – females at least. Some were pale as snow. Others were cat-eyed. Still more were giantesses – as tall as Brod, almost.

'Lake!' Two golden-skinned girls rushed into Lake's arms.

'Jasmine! Hibiscus!'

Brod demanded, 'A human girl. Beautiful. So high. Black hair – short. Is she with you?'

'There is another captive,' a Styxian girl said. 'She is in the hold beneath this one. We've heard them take her water and seen glimmers of light shine up between the planks.'

Lake made for the door.

'No.' Brod said. 'This way is quicker.' He stamped his heel down, hard. Planks split. Two more stamps and there was a hole big enough for Brod to drop into the darkness below.

'Pass me down a lantern.'

Lake handed a light down and then followed. The Heir of Water loosened Raven's gag as Brod took the easy way to release her arms – punching through the pillar she was lashed to.

'I always seem to find you when you're all tied up and helpless,' Lake joked as he lifted Raven to her feet.

Raven ran her tongue over parched lips. 'This time,' she croaked, 'I'd like some water, please, before you take your wicked advantage of me.'

Twenty-Eight

Captain Daud ap-Dan grinned like a mer-cat. He said, 'So now I have three of you Heirs in my protection.' He rubbed his horny hands together in glee. 'Three out of four, eh? Who'd have thought it? I set my sails for a wild-auk hunt for the Fire Heir, and I found me Earth, Air and Water. If Vixia knew, she'd be shaking in her iron-heeled boots.' He pushed back from a table that was littered with the remains of their meal.

'Are you well fed? We've provisions aplenty. Both *The Claw* and the *Blue Swan* were well-stocked. We've pork and biscuit and cheese enough to feed an army, and wine enough to get one drunk.'

Brod fondled Raven's smooth right thigh under the table. Lake's fingers stroked the tender skin behind her left knee.

'We've had our fill, thank you Captain,' Raven said. 'I think the three of us should get some rest now. Which cabin will be ours? This one?'

'Which cabin? You'll have a cabin apiece, of course. I thought Brod would stay here, on the *Serpent*, Lake would take *The Claw* and you, ma'am, would be safe and snug aboard the *Blue Swan*.'

Raven stiffened and covered both Brod and Lake's hands, stilling their subtle caresses. 'Separate? One of us on each of three ships? Apart from each other?'

'That was always the way of it, as I was taught by the White Lodge. In the good old days, before Vixia, when the Heirs travelled it was never two on the same craft. There might be some disaster, you see? They never took the risk of all four being lost at once.'

Lake squeezed Raven's leg. Brod's palm smoothed up under the brief skirt that Daud had found for her.

'You mean a storm or the like?' Lake asked. 'Fear not, Captain Daud ap-Dan. I am coming into my power, you see. I can likely promise you smooth waters – or at least good warning of foul.'

Daud frowned. One hand's fingers toyed with his beard while the palm of the other smoothed his shiny head. 'Like enough, Sir Water Heir, but can you also control the winds? There's typhoons in these parts.'

Raven leaned forward. 'Captain, I cannot claim to rule the zephyrs, yet. You see, this is the way of it. Heirs together have more power than when apart. I spent some time alone with Lake, and my powers grew. Put us three close together and we'll each be doubled in might.'

Brod added, 'And I had no power at all until I first met with Raven. It was that meeting that woke me.'

'So,' Lake said, 'It seems passing wise to keep us in close company, Captain. Let us sail in convoy, as you suggest. Lead the way, in *The Claw*, if you will. Let the *Sea Serpent*, with us three aboard, follow. Have the *Blue Swan* bring up the rear. Each day that passes our combined powers will grow. Today I can offer you calm seas. A few days from now, I am sure Raven will be able to whistle you up any wind you might desire, or still a storm, if need be. Should we be set upon by slavers or the like, Brod will by then be thrice as strong as he is now. He'll likely be ready to sink ships with his fists. Come now Captain, you see the sense in what I say. What say you?'

Captain Daud tugged at his chin's ringlets until his lower lip drooped. 'I like it not, but you three are the True Heirs, and I must bow to your command. Very well. I will have a cabin suitably prepared. You wish to share your quarters, you say?'

Brod's smallest finger found the moist heat in the crease of Raven's groin. Her thighs parted encouragingly. 'Oh yes, Captain,' he said. 'We most certainly wish to share.' He looked from Daud's wide bunk to his ample couch. 'This cabin will do for us, if it's no trouble, Captain?'

Daud sighed. 'No trouble at all. Well, I would rather stay and share a flagon or two with you three wonders, but I must see to the direction of my men. There's just two-score and five as are able-bodied now. I'll be grateful for that easy sailing, if it please you, Water Heir. With just fifteen men plus myself to sail each craft we'll be sore put to cope.'

'How about the female slaves we freed?' Raven asked. 'They seemed fit enough. Those giantesses looked strong as two men each. The felines would do well in the rigging, I've no doubt. Could you not put them to some simple tasks, overseen by your men?'

Daud grinned through his beard. 'I tried that. Those horny harlots have been kept without men for far too long. I set two of 'em to coiling rope, with my second mate to watch 'em. No sooner was my back turned than the big one was holding him down while one o' them tiger-women was raping him. Not that my mate was struggling none, mind, but if I was to set that randy parcel of minxes among my men I'd need a second set o' crews to man the ships, I would. I've confined the lascivious bitches below, but with every creature comfort, mind you.'

Brod said, 'Give us three till the morrow to – er – get to know each other, and then Lake and I will gladly give you a hand, Captain.'

Daud shook his head. 'Can't allow that, but my thanks. Heirs can stand and fight alongside my men, and welcome. That's only fitting, but I'll not have Arcadian royalty sweating next to my sea-scum, I'll have y' know. That would be unseemly.'

Lake chuckled. 'Oh well, Captain Daud, call on us if you need any miracles then.'

'My thanks. I will.' Daud turned to go.

Brod slapped his own forehead. 'Captain! One last request.'

'Yes? What is it?'

'My old cabin? Could you have a man look in? He should find Impah there still, bound to a chest. Have her fed, bathed and rested, if you will, and then tell her to join us here?'

When Daud closed the door Raven laid her slender hand on the massive bulk of Brod's thigh. 'Another woman, Brod?' Her nails teased his skin. 'I'd be happy to share you and Lake with the wench, later, but for now, for the sake of our powers we three should – er ...'

'Get very close?' Lake suggested.

Brod grinned. 'You don't understand. I have no intention of allowing another woman to come between us until our reunion has been consummated a number of times, Raven. It's in this wise, Air. I owe my present strength to Impah. She is the one who has succoured me, so far from land. I must repay her, but not as you think. She is a novitiate in the service of Sloona the Slave. Her greatest joy will be in attending to our every need while being ignored herself.'

Raven stood, unknotted her skirt, and asked, 'Is she pretty, Brod?'

'In the style of a sex-slave, slender and docile, yes she is. Her pleasure is in serving the pleasure of others, and she serves well. Impah will fetch and carry for us, mop our brows, cleanse us with her tongue if need be, and relish every moment of the most abject servitude.'

A wicked light came into Raven's eyes. She folded her skirt and laid it aside. 'Then let her attend us by all means, Brod. When we three have enjoyed each other to the full, I might well be tempted by softer charms, especially if they are submissive ones. It's an age since I enjoyed the taste of a woman.'

Raven paused, a far-away look on her face. She remembered her few days of captivity in Pasnar's villa, and the golden-girdled Tiblan slave, M'ree.

When she recalled straddling the girl's pretty face while the lustful slave was corded tightly to a hard bench, and the way that a long prehensile tongue had risen between her thighs, probed, entered, and then squirmed up into her vagina for such an incredible distance, her coynte ran wet and her mouth dried.

'I need love,' she husked, stroking both men's backs. 'I need it now.' Her nails hooked, and raked.

Lake stood and untied his loincloth. 'There'll be loving enough, and in many kinds for us all, I warrant. There are two lovely Island-girl friends of mine locked below, and a dozen more exotic beauties confined with them. There's blackest black and snowflake white, those as tower over me with their breasts level to my mouth and those who stand little higher than my cock, and there's a pair of pretty kittens to be petted.

'Between the lot, this'll be a hectic voyage, eh Brod? If you've a fancy for the love of a girl or two, Raven, we've all sizes and shapes to hand.'

Brod flung his one garment across the cabin and made to rise from the bench. Raven's tiny hand on his muscular shoulder restrained him.

She looked down between his thighs and said, 'You've grown Brod. You were big when first we met, more than a year past, in the days when neither of us knew who we really were. In those thirteen moons you've grown taller, and broader, but mainly . . .'

Brod grinned at her. Though he was seated, his head was level with hers. 'Yes Raven?'

'Mainly . . .' Her body shook deliciously. 'Mainly, Brod, you've grown so much longer and thicker. Where do you find the mates you need, Brod? Can a mortal woman take such a magnificent weapon?' She reached out without stooping and trailed her fingers wonderingly around the circumference of his shaft, just beneath its purple globe.

'I've been fortunate,' he said. 'Soon after you first introduced me to the joys of love I met up with as randy a pair of sluts as you could wish for. I was smaller then, but I've no doubt they'd find some way for us to couple if they were here with us now.

'Then there's been Rena, who is Rune-graven, and so capable of erotic feats that belie her size. There was also a visit that I enjoyed, from three demonic succubi. That trio of supernatural sluts almost defeated me, I admit.

'Then I made fast friends of a pair of hardy mountain amazons, either of them capable of breaking the backs of ten strong men.'

Brod closed his great fist over Raven's tiny hand and pumped it slowly down his stem. 'Raven, you underestimate your mortal sisters. Even Impah, who is but human, with no magic and narrower through the hip than you, managed to accommodate my cock's bulk, eventually.'

Raven ran the knuckles of her free hand up the underside of Lake's cock. 'And now it is my turn to be stretched. Order-be-praised the Air enhances my womanly skills, for I now attempt a feat such as heroic songs should be sung on. Prepare the way for your tongue, Brod.' She bestrode his knees and started to croon a soft song of lust.

Seeing that the succulent object of his desire was too low for his comfort, Brod took her kittenish hips in his broad hands and lifted Raven's core bodily to his mouth.

Joyous in her lust, Raven kicked both feet out sideways, pointed-toed, in a pose akin to a temple dancer in mid-leap. Brod held her suspended thus, contemplating his target. Her sweet coynte's nectared folds tempted his taste-buds, but the spread of her thighs had raised their inner tendons, leaving tremulous hollows beneath their bowstring tautness.

Brod knew how sensitive those shallow and shadowy indentations were, for either sex. Many a candle had burned to a stub and guttered out while he himself had quivered from the tireless attentions of Mahia and Leiala's tongues, the mother tantalising his right groin while the daughter teased his left, their soft hands linked the while around his shaft and working his foreskin with such patient slow caresses that the erotic tension had crinkled his balls down to the size of a fist.

That was a game for less urgent times, but even though all three of the Heirs trembled from their need, Brod did not want their first triple-coupling to be as mindless as that of dire-stoats in rut. He stiffened his tongue. Its tip vibrated in Raven's left groin. Brod wetted and flattened it, and drew it at a snail's pace from left to right. It tickled the stretched skin just beneath the closure of Raven's coynte and then moved to her right groin, and back. The slippery torture continued until the salt-sweet taste of her told him that her essence was spilling.

Rigid to its tip, his tongue stabbed, stabbed, stabbed.

Raven's hum deepened to a thrumming so low-pitched that it quivered the walls of her vagina. Securely sat upon Brod's wide palms, she let her body fold backwards at her waist. Her head dropped behind her. She saw Lake standing there, ready. Her kisses trailed down his broad chest, descended the ridges of his flat belly, and lower, to where his proud cock stood waiting.

Impah, naked but for a square of silk knotted low on her hips, entered the cabin unnoticed. She took a demure position in a corner. Her eyes were big with wonder. These three were not Gods, but neither were they mere mortals. The privilege of being present at their almost-divine coupling weakened her knees at the same time as it convulsed her vagina. Sloona was indeed good.

Lake's palms cupped Raven's shoulders. Supported by the four hands of the two male Heirs, the Heir of Air felt weightless as her element and infinitely malleable. At that moment Raven felt sure that they could have twisted her body into a spiral. Neither her bones nor her muscles would have resisted. There would have been no discomfort, just an overpowering joy at being manipulated for her men's pleasure.

Folded so severely that the close-cropped ebony hair on the back of her head tickled her own buttocks and her ribcage spread like an open fan, Raven parted her lips for Lake and swallowed him to the hilt.

With Brod's tongue deep in her coynte and the head of Lake's cock buried in her throat, Raven found herself crying with happiness. It was not just the erotic pleasure that racked her body with sobs of delight. No – it was the feeling of union. More – three of the Heirs were really together at last – and she was the conduit that joined them. Without her, it could not have happened. Brod and Lake were mystically sealed, joined together in eternal brotherhood, through her.

What would it be like, she wondered, when they found the Heir of Fire? The togetherness would surely be overwhelmingly beautiful. Earth, Air, Fire and Water. The four Elements. Together they made All.

Raven had an orgasm. Once, before she'd known who she was, such a wrenching climax would have devastated her. Now, as part of this enchanted trinity, she knew it was but the first plateau of an escalation that would take her higher than any woman had ever ascended. Or at least, higher than any had risen since the Thrones had been vacated by Vixia's cruel assault on Arcadia.

Raven gathered her senses. Thus far, she had been a party to the love-making by being passive, by being delightfully used by Brod and Lake. Now it was time for her to take a more active role. She let her throat vibrate on Lake's cock, trilling it in a manner that would have boiled any normal man over. Lake, she knew, was the Master of Bodily Fluids. His spending would come when he willed it to, and not a moment before.

She swung her legs down to plant her feet flat on Brod's thighs. Using the strength of her thighs and abdomen alone, she drew herself up off her twin impalements, Brod's tongue in her coynte and Lake's cock in her throat and mouth. She stood high, the top of her head brushing the cabin's ceiling.

Her hips made small, tight, tempestuous circles. Her vibrant pubes brushed across Brod's mouth. The trembling cheeks of her bottom grazed Lake's face. Still rotating, she bent her legs, lowering herself. Her thighs opened sideways, spreading like a frog's. She descended lower, and lower, bumping her mound on Brod's chest and her rear on Lake's. Neither man moved. This was Raven's dance of desire. It was their turn to wait with mounting impatience.

The soft cup of her sex settled on the dome of Brod's cock. The crease of her bottom found the head of Lake's. Raven stretched her arms sideways. She had no need of her fingers' aid. The Heir of Air had total control over her body. She commanded her sphincter behind and her coynte before. Both sighed open. Her hips rotated still as she lowered herself even deeper, welcoming both invaders. Lake's helmet plopped past the constriction of her anus, into her rectum. Brod's glans slithered into her vulva and beyond, forcing her vagina to stretch wide over his staff.

Raven twitched, once, twice, thrice. Both male maces-of-love were secure in her depths. Glee warbled from Raven's throat. She was distended like she'd never been before. Those mighty rods filled her entire being. All that remained was for her to abandon herself to them, totally.

She kicked her feet out to left and right and let her own slight weight sink her down, impaling herself. So full was she with maleness that her descent took all of ten jerking heart-beats.

When she could go no lower, when Brod's pubes were snug against hers, when Lake's were nestled in her buttocks' kiss, Raven let herself go completely limp.

The men knew what to do. As one, they surged out of her, and into her, and out of her. The pores on Brod's cock came alive, tingling and avid. They sucked at the wetness that coated Raven's vagina, drinking the slick portents of the orgasm that was yet to come.

Lake's mind caressed Raven, stirring the hot blood that pounded in her nipples and throbbed like a drumbeat in her clitoris. His power convulsed the walls of her rectum on his own flesh, and churned her womb until its deep and tiny mouth mumbled on the head of Brod's cock.

Lake's power was pumping Raven's fluids. Brod's cock was sucking at them. Their elemental powers flowed through her like a sub-oceanic river. She was everything, and nothing. Air was overwhelmed as Water pounded her onto Earth. She was defined by the lusty primordial forces that battered their energies into her.

Oblivion swirled inside Raven. She surrendered to it. Her blood was a raging tide of erotic passion; her body a maelstrom of sweet desire. She rose to another plateau, and yet another, until she entered a realm of reality that was far beyond the mundane. She soared on an escalating cadence of ecstatic climaxes.

Raven's final orgasm was not just of her body, even though it tingled the roots of her hair and vibrated through the nails of both her fingers and toes. No – her orgasm was beyond the merely physical – it echoed through her very soul!

Twenty-Nine

They laid Raven's limp sweat-soaked body on Captain Daud's couch. Lake tucked a down-stuffed linen pillow under her lovely head. Brod covered her with the supple pelts of snow-ocelots.

'Is she alive?' Impah asked. 'Is she well?'

Before either Brod or Lake could reply, they heard Raven's voice, clear and strong, though her lips didn't move.

'My spirit is more alive than it has ever been,' she said. 'My body is undamaged, just happily exhausted. I am rebuilding its vigour, but that will take time.

'Lake, Brod, there are females below who have been without the solace of male company for too long. Go and comfort them. Impah – Slave of Sloona – remain with me. Cleanse this body of mine with the kisses of your mouth. Seek out its secret folds with your tongue. Open me with the gentleness of your fingers. Dry me with your sighs. When my physical being is strong again, I will have tasks for you to perform.'

'It is the nature of Air to follow the tempest with calm. Calm is succeeded by soft breezes. Be my serene zephyr, Impah. Restore me, and when I stir once more I shall fall upon you like a typhoon, demanding of you all that you can give, and more.'

Impah knelt at the end of the Heir to the Throne of Air's couch. She folded the pale furs up from Raven's tiny feet and bent over them. Deliriously happy, Sloona The Slave's novitiate slavered between her new Mistress's pretty little toes with her wet and sinuous tongue.

Brod and Lake, both naked and damp from their exotic efforts, closed the cabin door behind them. One deep deck lower, they paused to unbar a massive portal.

Lake sniffed. 'Do you smell it, Brod?'

'Yes. Woman-smell.'

'The smell of many women,' Lake corrected. 'The sweet scent of women in heat. Raven was right. There is great need within.'

Brod opened the door. Both men entered the high-ceilinged chamber and stood in awe. Daud had been true to his word. The slaves that they had rescued were confined, but in sybaritic luxury. The hold had been constructed for storage. Now its only cargo was female flesh, in rich abundance and of the finest quality.

Daud had stripped all three ships to provide the most luxurious furnishings. A score of bronze, copper and silver lanterns swung from oak beams, casting ample light. The deck had been covered with precious rugs so generously that in no place did they lay less than three deep. A hundred pillows and cushions were strewn willy-nilly, offering the comforts of wool, linen, silk, satin, brocade and intricate tapestry.

Three walls had been hastily hung with velvet drapes and brilliant banners. Four enormous chests that had been filled with fine fabrics stood open now, their contents looted and scattered. Silks had been torn into squares, used as frivolous coverings, and then abandoned, having served the prime purpose of such – to tantalise lovers' eyes.

A board on trestles was laden with every kind of meat, cheese, bread, biscuit, sweetmeat, ale, wine and spirit-of-wine that a ship at sea could provide. There were five luxurious couches, each of a different size and style, from the narrow padded board that Isnotian courtesans favoured for their coupling to a massive fur-covered six-legged multi-curved Torimactic ceremonial love-bed.

Comfort, to a seaman, is a hammock. A dozen had been slung, four of them woven from silk cord and broad enough to sleep three men each.

Before being refurnished, the hold's bulkheads had been

hung with nets to retain small packages and bales safely. These webs remained, festooned with more precious and exotic goods than they'd ever held before – voluptuous women and lithe girls.

A supple female with a furry stripe down her spine was clinging to cords by her clawed fingers and toes. Her rump projected out into the hold. A tall and slender figure with coppery skin stood beneath the cat-woman, face upturned, mouth half-buried in the feline's musky sex. Behind the eastern beauty, Hibiscus stood rubbing her sex against the rigid back of the tribade's quivering thigh. Her loving arms circled a lithe back. The Island girl's fingers strummed the tips of gold-bound elongated nipples.

Beside the cat, Jasmine had hooked her legs into rope netting and hung herself upside-down. An ebony Styxian stood on the carpeted deck facing away from her, bent over, spread-legged to grasp her own ankles. Jasmine, dangling, was gripping the black girl's thighs, tugging the tiny slot in her arse onto the stiffened spike of her tongue.

Two more human felines hung from their arms, face-to-face. The outermost pulled herself up, rubbing the full sinuous length of her naked body over that of her companion, let herself down, and pulled up once more. Each had a long pointed tongue fully extended, slavering over whatever skin presented itself.

Two blonde giantesses lolled at the base of the bulkhead, gazing around, idly observing the lascivious display that surrounded them. Each had a hand in the other's lap, toying with a rigid clit the size of a grown man's finger. The third giantess, her breasts bite-mottled and nail-scratched, her pubes puffy and bruised, sprawled on her back, giving suckle to a pair of exquisite Mathrassian albinos who she held cuddled in her arms as if they were babes.

The last participant in this lesbian orgy was also a diminutive albino. She was lying between the third giantess's thighs, holding the blonde's fantastic clit in a tiny fist, pumping it as if it was a cock and masturbating herself at the same time. When the giantess's sigh signalled that the tiny one's attentions had achieved their aim, the translucent-skinned beauty ducked her head to the big woman's soft cup and lapped out its essence with a quick flickering of her tiny tongue.

The air was so thick with female musk that Brod thought he could likely squeeze drops of womanly essence from a fistful. The melodious voices of sex – yelping, squealing, trilling, moaning, grunting, sighing – almost drowned out the non-vocal sounds – the rhythmic slapping of flesh on flesh and the delicious wet noises that mouths make on mouths, coyntes make on coyntes, and each makes on the other when they are all both sopping and slack with lust.

Lake coughed.

For a heartbeat, all was still.

A dozen female forms erupted at the two men.

Lake let himself be bowled to the floor under a mewing, giggling press of limbs and bodies. Cat-women purred as they rubbed their bellies up the lengths of his sides. Four tiny translucent hands locked in his hair and twisted his face from the kisses of one pale-lipped mouth to the other. A long thin snaky body sprawled along Lake's back, wriggled down to the smooth hardness of his buttocks, pried them apart and insinuated a needle-long nipple into the tight knot of his arse.

Hibiscus and Jasmine each took one of his wrists and guided his hands to their mouths, their breasts, and between their thighs.

The three voluptuous blonde giantesses had Brod's massive body to themselves. The sight of a male who was so large that he made them look small by comparison overwhelmed their female sensibilities. Although they were almost as tall as he was, his breadth dwarfed them.

The first one to reach him smacked the firm pillows of her breasts into his chest. The shock of the cushiony collision didn't even rock Brod. He simply folded one massive arm around her and held out the other arm to scoop a second immense female form into his embrace. The third stood back in open-mouthed awe as Brod lifted the first two off their feet and shook them against his body.

One wrapped her legs around Brod's thigh and humped her pubes at the bulge of its steely muscles. The second threw her python arms around his neck and went for his mouth as if it was a cold spring and she four days without water. The third dropped to her knees, crawled into the tangle of limbs, and exulted in having to crane *up* to get her mouth to the mighty yard that jutted from between Brod's thighs.

The Heir to Earth held his two titanic captives clamped tight to his torso despite their joyful giggling wriggles. He raised and lowered them by the strength of his forearms, lifting first one and then the other to be kissed, or even higher, so that his avid mouth could suckle at the great rubbery polyps that crowned their prodigious breasts.

Each time he sucked his happy victim would press her breast against his face with all of her strength, urging him to take as much vibrant flesh into his mouth as it could encompass, and then draw back, increasing the force of his suction and drawing the enormous soft white mass of her breast into an obscenely elongated pear. Soon, all four nipples were darkened to the shades of bruised plums and were engorged to sizes no plums ever achieved.

Brod growled and gnawed and shook his head. Breast-flesh wobbled into vibrant concentric waves. Splay-lipped womanly cores humped moistly on his lips. Nails raked his back and chest, leaving livid weals that were then laved by the flats of broad wet tongues.

The giantess who was crouched between Brod's thighs slurped and slobbered the length of his cock until it stood with its purple dome higher than his navel. Brod set the two in his arms down, drew the third to her feet, cupped her ample hips in his palms, and raised her high above his head. Her coynte was a hot ripe water melon with the first slice already removed. Brod buried his face into wet pink flesh. The giantess's contralto climbed into the range of a soprano. Her hips bucked at Brod's face. His mouth clamped on her clit and drew on it, sucking out a long spike of tender flesh. Her belly juddered, fucking her clit between Brod's tight lips.

The other two sank to the floor at Brod's feet. Two massive soft hands stroked his cock as two more cupped and jiggled the enormous sack that dangled between his legs. Two tongues that would not have looked out of place lolling from the jaws of sabre-toothed tigers slithered into the creases of Brod's groin or lapped at the oozy eye of his cock, savouring the sweet dew that leaked from it.

Brod, exulting in his strength, tossed the woman his mouth had been serving into the air, caught her, turned her around, and set her down on her hands and knees. He too, knelt. Brod had no further need to move. A second magnificent blonde bent his springy cock down to its target. The third spread her sister's coynte wide and ready. The head of Brod's cock was rubbed up and down between sopping coynte-lips. The kneeling one lunged back, wriggled her plump rump, and settled Brod's rigid staff into her humid depths.

For Brod, it was a miracle. Even coupling with the bandit amazon queens, Gowan and Marl, he'd been used to holding back lest the enormous bulk of his weapon injure their delicate inner flesh. Now he had no need to take care, but it was not he who performed the lunatic gallop. It was the woman who battered back at him like a tornado, who revolved on his iron spike like a whirlwind, who humped and bucked and gyrated with such insane intensity that soon her coynte churned and gushed her scalding essence over this shaft, but kept on fucking and fucking, until his own molten lava jetted into her depths, filled her, and overflowed to run down her magnificent trembling thighs.

She slumped forward and rolled aside. The other two stood still, as if questioning what they should do next. Brod answered their unasked query by tugging the one to his left down into her sister's just-vacated position.

As his foam-smeared knob touched the inner surfaces of her pendulous sex-lips though, she reached behind herself and steered his cock higher. Brod had not surrendered himself to the clamping joys of buggery since he'd left the magical Rena, back in the rebel encampment. He let out a whoop, grabbed two fists' full of firm buttock and slammed the giantess along the full length of his rigid shaft to smack her dimpled cheeks back into his groin.

She bellowed her delight at the rude invasion. Her massive pendulous breasts shook with deep silent laughter. Delirious with the ecstasy of being, for once, a mere toy in the hands of a male who was stronger than she was, she juddered into the first of a long series of convulsive orgasms.

With one giantess slumped in exhaustion, another kneeling and the third clawing his buttocks as her tongue flickered beneath him over his balls, Brod was finally able to see what Lake and the rest of the rabid harlots were doing.

He'd been taken a prisoner of lust, though Brod was sure that the Heir of Water could have freed himself in a moment had he so wished. He had been borne bodily to the hanging net and tangled into its web, his back against the bulkhead.

Female forms crawled all over him. Jasmine had climbed high and spread her sex over Lake's mouth. The Styxian beauty was pressing an ebony breast into one of his hands, where it was mauled and twisted into obscene unnatural shapes, to her evident glee. Two feline mouths purred as one slobbered each side of his swollen glans, with occasional quick laps into each other's sharp-toothed wetness. A third feline had her face uptilted between Lake's thighs. Her purrs vibrated the testes that dangled into her gaping mouth.

Two albinos teased Lake's masculine nipples with tiny nips from diminutive teeth. The oriental girl was drawing patterns on the taut skin of Lake's belly with the point of one elongated nipple, squirming it into his navel and then drawing it up as high as his ribcage before returning it to its drilling.

Hibiscus was on the deck, arched into a wrestler's bridge, jerking her frantic hips at the air. Brod realised that the Island girl was not being neglected. No doubt Lake was probing the uttermost depths of her vagina with the magic fingers of his mind.

Brod came. As his sated victim slumped, before he could pull the third giantess from behind him for her turn to be impaled, the hold's door opened. Raven entered. Four crisp clean notes trilled from her lovely throat. The tune twined about itself, became a warbling chord, and soared.

The two resting giantesses sat up, renewed lust gleaming in their eyes. Hibiscus screamed an orgasm. Two cat-women thrust squirmy fingers into each other's sex. Throughout the hold, those who had been sated found that they were ravenous once more; those who had been close to their pleasure reached their climaxes, and rode over them, needing more. A fair giantess, a diminutive albino, a supple cat-woman and the eely oriental all rushed to Raven, slavering lust. The Heir to Air spread her lovely thighs, ready to receive their oral homage.

Thirty

The three ships anchored in a secret cove. Raven and Lake promised the six men who stayed aboard calm waters and clear skies.

The trek to the rebels' volcano took eight days of strenuous marching and seven nights of even more strenuous loving. Only Lake's magic made it possible. His command of body fluids ensured that his companions, when they slept, slept deeply and rose refreshed. When they tired, his mind found complex vessels in each one's body that could be coaxed into delivering reviving essences into their blood.

Brod carried the entire party's provisions in one massive bundle that rode easily on one mighty shoulder, though it was thrice his bulk and twice his weight. His free arm always carried one of the women who had become fatigued, while another sat in a canvas sling that hung down his broad back. Brod knew that their weariness was often feigned, but did not object. Their soft nibblings at his nape and into the hollow of his throat put a spring into his stride that he valued at ten times the slight effort of bearing their weight.

When they came to a narrow path that wound up the side of a mountain and some feared the precipitous height, Raven summoned up a stiff breeze to blow against the mountain's flank and support them.

They were met half a day from the volcano. Dendri and his men brought litters for the women and horses for the men. When they had wound their way through the secret tunnels to the green crater they found the sleeping volcano's cup asmoke with cooking fires and steaming with great pots of boiling water, for the sudorium could never hold all who needed cleansing.

Gowan and Marl's giggling amazons stripped and scrubbed the sailors. As soon as one was cleansed of the stains of travel, he was dragged aside and simultaneously fed gobbets of meat and tid-bits of girl-flesh. Most gulped the food as quickly as they might so that their hands and mouths would sooner be free for more luscious, living treats.

The three Heirs were taken up to the lip of the crater, to be greeted by Hypocrate's blind tears of joy. Once the tale had been told, with those portions that would have no relevance for the old man omitted, he dismissed them.

'Return to the crater, Brod,' he commanded. 'You have toiled hard and long for the rebel cause. It is time for you to revive your powers. Eat, drink and couple, lad. Always remember that your might is fed by the lust of women. Is there one below who is ready to serve that sacred end?'

Brod grinned. 'One at least, great mage. If I am fortunate there might be two.'

'Three?' Lake chuckled.

'If it serves the rebellion, *I* will sacrifice myself,' Raven added. Her nails raked across Brod's buttock, beneath his loincloth, for emphasis.

'Then go.'

Hand in hand, the three Heirs bounded down the side of the crater, eager to join in the riotous orgy that was being celebrated below.

Three of Captain Daud ap-Dan's crewmen had acquired special tastes during their long voyages, far from shore and woman-kind. Marl's amazons were accommodating even them. The three had been stripped and bent over trestles. Three of the muscular women had donned the strap-on dildos that had formed part of their uniforms back in their days of brigandage and were buggering the sailors with a lusty will. Three more warrior women squatted beneath the trestles, fellating the tars' cocks. The men, though boy or men-lovers by preference, seemed to have no objection to the feminine attentions. A mouth is a mouth.

Pohl, one of the Tiblan boy twins, waved to the descending Heirs from the mouth of a cave. 'Rena and our new friends await you in the sudorium,' he called.

Raven squeezed Brod's finger. 'Rena? I knew her when we both served Vixia. She was a toothsome little slut, as I remember, but somewhat timid.'

'She's timid no longer,' Brod grinned. 'I told you – she was Rune Graven into the wildest vixen a man could dream on. Tangle limbs with that one, Raven, and you'll need all the powers that Air has granted you.'

'Then let's at her! Come, I'll race you two sluggards for first choice of the lovers that await us.'

She tore ahead. Brod pounded and Lake loped after. Either by Raven's design or perhaps because all three were truly equal, they burst into the steamy sudorium side-by-side.

It was a scene fit to be painted as one of Vixia's living murals. Impah had persuaded someone to bind her to a stalactite. Two broad black leather straps circled the stone stele. Impah, facing outwards, had been restrained by having her forearms clamped behind her, tucked down under one strap, and her legs bent up at her knees and tucked under the lower. She was arched out, spread-legged, as helpless and available as her submissive heart desired.

The yellow-eyed cat-woman was taking advantage. Her cupped palm was slapping rhythmically up between Impah's thighs, spanking her sex. At the same time she had one of Impah's virginal pink nipples gripped between her feline teeth and was tugging on it, drawing the girl's barely-developed breast out into an extended tent of tender flesh.

Impah gasped, 'Harder, harder.'

Perhaps the cat-woman had learned some of the true speech during her period of confinement. If she had, 'harder' would likely be the first word she'd have learned. In any case, she responded. Her palm cracked up. Her head tugged back. Her free hand raked its claws down Impah's ribcage, leaving livid weals.

Impah strained and sobbed. The next slap landed in moisture, splatting on the swollen lips of Impah's sex. The cat mewed her delight, sniffed in Impah's odour, and buried her face between the slave's thighs. As her thin lips clamped to Impah's clit, the cat began to purr, sending her happy victim into a writhing delirium.

'Mmm,' Raven mused. 'Purring on a clit? I would try that. Where's the other randy feline?'

The other cat was fellating Captain Daud. Raven was only generous with sharing her lovers once she'd been sated. The Heir to Air strode across the floor to the sudorium, grabbed the feline by the stripped hair at her nape, dragged her off Daud and bore her bodily to a bench.

Sitting with her slender thighs spread, Raven thrust the feral face to her groin and instructed, 'Lap, cat. Get my clit hard and then purr on it.'

Whether the cat understood the words or not, she got Raven's meaning. Her pointed tongue set to work.

Daud was not left with his cock straining into air for long. A blonde giantess took him by his stem, dragged him to the floor and engulfed his member in her vast cavern of a mouth. Large though it was, when her lips pursed it seemed tight enough, for a look of utter bliss came to the Captain's face.

Lake told Brod, 'I've lain with slender sylphs enough, these past few moons. My taste turns to more ample pleasures. If you will excuse me?'

Though the giantess he chose was twice his weight, Lake was stronger. He lifted her up in his arms and bore her into the bubbling hot pool. Neither spoke the other's tongue, yet they seemed to understand each other well enough. He steered her to the far edge, leaned her back over it, and closed his thighs around the breadth of her ribcage. When his knees bent they drew him close. His cock jutted up between the two billowy cushions of her breasts. She smiled and pressed her bosom around his staff. Lake lay back on steamy water and thrust up into her soft valley. The giantess bent her head down so that she could catch the head of his cock between her lips on each upstroke.

Rena was with the third giantess, coynte-to-face and breast-to-coynte in a lop-sided lesbian frenzy. Any smaller opponent would have been devastated by the Graven One's erotic ravishing, but the big blonde seemed perfectly content to let Rena pump one bunched fist into the cavern of her sex and another in her rectum while returning the erotic attention with languorous long-fingered probes into the nymphomaniac's spasming coynte.

Brod was sated on watching, though the composition in black and white that the Styxian made when entwined with the two albinos was a work of erotic art. All it lacked was him.

He plucked the two tiny women off the black beauty's supine body with no more thought than Raven had when taking the cat-girl from Daud. He sank to his knees astride her. The ebony girl's breasts had fascinated him since he'd first seen them, but with so many women clamouring for his attention, and Raven taking first place, up to that moment he hadn't found the right time to pay them the attention they deserved.

They were perfect globes, glossy and black and ripe as the poisonous ahnn fruit that was a totem to certain Styxian tribes. Her nipples were stiff cones, a shade lighter than her breasts' skin, perhaps blue-black. Brod put the pad of his finger to the tip of one and wobbled it. The engorged flesh was solid enough that as he tilted it, it indented the surrounding halo. He wobbled harder, sending tiny ripples through the girl's breast.

He barely noticed the weight of the albino who climbed upon his back and humped her tiny coynte on the ridge of his spine while slobbering her kisses across his broad shoulders, nor that of her sister, riding his heel.

H'neeth smiled up at him. 'My nipple likes to be sucked,' she said.

'Soon,' Brod teased. 'My fingers want to explore further, first.'

'I've got two. Why not suck on one while your fingers discover the other?'

'Very well.' Brod's massive fist engulfed her left breast. It squeezed gently, thumb below and fingers above. H'neeth's flesh was incredibly resilient, but Brod was strong. His thumb indented deeply. His grip extruded her.

He bent low and lapped once, long and slow, enjoying the prod of her rigid spike across the flat of his tongue.

'Suck!'

Brod's lips closed. He found her nipple's point with his teeth and nipped playfully.

'Suck hard!'

He grinned around his mouthful of black flesh.

'Do it nice for me and I'll lick your pale arse while you fuck one of the others. I'll make you scream from it, I promise.'

Brod lifted his head against the straining of her hand on the back of his neck. 'You really like your nipples sucked, don't you?'

'I've been telling you. I enjoy my tongue-work, too.'

Brod let her drag his head down. He sucked. His mouth mumbled her flesh, gobbling more and more into his mouth until half of her breast was drawn in. His tongue worked. His left hand massaged her right breast, probing deep enough to feel the granular structure beneath the outer layer. His head shook. Her breast was lifted up off her ribcage and vibrated in his oral grip. Brod's mouth released it. Before H'neeth could protest Brod had swooped to the other glistening orb and was worrying at it.

'Bruise me, you bastard,' she whimpered. 'Crush my teat! make it hurt good, damn you. Yes!'

Brod could feel her hand behind him, frotting at her own sex. He sat back, shedding a pair of tiny bodies, pinched both of H'neeth's nipples in his fingers, and shook.

'Yes, yes, yes, yes, yes.' She half sat-up in her convulsion. 'Ahhh! Good. Now, what did I promise?'

At that moment Rena, her face slippery with a giantess's spending, threw herself at the pair. Brod set her aside, almost negligently, swung around off his Styxian lover, and dropped atop Rena, impaling her with the full length of his cock. Pumping slowly into the gasping, slobbering girl, he twisted his head and told H'neeth, 'Something about your tongue and my arse, I believe it was.'

Giggling, the black beauty crawled across and contemplated the knotting and unknotting of Brod's muscular bottom. 'A promise is a promise,' she said, wetting her lips.

Epilogue

Vixia stood naked and spread-legged with her head inside the circumference of her scrying ring. Laylanda knelt behind her. The girl's teeth nibbled at the firm pad of muscle at the base of her Queen's spine. Two fingers were exploring the rubbery texture that lined Vixia's rectum. Laylanda's other hand stroked the Vile One's clitoral shaft with oiled fingers.

Vixia withdrew her head from the iron ring. 'We must celebrate,' she husked. 'Three Heirs now dwell within the volcano's cup. I have faith that the fourth will soon join them. Then my Lord Havoc will stir. The volcano will awaken. The entire rebellion, and the four nuisances will be flies in a furnace. Send word to Krotor, my sweetling. He has fifty virgins saved for just such a joyous occasion as this. Tell him I would have each one bound in a different style, their nipples and clits Graved to aching need, and ten bowls of warm honey-essence at hand. I have a fancy for depraved virginity, and you no longer serve that hunger, do you?'

'I serve in any manner you command, My Queen,' Laylanda sulked. 'Tell me, Maleficient One, is it not perilous to summon Havoc to do your bidding?'

Vixia tousled her love-slave's cinnamon tresses. 'You serve? Of course you do, slutling. You always will, for the rest of your life. As for the peril of summoning Havoc, you are right. Even for me there is danger.' The Queen smiled down on Laylanda. 'There are ways to make it less hazardous, though. A human sacrifice is involved, as you might guess.'

'A virgin sacrifice?'

'Enough questions. Off about your errand.'

Vixia watched her pet human depart the chamber. There was a strange look on her beautiful face. In any eyes less evil it might have been seen as wistful sadness.

'Not a "virgin sacrifice",' The Foul One whispered. 'That would be too mundane. The only sacrifices that please Havoc are those that have meaning to the sacrificer. He only devours the souls of the ones His worshippers feel affection for, my sweet little love.'

NEW BOOKS

Coming up from Nexus and Black Lace

House of Intrigue by Yvonne Strickland
January 1996   Price: £4.99   ISBN: 0 352 33055 4
Karen cannot resist the lure of the depravity which surrounds Sonia's house but the ruthless disciplinarian Pauline has a score to settle with Karen, and an endless array of instruments with which to settle it. The effect of the punishment only serves to increase Sonia's disobedience, and the naughtiness intensifies.

Slave-Mistress of Vixania by Morgana Baron
January 1996   Price: £4.99   ISBN: 0 352 33054 6
Queen Vixia, now free to indulge her sadistic desires, focuses upon the virginal Lady Laylanda as her next victim. But Laylanda's resistance only increases the humiliating punishments inflicted on her. On the other hand, Brod must gain power by arousing as many orgasms in women as possible, and he has no problems finding willing candidates.

Bound to Obey by Amanda Ware
February 1996   Price: £4.99   ISBN: 0 352 33058 9
As the newly appointed servant, Caroline has more discipline in store for her than she expected, and a far less substantial uniform. As she learns more about her kinky employers she discovers she can be witness to even more deviant antics than she ever imagined possible.

The Island of Maldona by Yolanda Celbridge
February 1996   Price £4.99   ISBN: 0 352 33028 7
The women of Maldona are an ancient order devoted to physical perfection, Sapphic love and strict discipline. Their leader, Jana, and her slaves set out on a quest and recreate their passionate rituals of punishment and reward on a deserted island. But the goddess Aphrodite threatens their harmony and the rivalry comes to a head in their naked physical battle.

White Rose Ensnared by Juliet Hastings
January 1996   Price £4.99   ISBN: 0 352 33052 X
Against the backdrop of the Wars of the Roses, another battle is taking place. Rosamund, now recently widowed, finds herself at the mercy of Sir Ralph Aycliffe, a powerful knight who will stop at nothing to humiliate her and enslave her beyond redemption. Only a young squire will risk everything and battle over her body.

A Sense of Entitlement by Cheryl Mildenhall
January 1996   Price £4.99   ISBN: 0 352 33053 8
Angelique inherits a half share in a Buckinghamshire hotel, but this is a hotel with a difference. In it the clients behave strangely and the labyrinth of hidden passages reveals a secret room where the weirdest and wildest erotic fantasies can be acted out.

The Mistress by Vivienne LaFay
February 1996   Price £4.99   ISBN: 0 352 33057 0
Emma Longmore is very much enjoying her role as mistress to Daniel Forbes, and her salacious means of passing the time involves initiating the daughters of local dignitaries in the arts of lovemaking. But when it seems Daniel is tiring of this lifestyle and diverting attention onto the household staff, Emma becomes drawn to the flaunted libidos of Paris.

Aria Appassionata by Juliet Hastings
February 1996   Price £4.99   ISBN: 0 352 33056 2
The inexperienced Tess is about to play one of opera's most notorious roles, Carmen, in a production that promises to be as raunchy and explicit as it is intelligent. Tony Varguez takes on the task of educating her, setting the stage for unbridled erotic exploration and painstaking research. But like the character she is to play, Tess soon finds herself torn between two equally beguiling lovers.

NEXUS BACKLIST

All books are priced £4.99 unless another price is given. If a date is supplied, the book in question will not be available until that month in 1995.

CONTEMPORARY EROTICA

THE ACADEMY	Arabella Knight	
CONDUCT UNBECOMING	Arabella Knight	Jul
CONTOURS OF DARKNESS	Marco Vassi	
THE DEVIL'S ADVOCATE	Anonymous	
DIFFERENT STROKES	Sarah Veitch	Aug
THE DOMINO TATTOO	Cyrian Amberlake	
THE DOMINO ENIGMA	Cyrian Amberlake	
THE DOMINO QUEEN	Cyrian Amberlake	
ELAINE	Stephen Ferris	
EMMA'S SECRET WORLD	Hilary James	
EMMA ENSLAVED	Hilary James	
EMMA'S SECRET DIARIES	Hilary James	
FALLEN ANGELS	Kendal Grahame	
THE FANTASIES OF JOSEPHINE SCOTT	Josephine Scott	
THE GENTLE DEGENERATES	Marco Vassi	
HEART OF DESIRE	Maria del Rey	
HELEN – A MODERN ODALISQUE	Larry Stern	
HIS MISTRESS'S VOICE	G. C. Scott	
HOUSE OF ANGELS	Yvonne Strickland	May
THE HOUSE OF MALDONA	Yolanda Celbridge	
THE IMAGE	Jean de Berg	Jul
THE INSTITUTE	Maria del Rey	
SISTERHOOD OF THE INSTITUTE	Maria del Rey	

JENNIFER'S INSTRUCTION	Cyrian Amberlake	
LETTERS TO CHLOE	Stefan Gerrard	Aug
LINGERING LESSONS	Sarah Veitch	Apr
A MATTER OF POSSESSION	G. C. Scott	Sep
MELINDA AND THE MASTER	Susanna Hughes	
MELINDA AND ESMERALDA	Susanna Hughes	
MELINDA AND THE COUNTESS	Susanna Hughes	
MELINDA AND THE ROMAN	Susanna Hughes	
MIND BLOWER	Marco Vassi	
MS DEEDES ON PARADISE ISLAND	Carole Andrews	
THE NEW STORY OF O	Anonymous	
OBSESSION	Maria del Rey	
ONE WEEK IN THE PRIVATE HOUSE	Esme Ombreux	Jun
THE PALACE OF SWEETHEARTS	Delver Maddingley	
THE PALACE OF FANTASIES	Delver Maddingley	
THE PALACE OF HONEYMOONS	Delver Maddingley	
THE PALACE OF EROS	Delver Maddingley	
PARADISE BAY	Maria del Rey	
THE PASSIVE VOICE	G. C. Scott	
THE SALINE SOLUTION	Marco Vassi	
SHERRIE	Evelyn Culber	May
STEPHANIE	Susanna Hughes	
STEPHANIE'S CASTLE	Susanna Hughes	
STEPHANIE'S REVENGE	Susanna Hughes	
STEPHANIE'S DOMAIN	Susanna Hughes	
STEPHANIE'S TRIAL	Susanna Hughes	
STEPHANIE'S PLEASURE	Susanna Hughes	
THE TEACHING OF FAITH	Elizabeth Bruce	
THE TRAINING GROUNDS	Sarah Veitch	
UNDERWORLD	Maria del Rey	

EROTIC SCIENCE FICTION

ADVENTURES IN THE PLEASUREZONE	Delaney Silver	
RETURN TO THE PLEASUREZONE	Delaney Silver	

FANTASYWORLD	Larry Stern	
WANTON	Andrea Arven	

ANCIENT & FANTASY SETTINGS

CHAMPIONS OF LOVE	Anonymous	
CHAMPIONS OF PLEASURE	Anonymous	
CHAMPIONS OF DESIRE	Anonymous	
THE CLOAK OF APHRODITE	Kendal Grahame	
THE HANDMAIDENS	Aran Ashe	
THE SLAVE OF LIDIR	Aran Ashe	
THE DUNGEONS OF LIDIR	Aran Ashe	
THE FOREST OF BONDAGE	Aran Ashe	
PLEASURE ISLAND	Aran Ashe	
WITCH QUEEN OF VIXANIA	Morgana Baron	

EDWARDIAN, VICTORIAN & OLDER EROTICA

ANNIE	Evelyn Culber	
ANNIE AND THE SOCIETY	Evelyn Culber	
THE AWAKENING OF LYDIA	Philippa Masters	Apr
BEATRICE	Anonymous	
CHOOSING LOVERS FOR JUSTINE	Aran Ashe	
GARDENS OF DESIRE	Roger Rougiere	
THE LASCIVIOUS MONK	Anonymous	
LURE OF THE MANOR	Barbra Baron	
RETURN TO THE MANOR	Barbra Baron	Jun
MAN WITH A MAID 1	Anonymous	
MAN WITH A MAID 2	Anonymous	
MAN WITH A MAID 3	Anonymous	
MEMOIRS OF A CORNISH GOVERNESS	Yolanda Celbridge	
THE GOVERNESS AT ST AGATHA'S	Yolanda Celbridge	
TIME OF HER LIFE	Josephine Scott	
VIOLETTE	Anonymous	

THE JAZZ AGE

BLUE ANGEL NIGHTS	Margarete von Falkensee	
BLUE ANGEL DAYS	Margarete von Falkensee	

BLUE ANGEL SECRETS	Margarete von Falkensee	
CONFESSIONS OF AN ENGLISH MAID	Anonymous	
PLAISIR D'AMOUR	Anne-Marie Villefranche	
FOLIES D'AMOUR	Anne-Marie Villefranche	
JOIE D'AMOUR	Anne-Marie Villefranche	
MYSTERE D'AMOUR	Anne-Marie Villefranche	
SECRETS D'AMOUR	Anne-Marie Villefranche	
SOUVENIR D'AMOUR	Anne-Marie Villefranche	

SAMPLERS & COLLECTIONS

EROTICON 1	ed. J-P Spencer	
EROTICON 2	ed. J-P Spencer	
EROTICON 3	ed. J-P Spencer	
EROTICON 4	ed. J-P Spencer	
NEW EROTICA 1	ed. Esme Ombreux	
NEW EROTICA 2	ed. Esme Ombreux	
THE FIESTA LETTERS	ed. Chris Lloyd	£4.50

NON-FICTION

HOW TO DRIVE YOUR MAN WILD IN BED	Graham Masterton	
HOW TO DRIVE YOUR WOMAN WILD IN BED	Graham Masterton	
LETTERS TO LINZI	Linzi Drew	
LINZI DREW'S PLEASURE GUIDE	Linzi Drew	

Please send me the books I have ticked above.

Name ....

Address ....

....

....

.... Post code ....

Send to: Cash Sales, Nexus Books, 332 Ladbroke Grove, London W10 5AH.

Please enclose a cheque or postal order, made payable to **Nexus Books**, to the value of the books you have ordered plus postage and packing costs as follows:

UK and BFPO – £1.00 for the first book, 50p for each subsequent book.

Overseas (including Republic of Ireland) – £2.00 for the first book, £1.00 for the second book, and 50p for each subsequent book.

If you would prefer to pay by VISA or ACCESS/MASTERCARD, please write your card number and expiry date here:

....

Please allow up to 28 days for delivery.

Signature ....
